A Season for Scandal

A Season for Scandal

LAURA WOOD

■SCHOLASTIC

Published in the UK by Scholastic, 2024
1 London Bridge, London, SE1 9BG
Scholastic Ireland, 89E Lagan Road, Dublin Industrial Estate, Glasnevin,
Dublin, D11 HP5F

Text © Laura Wood, 2024
Cover illustration © Mercedes deBellard, 2024

ISBN 978 0702 32537 3

A CIP catalogue record for this book
is available from the British Library.

Printed and bound in Great Britain by Clays Ltd, Elcograf S.p.A
Paper made from wood grown in sustainable forests
and other controlled sources.

MIX
Paper | Supporting
responsible forestry
FSC® C018072

1 3 5 7 9 10 8 6 4 2

www.scholastic.co.uk

To everyone who asked me for another
book about the Aviary – you made me so happy.
I wrote this just for you.

PART ONE

London
March, 1898

CHAPTER ONE

The day that my life veered dramatically off course, you could taste spring in the air, clear and sweet like rain-soaked grass.

As I stood on the footpath in the cold sunshine listening to Simon Earnshaw break off our engagement, I was struck by the pool of golden flowers that surrounded us. Earlier, I had felt nothing but joy at the view of the smudged blue-grey sky hanging over London, at the sight of the cheery yellow daffodils blooming in Hyde Park.

Then I thought those daffodils meant brighter days were ahead. *Now* I saw the truth. As I should have done in the first place; after all, I understood the language of flowers better than anyone.

Daffodil. *Narcissus*. Meaning: unrequited love.

Nature was not troubling herself with subtlety today, and even in such a dire situation as this one, I could appreciate the sly humour: the way the flowers nodded their heads like matronly gossips delighting in calamity, as if to say, *We told you so.*

"You see, this is exactly what I mean, Marigold," Simon said with a put-upon sigh. He was frowning at me. "I'm trying to tell you that we're not suited, and you look as though you're about to burst out laughing. It's not right. It's not ... becoming."

Becoming. That was an interesting word, wasn't it? I could never be quite sure what it meant. Simon, on the other hand, had a *lot* of ideas about what sort of behaviour was becoming for a young lady. It seemed they could mostly be reduced to this: the absolute opposite of Marigold Bloom.

"I'm sorry, Simon," I replied, swallowing my

amusement because the situation really wasn't funny at all. "I promise I will try harder to—"

Simon cut me off with an impatient wave of his hand. "It's too late, Marigold. I've tried and tried, but there's no use... You're just not what a wife should be."

That was new. Something icy weaselled along my spine. "What should a wife be, then?" I asked, and I hated how small my voice sounded.

Simon's eyes ran over me, and I knew what he saw: a wild riot of curly rose-gold hair that stubbornly refused to behave, a pair of steady grey eyes in a round, dimpled face, and a body that drew attention wherever it went – a fat body, a voluptuous body, a generous body of soft, wide curves. Mine was a body that tended to inspire one of two reactions – a nose-wrinkling desire that I make myself smaller, or a salacious interest in getting under my dress. Simon had always seemed to feel both.

Perhaps that was the problem.

"You know, Mari, you're just..." Simon paused, considering. He waved his hands around in a gesture that encompassed all of me. "Too much," he exhaled finally.

I stiffened, blood rushing to my cheeks.

Too much. It wasn't the first time he'd said something like that, but it hurt nonetheless.

Because I liked myself. I liked my body. I liked my hair. I liked that I stood out in a crowd.

Once, I thought Simon liked those things about me too. He had certainly seemed to when he had been busy kissing me and telling me how lovely I was while trying to undo the back of my dress, making breathless promises for our future together, as his busy hands moved over me. Then, it seemed, I was perfect.

Now that we were past that part and into the bit where I was set to become his actual wife, things had changed. The rules were different, and they'd shifted so fast I couldn't keep up.

The comments had started a few months ago – small, innocuous observations about the clothes I wore (too bright, too gaudy, too extravagant), who I spoke to (the boy on the corner selling newspapers, the lady with the yappy Pomeranian in the park, really anyone who crossed my path), the way I laughed (too loudly, too easily, too often). All that soon piled up into a general sense of dissatisfaction.

At first, I laughed it off. Then, when the remarks continued, I told Simon that he was hurting my feelings. He was all sincere apologies, pointing out that he was only trying to help. That I must understand that I would need to behave differently when we were married, that his wife would be a reflection on him. That he was a serious man, a respected man.

I tried to listen. I wanted him to be happy. I wanted to make him happy. But I never seemed to get it quite right. That was when it had started – the hot, queasy feeling that had taken me weeks to identify as shame. Simon's words had planted that seed of shame, and then week after week I'd felt it grow.

Now, his handsome face was set in grim lines. His blue eyes were cold, his mouth pulled down.

My heart sank as anger and pride and hurt jumbled inside me. And just a sliver of fear. Because this wasn't only about me. Marrying Simon was a way to look after my family, and right now that plan was in serious jeopardy.

"Simon…" I cleared my throat, trying again, trying to keep the (unladylike) bite of anger out of my voice. "Please, I—"

"I've asked Sarah Hardison to marry me," Simon blurted out, and a splash of pink spread across his cheeks, even as he tipped his chin in a defiant gesture, as if daring me to have something to say about it.

"You've..." I blinked. "How could you have asked Sarah Hardison to marry you," I asked slowly, "when you're already engaged to me?"

Simon tugged at his collar. "You and I never had a formal arrangement—"

"You proposed a year ago, Simon. We planned an autumn wedding."

At least he had a tiny morsel of guilt left in him, enough to look uncomfortable. I racked my brain, trying to picture Sarah Hardison. She was nice, I thought. We had spoken once or twice when she had been in the shop. She looked like a tiny porcelain doll and her father was in quite a senior position at a bank.

Simon waved his hand. "That was only talk, Marigold. What we've had, it was good, wasn't it? Pleasant. A childhood fancy. But we're eighteen now – it's time to be serious; it's time to settle down and stop sowing wild oats."

I had the feeling Simon was parroting his father's words here. It certainly sounded like his father, who had made it clear that he thought his son could do better than the granddaughter of a florist.

"I thought we *were* serious."

The look he gave me then was pitying. He reached out and patted my hand. *Patted my hand!* A surge of fury blazed within me. I had never hit anyone in my life, but my fingers curled into a fist.

"This is for the best," Simon said, oblivious to the fact that I was fantasizing about squashing his head like a grape. "Now, let me take you home."

The whole situation seemed like a bad dream. Could this really be happening? Could things fall apart so quickly, so easily? A handful of words spoken on a walk in the park upending an entire life. Several lives.

I shrugged his hand off. "No, thank you." I ground the words out, determined to retain some shred of dignity. I was relieved to find I still had that thread of steel left inside me; I'm certain there was part of Simon that had been expecting a scene. Indeed, there was part of me that could happily have provided it, a part that wanted nothing more than to cry, to beg him to reconsider. I wasn't going to let that happen; instead I kept my face and voice expressionless, a mask of bland indifference that only a fool would truly believe.

He didn't even bother trying to hide his relief at my calm acceptance. "Oh, well then." He was already stepping away. "I'll let you get on your way. No hard feelings and all that. I'm sure I'll see you soon."

And on that incredibly anticlimactic note my relationship with Simon ended. Almost two years of my life, all my plans for the future ... gone.

I stood, absorbing the moment like a blow, and breathing deeply as I settled back into my body.

Here in the park, you could almost forget you were in the middle of the city. Here, green shoots were bursting through the dirt, flowers were starting to bloom – splashes of vibrant colour that wanted to spill over on to the well-trodden footpaths. I wriggled my toes in my boots. Under the earth, I knew that life whispered, gathering itself, preparing to blaze upwards, reaching tender, twining fingers towards the sun. The breeze stirred through the newly uncurled leaves over my head, bright and fresh and full of promise.

I've always loved spring the most. It makes sense, I suppose, for a florist. It's the time when the world seems to wake up and stretch, to shake off the dreariness of winter and come alive again. It is a time of new beginnings, fresh starts.

Nothing could be that bad, I reminded myself. Not really, not when the world was green and alive.

I tugged at my drab, grey coat. I'd bought it because Simon hadn't liked my old one, with its bright crimson lining and pretty trim. He'd said it was flashy. That it drew the wrong sort of attention. Surely, he had said, the only attention I really wanted was his?

That would change now. Everything would change now.

Bending down over the riot of daffodils, I snapped one carefully at the stem, threaded it through my buttonhole – a defiant flash of gold against my throat.

I needed to tell my family what had happened. I wasn't sure how I was going to do that, not when Simon's decision affected them almost as much as it did me.

I was going to need another moment before that, I thought on a ragged sigh. A moment to collect myself, a moment of steadiness.

There was only one place I wanted to be.

CHAPTER TWO

The sight of Bloom's flower shop in all its glory was like a balm to my soul. I felt some of the anxiety slip from my shoulders as I approached the building where I spent most of my days. Not every young woman could say they loved their job as much as I did.

The door to the shop was painted a gleaming black, the wide picture windows to either side filled with frothy, unruly displays of spring flowers that I had put together myself, and that – I was pleased to say – often stopped passers-by in their tracks, tempting them inside. The sign above the door was gold on black, *Bloom's Est. 1845*, with the shop's logo – a bouquet of marigolds, roses and daisies in reference to the given names of the Bloom women – twined around the words. Green palms stood proud in pots on either side of the door, and on the street in front was a small grocer's cart that we used to display posies and men's buttonholes.

"Hello, Jane." I kept my voice level, all signs of anxiety tucked away as I greeted the young girl who stood behind the cart, overseeing that side of the business. "Looks like you've had a good morning."

Jane nodded, pleased. "Those white tulip buttonholes you made have gone down a treat, Miss Bloom. You were right – they look very handsome against the dark suits."

"Lovely. We'll make sure to pick up more at the market later if Jack has a decent supply. What about the pink anemones?"

Jane frowned. "Not so good. I think they're drooping a bit."

"I'll have to see if I can do something better with the wire. They're so delicate."

"Right you are." Jane was distracted then by an approaching customer, and I pushed my way through the door. The brass bell above rang out a greeting – a bright, happy sound.

I loved this shop. I loved the tall windows that faced out on to the sunny street. I loved the banks of elegant, fine-leafed palms that framed the black-and-white tiled floor in front of the counter. I loved the ever-changing baskets of flowers: today, slender purple irises, creamy magnolias, star-like golden narcissus, filling the room with their heady scent.

I loved the enormous brass till that sat beside the tray of pretty chocolates – violet and rose creams that my sister Daisy and I made in our kitchen, all available to buy in cream boxes stamped with the Bloom's logo.

I loved the wall covered in different coloured ribbons, the vases spilling over with examples of the bouquets we could put together. I felt such a bone-deep sense of pride as I took it all in – a shop that I had helped to build. A shop that was so warm and welcoming that people wanted to linger.

Simon, on the other hand, did not care for the shop.

Or, at least, he did not care for the way I ran it. *Like a man*. I felt my spine straighten, my shoulders draw back. I wasn't going to let Simon Earnshaw or anyone else threaten this place.

Suzy, one of our shop girls, waved at me from behind the counter and then returned her attention to the gentleman she was serving.

"I need something that says, *I'm sorry I dislike your cat, but I really do love you*," the man said, desperation bleeding into his words.

Suzy's eyes drifted to me, a smile pulling at her mouth. She knew I'd never be able to pass up such a challenge. "What do you think, Mari?"

I glanced around the shop, pursed my lips. "Bluebells for humility, hyacinths to ask for forgiveness, arrange them with some of the olive branches as a peace offering, and tie it all with a blue ribbon," I said after a moment. "Oh, and some pink tulips too."

Tulip. *Tulipa*. Meaning: I declare my love for you.

Tulip season was always a busy time for us. There were plenty of declarations to be made at this time of year. Like I said, spring was a time for new beginnings.

At least for most people. The sour words rang in my head.

"I'm sure that will do the trick ... though I would consider buying a packet of catnip seeds as well." I gave the man a sympathetic smile. "I think it's probably a case of love them, love their cat. A gesture like that might go a long way."

"I think you're probably right," the man said with a doleful sigh. "I'll take the seeds as well."

"I'll go and get them for you," I said, leaving Suzy to put the bouquet together. I stripped off my coat as I moved through to the back of the shop. This was my kingdom – the space where I did most of my work – the cool, shady room with its drawers full of alphabetized seed packets, gardening tools neatly stored, florist's wire and pins and everything else I needed to grow, arrange, organize the flowers – and the small garden beyond, full of flowers I had grown myself. Running the length of the wall was a long, rough potting bench and in the air the warm, clinging smell of damp earth. A pair of doors opened on to my garden, and I propped them so they stood ajar, letting the spring air inside.

It was a special place. It was also the place that represented my biggest secret. Much as I loved the shop, when I slept, it wasn't the business I dreamed about: it was wide open spaces brimming with life that I tended and cultivated with my own hands. Not that I ever told anyone else that. Bloom's was my responsibility, and it was hardly a burden. Wide open spaces were hard to come by in London, and I had never been further from the city than Hatfield.

Any remaining tension fled as I busied myself, grabbing the catnip seeds and delivering them to the customer, then returning to the back with more anemones – holding my tongue between my teeth as I worked to create new buttonholes that would hold better while retaining their air of fragile prettiness. It was good work, work that busied my fingers and calmed my mind.

Pleased with my efforts, I rolled my shoulders and carefully gathered the posies in a trug, taking them outside to Jane, who gave her enthusiastic approval.

"They'll be gone in no time," she said, a glint in her eye.

"Ah, Miss Bloom, there you are," a voice came from behind us, and I saw Jane's smile drop. It was, I thought, perhaps the very last voice I wanted to hear at this particular moment.

"Hello, Mr Earnshaw." I pasted on a polite smile as I turned to face Simon's father, moving a step away from Jane, away from the shop as I did so. I didn't want him here, even if he had more right than anyone. All my hard-earned calm deserted me at that thought.

Geoffrey Earnshaw was a tall, well-built man. His hair was light blond and thinning, his eyes a dull grey-blue and darting, his skin pale as watered-down milk. He had narrow, grasping hands that I did my best to avoid. He had a reputation for putting those hands where they didn't belong.

"I understand that you and Simon had a difficult conversation this morning." The sympathetic grimace he directed at me made my stomach turn.

"I don't know about difficult," I said, keeping my tone steady and pleasant, pride kicking in once more. "I am sorry that the engagement has come to an end, but these things happen."

"How right you are." He sidled closer. "I must say, I'm relieved to hear that you are taking it so well, my dear."

"As well as can be expected," I said stiffly as those bony fingers closed around my elbow and squeezed in what I supposed was a gesture of sympathy. I felt the cold, heavy bite of the signet ring on his finger.

"Of course, now that your situation has changed, you must be afraid our business arrangement with the rent will be affected too." He purred. "It is a trifle awkward to break off your engagement to your landlord's son." He chuckled.

I lifted my chin, refraining from pointing out that I had nothing to do with the engagement being broken and that if anyone should be feeling awkward it was him. "Thank you, but I'm not worried, Mr Earnshaw. Whatever the new terms of the lease are, I'm sure we can meet them. After all, Bloom's has been in business for over fifty years."

Mr Earnshaw's nose wrinkled indulgently, but his hand remained on me. "Oh, Miss Bloom, how well that sounds, but we're all friends here... We know each other far too well for posturing. I hardly think one can call a flower cart a business."

I fought not to snap back. My grandfather had worked his way up from selling flowers on the street as a young man to running one of the most eminent florists in London. It was nothing to be sniffed at, particularly not by a mediocre man such as Earnshaw. *He* had simply inherited his father's shares in a shipping company, and his grandfather's shrewd property purchases, and then sat back like a satisfied pug and enjoyed the income. Geoffrey Earnshaw had never made a single thing for himself. Well, except for Simon, I suppose, and just look how well that turned out.

"But we're getting away from my point." His hand drifted higher up my arm, the touch slinking into a horrible, surprising caress. "What I was trying to say was that just because things are at an end between you and my son doesn't necessarily mean the business has to suffer. Perhaps the two of us could come to some *other* arrangement..."

My head snapped up and I met his eye.

I wished more than anything for the right words. Something pithy and cutting. But they didn't come.

He smiled, showing off teeth that seemed too big for his face. Unlike his lazy movements, the smile was sharp and predatory. His hand slithered back down my arm and around to my back. It was only a light graze, but I felt it cling to my skin like the trail a slug leaves behind. His fingers splayed, only for a moment, over the base of my spine and flexed. I felt each of his fingertips digging into my flesh.

I took a quick step back.

"Just something for you to think about," he said easily, while I stood and stared. "Good day to you, Miss Bloom." And with that, he lifted his hand to the brim of his hat and strolled off as though nothing had happened.

My blood was cold. That uninvited touch, brief as it had been, lingered, made me feel like scrubbing my skin with soap and water. Had that really just happened? Had Simon's father propositioned me? Here, in the middle of a busy street, outside my own shop? I rubbed my hands over the tops of my arms. It was still sunny, and people rushed by me, going about their business;

the scene was almost painfully ordinary, but I felt chilled, hollowed out.

I found myself walking back through the door. I took a deep, steadying breath. The cold feeling eased a little.

Home. I would go home.

CHAPTER THREE

"The man is a pig!" Daisy exclaimed, pushing her hands through her blonde hair, messing up the careful style that I knew would have taken a good hour in front of the mirror, demonstrating just how upset my sister really was.

She was speaking about Simon. I hadn't got around to telling them about his awful father yet. I was easing myself into it. (And it comes to something, doesn't it, when the fool who broke off your engagement for no good reason is only the second worst man you've dealt with that day?)

"Daisy!" my mother chided gently, pouring the tea that she insisted would make everyone feel better. "That language is not appropriate." There was a pause while she replaced the teapot in the centre of the table and turned it clockwise so that the floral design faced forward. "Although in this case it is not inaccurate."

The three of us were arranged around the sitting room in our home above the shop, and the pretty, feminine space was doing almost as much to soothe me as the righteous, fiery outrage that sparked in my mother's and sister's eyes. I was still unsettled about the scene with Earnshaw, but being here with them chased some of the shadows away.

Daisy's delicate fingers were already straightening her hair, but her blue eyes blazed as she gave a short, humourless laugh. "He's a pig and he didn't deserve Mari – and speaking the truth is never inappropriate."

"Well, it's done now," I said, trying to keep my tone light. "Perhaps Simon was right. Perhaps it was just a childish infatuation."

"If you feel like that, then it's for the best." Mother sighed. "You shouldn't marry someone unless the thought of them leaving shatters your heart into a hundred pieces. I want that for both my girls."

"You want us both to have our hearts shattered into pieces?" I asked over the top of my teacup.

"Yes!" Mother exclaimed instantly. Then she frowned. "I mean no, no, of course not. I meant…"

"I know what you meant!" I laughed. "I was only teasing. And you're right – I never had any great passion for Simon, but then I never expected to. I thought we'd be happy."

"Happy with a worm like him?" Daisy huffed. "Doubtful."

"Is he a worm or a pig?" I asked thoughtfully. "Or some sort of hybrid? A pig-worm, perhaps? A porm?"

Reluctantly, Daisy chuckled. Then she tilted her head to the side and observed me thoughtfully. "At least you're taking it well, Mari," she said. "I'm sure I'd be a weeping, wailing mess if someone broke off my engagement – even if I had been engaged to a pig. But that's you all over. You're just so … steady. Not like me."

It was my turn to laugh. I appreciated Daisy's self-awareness. At fifteen she was very pretty – small and slender with a mop of guinea-gold curls and wide blue eyes, and she existed on a steady diet of fashion periodicals and penny dreadfuls. The more gothic and ridiculous the love story, the better, as far as Daisy was concerned. She could happily make a melodrama out of the tiniest domestic wrinkle. (Take, for example, the time Mother denied her a new and quite unflattering hat and Daisy drew a straight line from this event to her untimely demise via several increasingly outlandish coincidences, including a seagull and a one-eyed man with a pipe. Needless to say, she wore the hat to church the following Sunday.)

I would have said it was something she'd grow out of, but she was so precisely a copy of our mother in both appearance and temperament that when they stood side by side they looked like the sort of little wooden dolls that stacked one inside the other.

"Well, exactly," Mother agreed with Daisy, only proving my point. "I, for one, would have taken to my bed immediately." She sighed again, heavily. "Probably wasted away, all pale and interesting." Her face looked a bit wistful at this, clearly imagining the picture she'd make lying prone across the bed in her nicest nightgown. "It's fortunate that you take after your father, Mari. He was such a dear, reliable man."

As my father had died shortly after Daisy was born, when I was only three, I would have to take Mother's word on that. I knew that my parents had loved each other deeply – Mother was always clear on that matter, had even written several flowery sonnets on the subject that Daisy and I had listened to with different levels of enthusiasm. My grandfather always said that when his son brought home a Rose, he knew their match was destined.

Even so, the way she often spoke about my father in relation to his similarities to me was not so much poetic as it was like a depressingly dull advertisement for a clock. Reliable. Steady. Dependable. Sometimes it made me feel more like a sturdy shire horse pulling a plough than an eighteen-year-old girl.

"Yes, well, I don't have much interest in wasting away." I took another sip of my tea, picked up a lavender shortbread biscuit and crunched into it with satisfaction. I had found the perfect balance of floral sweetness with this batch; it was time to offer them for sale in the shop. "And there's far too much for me to do to take to my bed." I hesitated but decided to take the metaphorical bull by the horns. "My engagement to Simon – or lack thereof – may have implications for the business."

Mother had been stirring sugar into her cup and the silver teaspoon halted in its lazy circles. She lifted her eyes to mine. "Do you think... Will his father..." She trailed off.

"Will he raise the rent on the shop?" I said. "Yes, I'd imagine so. He... Well, I ran into him before I came up here."

I gave a brisk account of what had happened. Mother's face was pale, Daisy's gaze murderous as she almost vibrated with anger.

"He would dare—" my sister started, but I wrapped my hand around hers, gently prising the teacup from her fingers.

"It's no good flinging Mother's best china at the fireplace," I said, setting the cup back on its saucer. "Yes, he did dare, and none of us can pretend to be surprised that the man is an awful, lecherous—"

"Pig-worm," Daisy finished.

I laughed, though the sound was forced. "Like father, like son, I suppose."

"I can't believe you're so calm about it." Daisy tilted her head to one side, observing me as though I was some mysterious new species.

"I'm furious about it," I said simply. "It was horrible. *He* was horrible. But as I'm not about to become his mistress, it's better to put my energy into finding a solution. We're going to have to raise a decent amount of funds, I suppose, if we want to stay."

The three of us fell silent at that. Because here was the real problem – Simon's father owned the building in which we were currently sitting: the site of Bloom's and our home above it.

My engagement to Simon had been seen as part of a long-term business arrangement – albeit one that his father had entered into reluctantly. Upon our marriage, Simon would own the building in which my family would continue to live and work, and when my grandfather died, the business would belong to Simon too.

As the shop was successful, and I was an extremely

competent manager who had grown the business as far as a person possibly could, this was hardly the act of benevolence that Mr Earnshaw made it seem. He and Simon stood to make a good amount of money from it, though both seemed completely baffled by my role as my grandfather's second-in-command, and heir apparent, and by the very idea that a business run by a woman could be turning a profit.

"I don't know how to tell Grandfather." I shifted uncomfortably against the pretty though worn sofa cushion. "Not about Mr Earnshaw," I said quickly. "There's no need to trouble him with that."

My mother and sister both nodded in swift agreement. It was all too easy to imagine Grandfather calling for pistols at dawn, which would, I thought fondly, appeal to his own romantic nature but – as this was 1898 and no one had duelled for almost fifty years, *and* the man had never so much as fired a gun in his life – could only end in some fresh disaster.

"You know he was never thrilled about the arrangement with Simon in the first place," Mother began tentatively.

"I do know that," I agreed, "but he understood it was necessary. Practical. Without the agreement in place, Mr Earnshaw has no reason not to drive up the rent, let alone reduce it as we had planned. We're in the fashionable part of town. He knows he can get more for the building. He would have squeezed us out a long time ago if it hadn't been for the engagement."

I looked around at the sitting room, the one that I had grown up in – the one my father had grown up in, and a fragile connection to him that had always felt so important. To be forced to leave would be a terrible wrench for all of us, and Grandfather was older now, his health not what it once was. I couldn't see him leaving his home, the one he had built and shared with his wife, without a fight. And despite what he might have to say about the matter, I worried that such a fight might be asking too much of him.

"How could we move?" Mother's hands twisted fretfully in her lap. "Not just the house but to move the family business, the one that your grandfather built..." She trailed off again, tears brightening her eyes.

I tried not to let it bother me that she didn't mention

my contribution to the business. In the eighteen months since Grandfather had turned the day-to-day running of the shop over to me, our income had grown significantly. I had taken on several big accounts, working for some of the most prominent families in the city, and – perhaps most importantly – I'd established our own small nursery with a thoroughly modern greenhouse on the once-scrubby strip of land at the back of the house.

The greenhouse. At the thought of that, I winced. It had been a big investment: one I had made based on the certainty of a future with Simon. It had changed everything for Bloom's – we'd been able to produce a small but carefully curated contribution to our stock without being reliant on the local nurserymen and their changing prices. In addition to that, we could experiment with different growing methods, cross-breeding new varieties – particularly roses.

I had high hopes for several of my experiments. Grandfather and I had even talked about flower shows, about the possibility of stocking prize-winning blooms for our customers – the ones who demanded the rare, the exclusive, and who would pay well for it.

"It won't come to that," I said with a certainty I didn't precisely feel, but Mother's face cleared instantly. Her complete faith that I would fix everything was both gratifying and infuriating. "I'm sure I'll think of something," I added, trying to eradicate any hint of doubt from my tone.

"You always do," Mother agreed warmly. "Honestly, Mari, what would we do without you?" She reached over and squeezed my hand in hers. "You're a treasure."

For some reason this had tears prickling at the back of my eyes and I blinked rapidly. I never cried, and I wasn't about to start now. I simply had to be practical, make a plan. People were depending on me. If our outgoings were going to increase, then I would just have to find ways to boost our income. It was only a matter of balancing numbers. I could do that.

"And here are my little blooms, pretty as a picture!" a deep voice boomed from the doorway.

"Gramps!" Daisy got to her feet, rushing over to take his hat from him, while Mother fussed about getting him to sit in his favourite armchair and I poured him a cup of tea, setting a biscuit on the plate beside it.

Horatio Bloom was – unquestionably – a darling. Small and spry, well into his seventies, with a thick silver moustache that tickled when he kissed your cheek, and green eyes that sparkled with humour, he could charm the birds down from the trees. He took over his father's flower cart as a young man but had secretly dreamed of a life on the stage, and he certainly had the presence for it – which is a polite way of saying that all my sister's flair for the dramatic came from him.

His health had started to decline over the last couple of years, and he was easily tired, had dizzy spells and suffered heart palpitations that he would never admit to. Fortunately for him, he had a daughter-in-law and two granddaughters who watched eagle-eyed for any sign he was overexerting himself. He pretended to hate us fussing over him, but really he responded to attention like a flower to sunshine.

"Marigold, my love," he said, biting into his biscuit with an expression of bliss, "these are wonderful. The lavender is just right... Are you going to put them out downstairs?"

"I thought so." I nodded. "And the rosemary ones if I can get the balance right with the salt."

"A Bloom through and through." Grandfather sighed, content. "Always thinking, always growing. A man can retire happy when he has a granddaughter like Marigold, isn't that right, Rose?"

"Yes," Mother said, casting a glance my way. "We're all lucky to have Mari. We were just saying so."

"Mari can take care of anything," Daisy said staunchly.

I wondered why their supportive words felt like wearing a corset tied too tight. Clearly, they were waiting to see if I was going to reveal all to Grandfather, but I found myself desperate to put it off for as long as possible. I'd have to tell him soon; I was horrible at lying, but I needed a moment's pause, a respite from the bleakness of this morning's events. I wasn't sure I had it in me to go through it all again just now. Suddenly the room felt airless, the crawling sense of panic that I had pushed down returned with even greater force, taking me by surprise.

I placed my teacup back on the tray with an almost steady hand and got to my feet, dusting off my skirt.

"I think I'll head off to the library," I said, forcing a smile. "I have time before my meeting this afternoon with Mrs Birch about the arrangements for her dinner party, and there's a new book on landscaping I wanted to borrow. Time to start looking for some more new ideas."

Mother looked relieved by my decision not to tell Grandfather just yet, flashing me a look of agreement. He only rubbed his hands together and started telling me that the last book I'd taken out on propagating roses had clearly been written by an imbecile, with the cheerful confidence of a man who knew everything there was to know about flowers.

"Oh, Mari, you're so clever, filling your head with all those gardening facts," Daisy cut in, beaming at me, and even going so far as to bat her eyelashes.

"And what are you after?" I asked suspiciously.

Daisy's finger traced a pattern on the sofa. "Nothing, really – only if you're going to the library anyway, I wondered if you could pick up a book for me."

"After the fine you cost me last time?" I bit my lip, trying to look stern.

Grandfather chuckled.

"It's not my fault I dropped the book in the bath." Daisy pouted. "Honestly, I was just so scandalized." She shivered with gleeful appreciation. "Rodrigo had just come across Isabella's hiding place in the woods and..."

"Stop! Stop!" Mother held her hands to her ears. "You know I haven't got that far yet. It's taking me much longer to read, with the words smudged as they are. I spent several pages convinced they were discussing radishes rather than the potential ravishing of the heroine, and I found the sudden interest in root vegetables to be most confusing..."

Her complaint was cut short by Grandfather and Daisy's abrupt shouts of laughter. After a moment, Mother joined in too. I tried to laugh as well, and watched the three of them guffaw, spurring each other on, with a giddy mixture of love and worry. My family. They were depending on me.

"Radishes!" Daisy snorted from her position sprawled face down on the sofa, which only set the others off again. The fist that had wrapped around my heart gripped harder.

Trying not to draw attention, I slipped out with a

murmured goodbye, the sound of their laughter chasing me down the stairs.

I wouldn't let them down, I swore, remembering the feeling of Mr Earnshaw's fingers on my skin. I would find a way to fix this.

CHAPTER FOUR

Mudie's, the circulating library, was busy as ever with a seemingly endless stream of people moving through the doors. These stood beneath a discreet sign, in an unobtrusive building on the corner of New Oxford Street and Museum Street, and gave little indication of the dizzying space tucked behind them.

As I stepped inside, I was greeted not only by the sight of hundreds of thousands of books but that blissful, comforting smell of them – the sweet mustiness of crackling, ageing paper and leather binding.

The central hall in the library was a vast circle, with a soaring, domed ceiling. It felt almost like a theatre with its gilt and decorative plasterwork, but instead of stalls and velvet seats, the walls were lined with polished, wooden shelving extending up, up, up to the roof. A balcony ran round the room so that the shelves were split into two separate floors, though the rows stretched so high that you needed ladders to reach the books at the top.

In the middle of this space were a number of desks in a maze of concentric circles, at which librarians assisted readers with enquiries or checked out their books. To the sides were more desks, dark and heavy, where people could sit and read or study. Off to the left of this central room was a warren of other shelves, labyrinthine stacks twisting away into the rest of the building.

People from all walks of life frequented Mudie's, and I passed quickly between the group of young girls gossiping over the latest titillating three-part novel, and the gentleman who was arguing with a clerk about the historical records for one of the city's fish markets. I was greeted, casually, by one or two of Bloom's regular customers, who were browsing.

It was one of the things I valued most about Bloom's, the feeling that it was part of a community. We lived in a vast and ever-changing metropolis, a sprawling city that grew bigger every day, and yet here people knew my name. They bought flowers from me, and flowers – to my way of thinking – were deeply personal. I didn't just know the customers' names; I knew their birthdays, the names of wives and lovers, and I knew when they fell into infatuation or wanted to impress their in-laws. I knew when they argued and made up, when they lost the ones they loved and were grieving, and when new life arrived and they celebrated. It was a gift: all of life came through our doors.

I was smiling over the thought as I slipped deeper into the maze. I didn't need to consult the floor plans to know in which corner the horticulture books were squirrelled away, and I made my way unerringly to the correct section. It was quiet here, empty – a rather neglected bit of the library, but that suited me just fine. The buzz of conversation receded. Calmness reigned and to my busy mind it was as welcome as a cool, clear draught of water.

I hadn't lied about wanting to borrow a book – there

was a new title on the theory and practice of landscape gardening that I was keen to pick up, despite the fact that I had done as much as I could to create the garden space at Bloom's. We simply didn't have the room to keep up with all my ideas, but it was nice to dream, wasn't it? I scanned the shelves, running my fingers over spines.

The solution would come, I told myself. There was always something that could be done, some plan to be hatched, some scheme to set in motion. I simply had to find it.

I had a brief flash of memory, back to two years ago, when my grandfather had had his first dizzy spell and ended up falling down the stairs, breaking his leg. Everything had been chaos, Mother had been hysterical (which naturally wound Daisy up as neatly as a clockwork mouse), and Grandfather had been cross and pale and helpless, confined to his bed. It had been a difficult, overwhelming time ... and yet the world didn't stop spinning. The business had to go on, day by day.

And that meant I had to take care of it. I had sat beside Grandfather's sickbed and drawn up a list with him, and then I had crossed each item off it. Once that was done, I made my own list and crossed everything off that one too. I had fixed things before. I would fix them again. And perhaps the answer lay in the garden, some clever way to bring in more money ... something one of these books could help with.

Of course it came as no surprise, given the way that my day was going, that the book for which I had come in was on one of the highest shelves, and there was no clerk in sight. Glancing around to make sure the coast was clear, I rolled the ladder along to the spot where I needed it and clambered up. You weren't supposed to, and I knew it was precisely the sort of thing Simon would call unbecoming behaviour, but it seemed foolish to waste my time and somebody else's when I could simply do the task myself. I was perfectly capable.

Although...

Now that I was up here, it was quite a lot higher than I'd thought. Very high, in fact. And – truthfully – I wasn't keen on heights. I made the mistake of looking down and the floor (which was suddenly quite far away) seemed to tip a little.

I stood frozen for a moment or two, had a firm word

44

with myself and then, carefully, I withdrew the book and began to climb back towards earth. My knees were trembling pathetically, and my free hand clung so hard to the side of the ladder that my knuckles were raised white peaks. My progress was humiliatingly slow.

I was concentrating so intently on the steps that the angry voice below me took me more by surprise than it should have done.

"This whole damn place is a maze! My God! What section is this? Why are there books on growing potatoes now?"

The unexpected bark of bad temper made me stumble on the ladder, my foot sliding, hand grasping. The book slipped from my fingers, and I watched in dull horror as it headed straight for the head of the man who had spoken.

Time seemed to slow to a crawl as he tipped his face up at my gasp of shock. I had a brief impression of cheekbones, a strong jawline and dark, furious eyes before his hand flew up. Too late.

The (unfortunately heavy) book caught him square on the forehead. He let out a grunt of pain and I watched in appalled silence as the man collapsed into a dead heap on the ground.

Wonderful, I thought with a flicker of hysteria. This day just kept getting better and better. I came to the library to relax, and instead I had accidentally murdered someone.

CHAPTER FIVE

I climbed down the remaining steps, my heart in my mouth, and approached the body. What was the prison sentence for murdering someone with a book? Did it have a name? *Libercide*, I supposed, my brain happily supplying the Latin when it should probably be more focused on how best to flee the scene of the crime. Just as I was kneeling beside him, readying myself to feel for a pulse, the man groaned and propped himself up on one elbow. His eyes blinked owlishly into mine, his expression one of dazed bewilderment.

"Oh, thank good—" I began shakily.

"What just..." The eyes narrowed, his brows dropped into a thunderous frown, and he pushed himself up to his feet, towering over me. "You! Did you just throw a book at me? What the bloody hell do you think you're doing?" the man yelled.

I don't know which of us was more surprised when I burst into tears.

I so rarely cried that I wasn't sure what to do with myself, but really at this point I thought no one could blame me. Men! Why must they be so relentlessly awful?

Curled in on myself, still on the floor, the tears streamed hot from my eyes, and my upper body shook from the sudden, unexpected onslaught of emotion.

"Oh, God," the stranger groaned. "Just ... get up off the floor, you little fool." With that, he wrapped his fingers around mine and tugged me unceremoniously to my feet.

Come on, Mari, I told myself sternly. *You nearly killed him – you could at least apologize.*

I took several shuddering breaths, wiped my eyes, then forced myself to look up at the person in front of me.

Any progress I had made on catching my breath was lost in an instant.

Because that's what he was: *breathtaking*.

It sounds foolish, I know, to be winded by a man's perfect face. It was a phenomenon I had previously thought was confined to Daisy's favourite novels. But this man was a romance writer's fantasy come to life. A handful of years older than me, quite a few inches taller, and lean but with shoulders broad enough to fill out his coat very nicely. He had curling, artfully dishevelled midnight-dark hair, and warm golden skin the colour of sand. His face was made of hard, uncompromising edges, which contrasted wildly with his full, sensual mouth. His eyes were dark and flashing, his brows heavy.

These perfect features were arranged in a furious scowl as he glared down at me. The scowl did nothing to detract from his handsomeness. He looked like one of those terrible anti-heroes, all brooding and stuffed full of dark secrets, the kind of man the heroine longed to reform, or die trying. (In the books, I knew they usually took the second option. And they typically died from something easily avoidable like catching a fever after walking in the rain, because none of them had a crumb of common sense or thought to carry an umbrella.)

A long and awful silence hung in the air as I gawped hopelessly at him, before the man with the face of a fallen angel broke it. "I don't know what you're crying about. You're not the one having projectiles flung at your head."

I sniffled. Blinked hard. A few more tears slipped out.

"Stop that at once!" The man's eyes widened. "Just. Stop. Crying." He reached into his pocket and thrust a handkerchief in my direction.

He looked so aghast that I couldn't help it: I laughed. It was a strange, watery gasp of a laugh, but it loosened something in me. I felt, thankfully, as though I were back in control of my own body, and the tears stopped, my breathing eased.

"Thank you," I croaked, accepting the crisp white handkerchief and dabbing my eyes. "I'm sorry for dropping the book on you. You startled me. And as for the tears, I'm afraid that there, too, you were simply in the wrong place at the wrong time. I don't usually cry."

"Hmmm." The man made a noise to indicate that he was dubious about the veracity of this statement.

I held the damp handkerchief out to him, and he accepted it with obvious distaste, using only the tips of his fingers. It was a nice handkerchief. Good quality. The initials OL were embroidered in the corner in black thread.

"I really don't," I told him, having composed myself at last. "It's been a terrible day, and I suppose when you fell down and then shouted at me it was the final straw. Not that I blame you, of course."

"Oh, that's big of you," he said sulkily. "Assaulting me was the last straw, was it? And what, pray tell, were these other straws weighing down on you? How have you spent your morning? Accosting old ladies? Kicking dogs? Knocking down small children, perhaps?"

That drew another gurgle of laughter from me, though he didn't really look like he was joking.

"Well," I found myself saying, "first of all, my fiancé broke off our engagement because he thinks I'm not ladylike enough and he's marrying someone else instead, and then his father, his awful father – who happens to own the building I live and work in – propositioned me in the street. When I refuse to become his mistress, I should think he'll happily destroy my business and evict my entire family."

Once again, I had surprised us both. I hadn't been planning to say any of that. The words had simply come out. And saying them made the whole thing real.

The impressive frown on the man's face had deepened. "You're not going to cry again, are you?" he asked gruffly.

I shook my head. "No. But I am worried." I was, I finally admitted to myself, out of my depth and afraid. "I don't know what to do, you see ... and I always know what to do."

There was another pause, and it suddenly struck me how awkward the situation was. Funny that it hadn't done so before.

"Anyway," I said, reaching down to collect my book from where it lay on the floor. I winced because it really was a generous tome – seemed there was a lot to be said about landscaping. "I apologize again about the book. And for crying on you. I'll leave you to your browsing."

"Wait." The man held up his hand as I walked past

him. His voice was a clipped command. I turned and he was reaching inside the pocket of his dark coat. He pulled out a pen and card, flipped it over before I could read it and then wrote something on the back.

"Here." He held it out. "They can help you."

I took it and looked down. On thick, white card, embossed with uncompromising black ink was a name and address:

The Aviary
Mrs Finch
Proprietress
1 St Andrew's Road
London

"Why are you—" I began, but the man was already pushing past me, his hands stuffed in his pockets, his long strides eating up the ground.

"Just go," he growled over his shoulder. "And give them that card." With that, he stalked out of view, his coat flaring out dramatically behind him and I stood alone once more between the stacks, dazed.

"What on earth?" I murmured to myself as I turned the card over in my hands. There, in a scrawling hand, was another message.

Oliver Lockhart sends his regards.

CHAPTER SIX

In fact, I knew the Aviary on St Andrew's Road. It was a haberdasher's, a particularly nice one. I had shopped there several times for buttons and trim for my dresses. I remembered admiring the golden bird cages full of silk flowers hanging from the ceiling, thinking that something similar with fresh flowers would work well for a party. Now that I was reminded of it, I had a client who usually threw a spectacular ball in the summer, and the cages would look perfect hanging in her orangery.

Floristry inspiration aside, the real question was: why

had an extraordinarily handsome and extremely grumpy man thrust a haberdashery owner's business card at me, told me they would help with my situation, and then swirled off like Count Dracula disappearing into the night? (This was, I supposed, not a good analogy because it had been the middle of the day, but there was certainly something of the otherworldly vampire about Oliver Lockhart, and the whole dramatic coat-swirling moment had felt very I'm-about-to-turn-into-a-bat-and-crawl-inside-a-maiden's-window.)

Perhaps it was foolish to go. No, there was no *perhaps* about it. The man was probably a lunatic. Or maybe he wanted to take his petty revenge over the book-dropping incident by sending me on a wild goose chase.

But I went anyway.

The haberdasher's was just as I remembered. Above the door was a sign, painted in curling golden script:

The Aviary
For all a lady requires

It was late afternoon now. The windows gleamed; large glass vessels filled with buttons were arranged on a swathe of velvet, a rainbow explosion of different colours. The display made me think of jewels or jars of sweets – both an appealing prospect. When I pushed the door I recognized the music of the bell, and I felt the same good feeling I got when I entered Bloom's. This was a place that someone cared about, and it showed.

Polished wooden cabinets lined the walls, while ribbons and trims were arranged on stands, making it all too easy to run them through your fingers, to enjoy that seductive slip of silk against your skin. The bird cages I remembered hung from the ceiling, and I smiled at the clever nod to the shop's name. There were no birds though, only silk flowers made from materials you could buy in the shop. In my mind I found myself twisting jasmine round the gold bars, filling them with a spill of crimson roses. You'd get the perfume then too – heady and romantic.

"May I help you?" a voice asked, and I saw that there was a girl standing behind a desk at the back of the shop. She had red hair and wore a dark dress and a white lacy cap and apron. Her smile was easy, and she looked as neat and well cared for as the shop.

"I'm not sure," I said, stepping towards her. "This is probably going to sound peculiar, but a gentleman gave me a card and told me to bring it here—"

"May I see the card?" the girl broke in.

"Of course." I handed it to her.

When she flipped it over and saw the note from Oliver Lockhart, her eyebrows twitched in the faintest hint of surprise. "Would you mind waiting here for a moment?" she asked smoothly.

"Not at all," I replied.

The girl lifted the heavy velvet curtain behind her to reveal a door, which she opened. Beyond the doorway I spied a small hallway with a staircase running steeply up one side. With a quick reassuring smile, the girl slipped through the curtain.

I was left alone to wait. That was no hardship in a place like this. I moved to a small table, examining the lengths of trim laid out on it with pleasure, choosing a braided mossy green velvet and a jaunty cherry-red silk that I knew Simon would hate but that made something inside me sing.

I chose another trim – shell pink this time – as a gift for Daisy. It would make up for me forgetting to collect her library book. (I had been a bit distracted after the almost-murder/run-in with a possible vampire prince.)

"I'm sorry to have kept you." The shop girl reappeared from behind the curtain, her eyes carefully watchful. "I'm afraid Mrs Finch isn't available at the moment, but she'd be happy to meet with you. If you could leave your name and address with me, then someone will be in touch with you to make the arrangements."

"Thank you." I still had no idea who Mrs Finch was or why this meeting was even taking place, but I supposed I had come this far. I wrote down the address of the shop.

"Oh, Bloom's!" the girl exclaimed, already wrapping up my purchases with deft hands. "I love it there. Sometimes I go out of my way just to walk past and peek at the displays. Such beautiful flowers."

It was my turn to smile with pleasure. "Make sure you stop in next time." I fished out one of my own business cards from my reticule. "Give them this and ask the girls for some of the lavender shortbread. It's delicious."

"I will, thank you." With that, she handed me my parcel and we said our goodbyes before I left.

It was only when I was outside again that I realized that Mrs Finch had kept the card that Oliver Lockhart had given me.

And I wondered why I cared that I didn't have it any more.

CHAPTER SEVEN

Late that night I headed out to buy produce for the shop at the flower market, trying not to dwell on my problems, which was easier than I had expected as my mind seemed only too happy to dwell on Oliver Lockhart instead. It had been a strange encounter, brief but compelling. There was something about him – and not only the fact that he was so devastating to look at – that I couldn't put aside. He had been grumpy, almost rude, and yet he'd sent me to the Aviary... I didn't understand it yet, but I felt instinctively that he had tried to help me. It was a puzzle. Something to think about. So I did.

If you didn't get to the flower market by midnight, then you'd find yourself in real trouble. The narrow lanes were so crammed with stalls and carts, as people prepared to barter into the early hours, that by one o'clock in the morning you couldn't move an inch, and selling was already at its height: a frenzied cacophony of sound filling the air as vicious haggling broke out on every corner.

Fortunately, I had been coming here for as long as I could remember, and so Robbie – the boy who took care of our cart – and I were settled in a prime spot the moment the sellers opened for business.

If anything else were needed to wipe away the troubles of the day, then being here would do the trick. There was nowhere like it and I fell quickly into the rhythm of the place, all other thoughts melting away.

Over the last century, the market had grown and grown, until now it stood, sprawled across the centre of the theatre district. It was right next door to the opera house, but we florists knew where the true drama was to be found.

The front of the covered market was like a temple, all graceful stone columns, and the inside – for me, at least – felt like a cathedral, enclosed by a ceiling of soaring glass and iron. The arcade was lined with sellers who loaded their stalls with flowers from local nurseries and further afield. Thanks to the railways and greenhouses, the flower trade had changed significantly since my grandfather's heyday, and now the press of people found themselves in a fairyland of bright hothouse flowers: blooming orchids, feathery ferns and fat, pungent roses. It was something to be proud of, the way that flower selling – after all, such an ancient tradition – was really here at the sharp edge of modernity, changing almost faster than we could keep up with.

The noise was tremendous, and the sounds, the smells, the frantic pace of it all stirred something inside me. Grandfather had been bringing me to the market since I was a young girl and I felt nothing but delight as I left Robbie in our spot, and weaved confidently between the stands, savouring the day's offerings, a bounty laid before me like a feast.

I was making a show of looking over some sweet

tea roses, preparing to grind the price down, when it happened.

A yell went up, an angry roar that had the hairs on the back of my neck standing on end, and then I was shoved aside by a small girl. I saw only a blur of spindly limbs, a thatch of straw-coloured hair, before she was gone, darting into the crowd.

The next shove that I took was more serious. An enormous meaty hand closed round my upper arm, almost throwing me out of the way as the burly mountain of a man who was attached to it pushed past.

"Thieves again." The flower seller sighed, coming round to help me, but I was already on my feet and in pursuit, sweaty palms holding up my skirts as I flew into the sea of people.

The man who had pushed me out of the way was called Scullen, and he sold greasy-looking pies of dubious origin from a stand that he ran with his pugnacious son. He was also a terrible bully with a reputation for violence (a reputation in which he took great pride). No one was foolish enough to steal from him, because the punishment was severe and had absolutely nothing to do with justice or the authorities, and everything to do with those raw-boned fists of his. The girl must not have been here long if she'd made the mistake of filching a pie from Scullen's stand, and she was about to pay a terrible price for that ignorance.

Busy as it was, it was easy to follow Scullen's progress because he stood a head taller than most of the crowd, and from the way he was moving, it was obvious he still had the girl in his sights. I was breathing hard by the time the crush began to thin. With a muttered oath, I saw the girl slip down a darkened alleyway, Scullen gaining on her and still bellowing like an enraged bull.

I sped up, much to the appreciation of one of the street sweepers who wolf-whistled as I flew past. I had no time to do anything but lift my hand in a rude gesture in return as I dived into the shadows.

Just in time.

When I reached them, the girl was sprawled on the ground, her face a pale moon against the cobbles in the light coming from the building behind her, Scullen towering over her like a monster from a fairy tale. The girl let out a whimper of fright. I would put her age anywhere between seven and eleven, and she had the gaunt look of one whose belly had been kept empty for more than one night.

"Stop!" I shouted. Or I tried to shout. My chest was heaving rather spectacularly from the running, and the word came out as more of a wheeze, but it was enough to cause Scullen to swing round.

He had his arm raised, and almost struck me as he spun.

"Miss Bloom," he grunted, his eyes narrowing as he took me in. "Don't know what you're doing here. No place for a lady. I'm handling some business."

His gaze flicked to the girl, who through some instinct had started to crawl in my direction. In Scullen's eyes there was a heat that told its own story. He would hurt the child, and he'd enjoy doing it.

I straightened up, undoing the clasp on my capacious leather handbag, curling my fingers around the small pair of secateurs that I kept in there habitually. They weren't much of a weapon, and I was very aware that my knees and my hands were trembling, but it was better than nothing.

I forced my voice to remain calm and even. "I think there has been some mistake," I said.

The glower on Scullen's face deepened. I was clearly becoming an inconvenience.

"No mistake when there's no-good thievin' bastards about." Scullen spat on the ground next to the girl, who let out another sound of distress.

"But this girl isn't a thief," I said, injecting my tone with surprise.

Scullen's eyes snapped to mine. "Saw her myself. And this is none of your business, you nosy bi—"

"*Mr Scullen*," I snapped frigidly, and it was enough to make him pause in the step he had unthinkingly taken in my direction. "If my employee forgot to pay you for your goods, then I'm sorry. I will rectify the matter immediately."

Hoping I wasn't making a mistake, I let go of the secateurs and instead withdrew a couple of coins.

"I believe this should cover it, with a little extra for the inconvenience, of course." I held the coins out in the palm of my hand.

Scullen's glare moved between my hand and the girl.

I could see the dilemma playing out on his face. He wanted the money, but his blood was up now. He wanted the fight too. He was like a shark moving in for the kill, and I saw, too clearly, the realization dawn that he could have both.

Should have gone for the secateurs, I thought as a slow, cruel smile spread across the man's face. I knew a moment of utter helplessness, a feeling I was not familiar with, and one I didn't care for at all.

"Is there a problem?" a cool voice asked from behind me, and I swung round to see a slight, well-dressed woman emerging into our pool of light.

She was around my age, with light brown hair and a sweet face dusted with a smattering of freckles. She stood easily, poised, but there was a sharpness in her dark eyes. The sight of her squaring up to Scullen would have been laughable if the moment wasn't so terrifying.

"More meddlesome baggage," Scullen rumbled. "Why don't you interfering females just f—"

"I believe my wife asked if there was a problem," came another voice. This one was clipped and cultured, and it belonged to a man of such golden beauty that I swear he illuminated the dingy alleyway with the force of his good looks alone. He was also built like a Greek god, and more than matched Scullen in height. His tone was frostily polite, but his face was set in firm, dangerous lines.

Clearly deciding the odds had shifted, Scullen spat on the ground again, snatched the coins from my hand and stomped away, muttering a lot of uncomplimentary words under his breath.

The woman let out a huff of annoyance. "I had it under control."

The man chuckled, his arm going round her waist. "I knew that, and you knew that, but I thought I'd just expedite the process."

I was distracted from this interesting scene by the young girl, who had scrambled to her feet and was about to take to her heels again. I wrapped my hand round her arm and felt her flinch.

"No, no," I said gently, removing my fingers. "You're not in trouble. What's your name?"

She looked up at me with wide brown eyes brimming with suspicion.

"They call me Scout, miss," she said finally.

"Well, Scout, as a general rule around here, it's not a good idea to try to steal from Scullen."

"He's a bad man," Scout said, rubbing her hand absently along her arm where I'd touched her.

"Yes," I agreed. "And I would keep out of his way if I were you. Now, do you know Bloom's on Oxford Street?"

If she was surprised by the change of subject, she didn't show it. "Place with all them flowers?" She pursed her lips.

I nodded. "That's right. Be there in the morning at eight sharp. Ask for Suzy."

"Why?" The suspicion was back.

"Because you need a job, and I need a delivery girl who is fast on her feet."

Scout's head dipped so that I couldn't see her face. "S'pose I could do that," she said gruffly, "if the price is right."

"Good. Mind you aren't late." I tucked a coin into her hand. "Now go and get yourself something to eat … from a different stall, I think."

Scout flashed me a brief, wary look, then dashed

off. I hoped she would come to the shop, but at least for tonight she would be well fed.

I turned to the two strangers who were watching in silence.

"Thank you for your help," I said, trying not to be too dazzled by the handsomeness of the man before me. "I think that was about to turn ugly."

"Horrible man." The girl sighed. "You should have let me punch him." This was directed at her husband. "Still" – her eyes narrowed thoughtfully – "I suppose there are more *creative* ways to deal with such bullies..."

She turned her attention to me, and the calculating look dropped from her face, her expression crinkling into a grin that was pure mischief. "I'm Izzy." She held out her hand for me to shake. "This lovely bit of window dressing is my husband, Max."

Max's eyes lit with fond amusement as I shook Izzy's hand and then his.

"Marigold," I said.

"Oh, we know." Izzy's look was measuring. "I've come with an invitation."

"An invitation?" The adrenaline from my

confrontation with Scullen was wearing off, and I was starting to feel dizzy.

"From Mrs Finch." Izzy's smile grew. "What time can you be free tomorrow?"

CHAPTER EIGHT

The next day I was back at the Aviary, wondering just what, precisely, I was getting myself into. This time, the red-headed girl behind the counter greeted me with a grin of recognition.

"You're to go straight up," she said, holding the velvet curtain to one side. "Just follow the stairs to the top; you can't miss it."

When I hesitated for a moment, the girl's smile softened. "It will only be a short meeting. We know you're busy. I think you'll be glad you came when you hear what Mrs Finch has to say."

Still not sure what to think, I nodded, then I stepped past the curtain and began the climb.

The stairwell was bare and dark, though it smelled pleasantly of lavender. When I reached the top, I was met with another door: this one had a brass sign nailed to it with no words at all, only the image of a small bird.

I knocked.

"Come in," a woman's voice called, and I turned the handle.

I had been expecting some sort of office, but the room into which I stepped was more like the inside of a gentleman's clubhouse. An enormous chimney breast dominated the centre of the space and groups of moss-green chairs and velvet sofas the colour of violets were arranged cosily around the double-sided fireplace. There were also tables holding chess sets, bookcases brimming untidily with books and periodicals, and a slightly battered piano in one corner. The whole room felt like an invitation from a host who cared only about warmth and comfort.

My attention turned to the walls. They had been

painted white, but someone had covered them in tall, twining murals of plants and flowers. I saw splashy flame lilies, saw-toothed succulents, dancing lady orchids, delicate pink-tinged caladium leaves – all so beautifully rendered that they seemed to move, rippling across the paint.

Along the back wall, the flowers vanished, replaced instead with the words:

> *I am no bird; and no*
> *net ensnares me:*
> *I am a free human being*
> *with an independent will.*

It was painted in tall, bold black letters. I knew the quote – *Jane Eyre*. It stirred something inside me: not comfort but something sharper, spikier, something that felt like those plants – hot and alive.

I was so distracted by the artwork that I didn't notice the other people in the room until someone cleared their throat behind me.

Whipping round, I saw Izzy, the young lady from last

night, standing beside another woman. This must be Mrs Finch.

I don't know what I had expected, given the strange way her name had suddenly popped up in my life, but it wasn't the woman in front of me. She was – I would guess – in her late thirties, extremely pretty, and we shared the same soft, generous figure. She was clad in a shimmering blue silk gown that I coveted immediately, and she dressed in a way that highlighted and accentuated her ample curves, drawing the eye to the dip of her waist, the spread of her hips. She was not even trying to blend into the background. I wondered what Simon would think about that.

Her light brown hair was pulled tidily back, and her face was dominated by a pair of eyes the same colour as her dress. Those eyes were focused on me now, and despite her softness and the feminine prettiness of her appearance, her gaze was direct, almost fierce in its concentration. I felt myself standing straighter under her scrutiny, and although she didn't actually smile, there was amusement in her expression.

"You must be Mrs Finch?" I asked, moving forward with my hand outstretched.

"Yes." Mrs Finch took it, squeezed my fingers. "And you are Miss Bloom. I understand you've already met Her Grace, the Duchess of Roxton."

I blinked. "I don't..."

"She means me," Izzy said with a sigh. "But don't let the title throw you. It's new and I'm not at all used to it either. I believe Mrs Finch is teasing you. And me."

The woman in question only smirked.

"Oh – I mean, yes, Your Grace," I said, stumbling over my words. Izzy, the woman who had stood with me in a dingy alleyway last night was a *duchess*? Wait – did that mean Max was a duke?

"Definitely not 'Your Grace'." Izzy grimaced. "We don't go in for ceremony at the Aviary. Izzy is fine, thank you."

"Izzy," I repeated, dazed.

"Why don't we sit and have some tea?" Mrs Finch gestured to one of the clusters of armchairs, and I noticed a tea service set up on a table between them. "I find that matters always seem so much less awkward when there's tea. I think it's because it gives you something to do with your hands."

I managed a smile at that. "Tea would be lovely."

Izzy and Mrs Finch both seemed utterly at ease, so I decided I wasn't going to let the combination of this bizarre, clandestine meeting and the casual introduction of the upper echelons of the aristocracy throw me either.

"We were surprised to receive your card," Mrs Finch said, once the tea had been served.

She was right: it was better to have something to do with my hands, and I swirled the silver teaspoon, slowly dissolving the lump of sugar in my amber tea.

"May I ask how you are acquainted with Oliver Lockhart?" she continued.

"I'm not," I said, tapping the spoon gently against the side of my cup and laying it on my saucer. Not for the first time, my mind flashed to the man in question. In fact, his sulky, beautiful face had popped into my thoughts with worrying frequency over the last twenty-four hours. "I met him yesterday. At least, I assume it was him. The gentleman didn't introduce himself."

"Tall, fantastically handsome, stalks about like an ill-tempered cat?" Izzy lifted her brows.

"Yes." I laughed at the perfect description. "That was him."

"But you only met yesterday?" Mrs Finch's question was cool.

"At the library." I nodded. "It wasn't exactly an auspicious meeting. I accidentally dropped a book on his head, and he was – understandably – displeased."

"I'm surprised you ended the encounter on cordial terms," said Izzy. "Oliver is not exactly known for being gracious."

"I'm not sure what terms we left things on," I admitted. "But I … poured out my problems to him, and he gave me the card, sending me here."

"Hmmmm." Mrs Finch tilted her head thoughtfully. "Perhaps you could tell us about the problems you shared with Mr Lockhart?"

I hesitated at that, my teacup lifted halfway to my lips.

"I realize it is a strange request." Mrs Finch sat forward, her voice gentler now. "You don't know us, but I assure you that you were sent here for a good reason. Whatever it is that troubles you may be something that we can assist with."

"I truly don't see how," I said doubtfully, but after looking into their faces for another long moment, I decided to trust my instincts and lay out the whole sorry tale.

Neither of them interrupted until I reached the end of my story, and they showed no sign of shock regarding its contents. Instead, they shared a glance I found hard to read and Mrs Finch sat back in her seat, her eyes half closed – an expression that was distinctly feline.

"Geoffrey Earnshaw," she said meditatively. "The name is familiar. Though I don't believe we have run into him directly … yet?" This question was directed at Izzy.

"Not as far as I'm aware, but Sylla would know better than me." Izzy pursed her lips. "A man of his character however… It should be almost too easy to find something he would rather not be found."

"That much is certainly true." Mrs Finch turned back to me. "Miss Bloom, I believe we will be able to help with this matter, though it will take us a day or two to gather the information that we need."

I must have looked as baffled as I felt.

"Perhaps," Izzy said slowly, "you should tell Marigold more about the Aviary now?"

Mrs Finch assessed me for another long moment. "I think you're right," she said at last.

"The shop?" I said. "It's lovely."

"The shop is only a small part of our business," Mrs Finch said. "The true work of the Aviary is conducted upstairs."

"Here?" I asked. "It is some sort of … society for ladies?" I hazarded. "It reminds me of a gentlemen's club – I have visited one or two to attend to the flowers."

"It is something like a society, I suppose." The cat-like look was back on her face. "The Aviary is an organization run by women, for women. The work we do takes on many different forms, but in its broadest sense we act as a layer of protection that is not always provided by the law. Take your situation, for instance." She gestured to me. "You find yourself at the whim of a dishonourable man. Your home and your livelihood are dependent upon his goodwill. While the proposition he made is abhorrent, it is not something that the law can prevent. Earnshaw has every right to expel you and your family from your business and your home if you don't comply with his demands. We at the Aviary take issue with that." There was a dangerous spark in her eye. "No, we do not care for that at all."

I felt something shimmer inside me in response to her words. The anger and the frustration I felt at my situation rushed to the surface.

"I can't say I care for it either," I said tightly. "Yet I don't see what can be done about it. Had I married Simon, then perhaps..."

"Had you married Simon, then the business you have built would have belonged to him." Izzy's words were heated. "You would have married for duty to a man who is clearly a colossal—" Mrs Finch delicately cleared her throat. "Right, not the point," Izzy muttered. "The point *is* that we can help you. And when we do, you won't have to give up the shop either."

Something thumped in my chest. "What do you mean?"

"I told you that our work is about protecting women," Mrs Finch said. "We are most easily described as an investigative agency. Women come to us when they have a problem that requires solving. We have found that the most effective way of doing so is often to acquire ... *leverage* over the men who are threatening them."

"Some people might call it blackmail," Izzy said sunnily. "If they were being vulgar."

She and Mrs Finch shared a smile, and I felt as though I had missed an inside joke.

"You're going to blackmail Mr Earnshaw?" I said slowly, my eyes moving between them. "If we're being vulgar?"

The smile on Mrs Finch's face blossomed. "Yes."

"How?"

"The Aviary is comprised of a network of agents who we call the Finches. These are women who come from all walks of life and who possess different skills. They work in secret." Mrs Finch inclined her head towards Izzy. "The duchess is one such agent."

"Finches are split into smaller groups – typically groups of four, so that we can be assigned to cover different cases," Izzy explained. "These groups are called charms. I recently took charge of my own charm." She said the words with obvious pride. "One of our charms will investigate Mr Earnshaw through whichever means seem the most appropriate, and we will then apply pressure to him so that he meets our demands."

"Do you mean to tell me that *you*" – I pointed to Izzy – "the *Duchess of Roxton* are part of a shadowy organization of women that blackmails men?"

"Well, I wasn't a duchess when I started, but in a nutshell, yes. That's it."

"But that's..." I trailed off for a moment, assaulted by too many feelings at once. "Incredible!" I finished finally, with a laugh.

Izzy beamed at me, and something flickered between us, a shared moment of glee. I couldn't believe such a group of women existed, but I found already, even without proof of what they could do, that I was glad to hear it.

"There are only a handful of people who know about Isobel's involvement," Mrs Finch said. She wasn't smiling any more and there was steel in her voice now. "It is a secret we are relying upon you to keep."

"Why did you tell me?" I asked. "You didn't have to. I'd never have realized who Izzy was."

The two women exchanged yet another look, and again I got the distinct feeling I was missing something.

"When you arrived with Oliver's card, you piqued our interest," Mrs Finch said finally.

"Oliver is … important to us," Izzy added. "We consider him a friend. Though I'm sure he would object to the description."

"And so we looked into you, Marigold Bloom. We had someone follow you." Mrs Finch nodded to Izzy. "We liked what we found."

I didn't know whether to be annoyed or pleased by this information. "Thank you, I think."

"As a matter of fact, I had already taken something of an interest in Bloom's." Mrs Finch leaned back in her chair. "You frequently employ women who may otherwise struggle to find employment."

I jolted in surprise. The fact that Bloom's often hired women with backgrounds that others might find … *unsavoury* was not common knowledge. Scout was hardly the first employee I had taken off the street. I pursed my lips. "My employees' past is their business and no one else's," I said firmly.

Something like approval flickered in Mrs Finch's eyes. "You are a hard worker who has built something extraordinary using your skill and brains," Mrs Finch continued. "You are loyal to your family. Your work takes you to many … interesting locations around the city."

"That is true, I suppose," I said slowly.

"You are a keen businesswoman too. Your accounts are perfectly balanced," Mrs Finch mused, and I didn't even bother wondering how she knew that. "You have a good eye when it comes to your clients," she continued. "There doesn't seem to be much trouble with extracting payment on time."

"I tend to know if a customer will be a problem," I admitted with a shrug.

"You read them well." Mrs Finch nodded. "And you're a saleswoman: you're good with people, with getting them to talk, to open up to you."

I thought about what she said and knew it was true. It wasn't only in business either. How often had Simon criticized me for precisely that, for wanting to talk to people, to find out about them, for being too friendly, too interested?

"I saw what you did in that alley last night," Izzy reminded me.

"Nearly got myself killed, you mean?"

"You protected that young girl," Izzy said quietly. "I

saw the man who chased her. If you hadn't intervened, I truly think she might be dead. You read his intentions. And you offered her what she needed too."

My stomach lurched. It wasn't as though I didn't know that, but I hadn't wanted to look at the idea head on. "I hardly think he was being subtle about his intentions."

"You ran in, unarmed and untrained, ready to defend someone in need. You measured his response and initially tried to dispel the situation with tact and diplomacy, which showed calm, clear thinking under pressure," Izzy continued.

"I wasn't unarmed," I said weakly. "I had my secateurs."

This startled a laugh from Mrs Finch. "Yes, Izzy," she said softly. "I think you might be right about this one."

Izzy sat back, looking smug.

"Right about what?" I asked.

"That Marigold Bloom has the makings of a Finch," Mrs Finch said. "That I should offer you a job."

CHAPTER NINE

I spent the next two days in a trance of indecision, thrown by Mrs Finch's offer of a job at her agency. She told me to take some time to think about it, and I had been doing little else.

I was still thinking about it in the back room at work when Grandfather's head popped round the door.

As much as I loved the shop, this room and the garden on to which it backed was where my heart lived. I might have convinced everyone, including myself, that adding our own small garden was to the advantage of the business – it even had the benefit of being true – but had it not made us a penny I would have pushed for it anyway.

Selfishly, I had carved out this tiny green space for myself. A place I could have my fingers in the dirt. A place where I loved to tip my face towards the sunshine, basking in it as much as any flower, and where even the grey London rain became something vital and life-giving.

"Are those the early rose cuttings?" Grandfather asked, interested. I stood at the potting table, carefully labelling the tiny cuttings I had planted, ready to be placed in the greenhouse. At my back, the doors to the garden stood open, spilling the pale light of spring across the stone floor. A gentle breeze ruffled my hair, lifting the heavy curls away from my neck. I wiped my hands on the apron I wore over my dress.

"Yes, I have high hopes for these beauties," I said. "But next week we can begin the cross-pollination on the new hybrids." I felt a tingle at this. Twenty years earlier, a gardener called Henry Bennett had found a way to create new breeds of roses by meticulously transferring pollen from one flower to another, producing seeds that combined aspects of both blooms.

It was only possible thanks to the constant warmth of the greenhouse, and it was an exciting undertaking – an experiment with unpredictable results: whether the seeds would thrive in the first instance, and then which features would be taken from each of the flowers involved. I found it fascinating.

"Well," Grandfather said, "as I've said to you before, Mari, don't run away with yourself, investing too much time or effort into it. I'll admit it's interesting work – but we'll never be able to grow on the scale of the nurserymen, so there is not much point in distracting ourselves from the running of the shop."

His words were like being doused in cold water.

"I won't disturb you," he continued. "I just wanted to let you know that I had a strange visit from Geoffrey Earnshaw this morning."

I stilled. "Mr Earnshaw?" I murmured. "What did he want?"

"He wanted to assure me that the change in circumstances between you and that good-for-nothing son of his..." Here Grandfather sniffed. He had been less than impressed by Simon breaking off the engagement, and I had only barely managed to talk him out of challenging Simon to fisticuffs. As a young man, Grandfather had apparently trained with Gentleman Jackson himself, although he became hazy if pushed for details on his illustrious fighting career.

"That disgraceful young turnip," Grandfather continued with a growl.

"What exactly did Mr Earnshaw say?" I prompted gently, my heart hammering.

"Oh, yes." The anger cleared from Grandfather's face, replaced with a puzzled frown. "He said that he didn't want us to be worrying about the rent. That as a gesture of goodwill he was even going to reduce it."

"Reduce it?" I managed, stunned.

"Least he can do in the circumstances. I have to admit I didn't think old Geoffrey Earnshaw had that sort of decency in him. And that's not all..."

"No?" I said weakly.

"He's offered us a twenty-year lease with the rate set, all legal-like. Now what do you make of that?" Grandfather tucked his fingers into his waistcoat pockets and rocked back on his heels.

"Twenty years!" I exclaimed. "But that's ... wonderful. An incredible offer. Even better than we'd have got if—"

"Better than if you'd married the turnip," Grandfather finished succinctly. "And I tell you, Mari, I'll be thanking my lucky stars you avoided that fate for the rest of my days, I truly will."

"Well," I said mechanically, still trying to digest the news. "He didn't..." I hesitated. "Mr Earnshaw didn't make any kind of demands?"

"Not a thing," Grandfather said. "Man was pale as a ghost, begging my forgiveness, practically crawling. Don't know what came over him."

I did. I felt a shiver tingle up and down my spine, a wide smile growing across my face. The Aviary had triumphed.

Part of me (quite a big part, I had to admit) had doubted it. As much as I *wanted* to believe what Izzy and Mrs Finch had told me, the whole thing had just seemed so ... far-fetched. And yet here we were; the Aviary had clearly found something Mr Earnshaw didn't want found and applied pressure to fix my problem. It had worked – exactly as they had told me it would.

I felt dizzy. The relief, as it finally seeped in, was enormous.

"Mari?" Suzy appeared in the doorway. "Can you come out here? There's a delivery for you."

"That's fine, Suzy – you can sign for it," I said.

"That's just it. Someone gave it to Scout to deliver to you. They said it had to go to you directly." Suzy's voice was uncertain.

"They gave it to Scout?" I asked. I had been pleased when the girl had turned up promptly the morning after our encounter with Scullen and accepted the job at Bloom's. So far she had proved a hard worker, and it was a relief to see more colour in her cheeks and that haunted, hungry look easing from her eyes. "What is it?"

"Well, it's curious..." Suzy gave a bewildered chuckle. "It's flowers."

"Flowers?" I blinked.

"Why would someone send *you* flowers?" asked Grandfather.

"I suppose we'll find out." I quickly untied the back of my apron, slipping it off and hanging it up before following them out to the front of the shop. It was quiet, with no customers currently browsing – only Scout, standing in the middle of the shop, clutching an enormous bouquet of flowers.

"What on earth...?" I moved closer, reaching out with my fingers to touch the petals of a tiny starry white flower.

"Edelweiss?" Grandfather bent closer. "Where has someone got hold of that in March?"

"It's a very ... *unusual* bouquet," Suzy said diplomatically.

She was not wrong. It was a curious thing, full of greenery and flowers that didn't quite go together. Not unless you spoke their language anyway. I lingered for a moment, cataloguing the contents in my mind:

Laurel. *Laurus*. Meaning: victory, success.

Edelweiss. *Leontopodium*. Meaning: courage and daring.

Clematis. *Clematis*. Meaning: ingenuity and cleverness.

Fern. *Adiantum*. Meaning: secrecy.

And finally: Dahlia. *Dahlia*. Meaning: commitment.

A laugh escaped my lips at the message. The Aviary

were celebrating a job well done, and now they wanted to know if I had considered their job offer.

"Weighs a bloomin' ton," Scout huffed, and I rushed forward to take it from her, but she pulled back out of my reach. "No, no." She shook her head. "She said first I have to ask if you'll take it with your right hand or your left."

Grandfather frowned. "*Who* said so, Scout?"

Scout's eyes darted to mine. "Lady from the other night. She gave me a shilling to bring these to you, but she said I have to go back and tell her if you took it with your left hand or your right." She rolled her eyes at this and muttered something under her breath about toffs and their strange ways.

"What lady is this, Mari?" Grandfather looked increasingly baffled.

"Just a friend," I replied. "It's a little joke of ours."

But it wasn't really. It was a proposal and, in the language of flowers, taking the flower in your right hand meant yes, and your left hand meant no. I appreciated the attention to detail.

I also appreciated what the Aviary had done for me

and my family. I thought about that overwhelming rush of relief I had felt only minutes ago. I could help someone else feel that way.

Beyond that, something else stirred too. The same feeling I'd had in the garden, a feeling of space to grow and truly *be*. It was adventure, the promise of *more*.

"Thank you, Scout," I said, finally taking the bouquet from her. I felt the smile spreading across my face. "You can tell the lady I took it with my right hand."

CHAPTER TEN

The third time I arrived at the Aviary in the space of a single week, I felt a curious mixture of nerves and excitement. The summons I had received from Mrs Finch had been brief and to the point, asking me to come late in the afternoon – this was usually my free time when I would sleep before going to the market. I supposed that running a secret agency of female detectives meant the task of working out my schedule was fairly easy, but I was still impressed by her efficiency.

On this visit I found myself taken even higher up in

the building – to the floor above the salon and into a well-ordered office that felt warm and inviting, lined with shelves full of books and various interesting objects – vases, paintings, a red jewel in a small glass case. An iron ring hung from a hook in the wall, and while I wasn't an expert, I'd guess that the long thin pieces of metal hanging from it were lock picks.

Mrs Finch sat behind an enormous desk, sifting through a stack of important-looking papers. The red-headed shop girl I had met before perched in a tall, straight-backed chair, and jumped to her feet when I entered.

"You're here." She grinned. "I'm glad you said yes. I thought that you would. I'm Maud, by the way; I should have introduced myself earlier." She held out a hand to me, and I shook it.

"You're one of the Finches too?" I asked.

"Oh yes, everyone who works in the shop is a Finch," Maud replied. "It makes life much easier, having an employer who doesn't mind about you coming and going."

I was relieved to hear that not everyone who worked

for the Aviary was a duchess – that some of them at least were more like me, and that they had to balance the Aviary with other work.

"I'm in your charm, actually," Maud continued. "They explained the charms to you?"

I nodded. "Four people who work together."

"That's right. We've been down to three since Izzy started running her own group, and it's a relief they finally found someone to fill in."

"Why don't you take Marigold through to the lab and see if you can extract Winnie while we wait for Sylla to arrive?" Mrs Finch said, not lifting her eyes from the papers in front of her.

Maud scoffed. "Wish us luck with that. Win has been muttering something about electrical pulses all morning; I haven't got any sense out of her yet today. Still" – she turned to me – "might as well give you the tour, now that you're going to be one of us."

Before she could herd me back through the door, I stepped towards the desk and dropped the small bouquet I was carrying next to Mrs Finch's papers.

Her gaze flicked to the flowers and then up to me.

Her mouth softened into that almost-smile. "Sweet peas? How lovely. Now, let me see if I remember..." She tapped a finger against the desk. "Thank you for a lovely time?"

I nodded. "That's right. Or in this case, simply thank you. Thank you for what you did for me. And for my family."

"It's what we do," Mrs Finch said, eyeing me steadily. The words carried an extra weight, and I knew now that the *we* included me.

"Go on," she said with a shooing gesture. "Go and get Winnie before she blows something up."

"Is she joking?" I asked Maud in a low voice as we left the room.

"Oh no," Maud replied cheerfully. "Win blows things up at least twice a month."

On this reassuring note, she led me back out on to the landing and down a narrow corridor.

"That's just a storage cupboard," she said, gesturing to the door beside Mrs Finch's office. "Then this is the training room." She pushed open the next door along.

I opened my mouth to ask what sort of training,

but stopped when I took in the scene in front of me. It looked as though I'd be gaining a better understanding of Grandfather's boxing slang, after all. In the middle of the room was a small roped-off boxing ring. Leather punching bags hung from the ceiling on iron chains. My eyes widened when I noticed the large glass cabinet against one of the walls.

"Are those ... swords?" I asked faintly.

Maud's cheerful demeanour didn't slip. "Fencing foils mostly. The odd sabre. I take it you don't fence yet? You'll learn. You'll learn a bit of everything here. Mrs Finch has some of the best instructors in the country to give us lessons. Fencing, boxing, knife-fighting..."

"Fighting ... with knives?" I managed, the words an embarrassing squeak.

"Much easier to carry about than a sword," Maud pointed out practically. "What about shooting? Can you shoot?"

"No," I said, feeling as though I was already an enormous failure. But, really, how many young women knew how to win a knife fight or shoot? I was a florist for goodness' sake; I could tell you the flowering season for carnations or when to deadhead your roses, but I'd hardly been filling my non-existent spare time with target practice.

"Not to worry," Maud said, clearly reading my expression. "Most of the girls don't know how to do these things when they arrive. Within six months you'll be able to disarm a man and neatly slice out his kidney should the need present itself."

I didn't know whether to be thrilled or deeply disturbed by this information.

Both, I decided. *Definitely both.*

"And this down here is Winnie's lab. Winnie's in our charm too." Maud pulled me along to the next room.

This, it turned out, was a fully working science laboratory, and a slim, pale-haired young woman stood at the long wooden work surface that ran the length of the room. She was bent over a microscope, which she was using with intense concentration.

The walls above the work surface were piled high with hefty-looking scientific tomes, and I spotted several I had read on the subject of botany. The rest of the walls held mahogany cabinets similar to the ones in the haberdasher's downstairs, only these were labelled with the names of various chemicals.

"Win?" Maud said loudly. "Win, Marigold Bloom is here." She repeated herself three times, and finally the woman looked up, blinking huge blue eyes behind wire-rimmed glasses, as though she was waking from a nap.

"Maud?" she murmured. "When did you get here?"

"Ages ago." Maud laughed, stepping forward and rubbing gently at a smudge on Winnie's cheek. There was something in that touch – something tender and easy that spoke to a relationship that went well beyond friendship. *Lovers*, I thought.

Winnie leaned into Maud's hand and looked at her adoringly. "You should have given me a shake."

"And risk blowing up our newest recruit?" Maud teased.

At this, Winnie's eyes turned to me. "You must be Miss Bloom!"

"Marigold," I corrected her, reaching out to shake her hand, which was soft and white but stained with black ink. "Mari, usually."

"The botanist," Winnie said.

"Florist," I replied.

"Your family owns Bloom's, don't they? I saw some fascinating hybrids on display in a friend's home from there last year. Would they have been your work?"

"Yes, I'm interested in breeding new roses. It gives us a competitive edge with our clients."

Winnie nodded. "A botanist then. And do you use Bennett's methods?"

I started in surprise. "Yes." I nodded, identifying a fellow enthusiast by the gleam in Winnie's eyes. "Although recently there has been some interesting research out of—"

"France," Winnie cut me off, her excitement clear. "I know, I read only the other day—"

"That's enough, you two," Maud broke in. "I can tell there's going to be plenty for you to discuss but we have other priorities at the moment."

Winnie beamed at me. "I must say I'm pleased to have someone to talk to about my experiments with the healing properties of plants ... and their potential use as weapons too."

"Poisons, do you mean?" I asked, intrigued. "Because

I've been focusing on herbal remedies, but—"

"Stop! Stop!" Maud laughed. "Sylla will be waiting and you know how she is."

Winnie made a quick sound of agreement at this, and the two of them ushered me out of the room.

We returned to Mrs Finch's office, where we found the final member of my new charm deep in conversation with Mrs Finch.

And just like that, any small amount of confidence I had felt grow during my brief conversation with Winnie wilted.

"Ahh, Marigold, let me introduce the leader of your charm – Sylla Banaji," Mrs Finch said.

I blinked. I knew Sylla Banaji. Well, I knew *of* her. Most people who came into contact with high society or the newspapers did.

The daughter of Lady Anne Stanton and Sir Dinshaw Banaji (she a member of a prominent family whose aristocratic roots can be traced back to the Norman conquest, he the Bombay-born, Oxford-educated, close personal friend of the Prince of Wales), Sylla was practically royalty. She was famous among the society gossips, an imperious beauty with a large following. Izzy may have been a duchess, but her unassuming manner had disarmed me. Sylla had all the regal bearing you'd expect of the queen herself.

I felt as though I should drop into a ridiculous curtsey but forced myself to stand straight under her scrutiny. And there was plenty of that.

Sylla stood in her beautiful ice-blue gown and eyed me the same way I scrutinized flowers at the market – weighing up if I was worth the asking price.

"So you're Izzy's florist," she said finally. "I suppose we shall see what can be made of you."

With that, she dropped gracefully into a chair, leaving Maud, Winnie and I to perch on the long, battered chesterfield sofa that took up one wall of the study. I exhaled slowly, knowing that I had just about scraped through some sort of test.

Mrs Finch settled herself behind her desk.

"As you know, we have been on the lookout for a new recruit to take Isobel's place in the charm." Mrs Finch twirled a pen between her fingers. "I feel confident we have found that person in Marigold. She has a unique set of skills that I think will add much to our organization."

I felt myself straighten at that, even as Sylla made a small scoffing sound.

"To begin, Mari, we offer all new members a six-month probationary period, during which they undertake any training we deem necessary – shooting, fighting, lock picking, basic medical skills, et cetera," Mrs Finch continued, as off-hand as if she were discussing the weather rather than arming me with weaponry. "During this period, the charm will take on smaller-scale jobs."

Sylla gave a disgruntled murmur at this, and Mrs Finch's eyes snapped to her. "A new recruit must be trained, Sylla. As *you* were."

Sylla gave an elegant shrug. "I certainly didn't require half a year before I could be put into the field."

"Yes you did," Mrs Finch replied neutrally. "And we will extend Marigold the same courtesy. Now." She turned to me. "You must have questions."

"Thousands," I said, glancing nervously at Sylla. "But I suppose the one weighing heaviest on me is how I will fit all this in. I have a business to run. My hours are not precisely my own, you see."

"Many of the Aviary's agents have other commitments. There is always a solution." Mrs Finch steepled her fingers. "Our suggestion is that Izzy, as the new Duchess of Roxton, will open an account with Bloom's. An *extremely* lucrative account that will require your personal attention and availability. And that will also account for your new salary." At this, Mrs Finch named a figure that had my jaw falling open.

Winnie and Sylla seemed unmoved, but Maud met my eye with a knowing smirk.

"Of course, this will mean you relinquishing some of your duties at the shop, delegating to others. Do you feel comfortable with that? It is no small thing for a woman to have built up the business you have, Marigold."

I thought about that. She was right: giving up some of my control at the shop would be difficult, but the challenge that the Aviary represented felt like an opportunity I hadn't even known I was waiting for. "I have employees I can trust to take on more responsibility." My mind went instantly to Suzy. "And with the increase from this ... *new account* ... I could even hire another if need be."

"If that is the case, please inform me," Mrs Finch said crisply. "The Aviary will absorb any cost in that area."

It seemed that working for the Aviary was also going to help Bloom's grow too. It felt almost miraculous given the state of affairs only days ago.

"I know that Izzy is a duchess, but will people really believe she needs Marigold running around at all hours on some sort of flower emergency?" Winnie said, wrinkling her nose.

I laughed. "That part is absolutely foolproof. You wouldn't believe some of the requests we get from the aristocracy, and the higher up they are, the more eccentric they can be. A duchess with a personal florist on retainer for all hours of the day and night? If anything, she'll set the fashion." An idea occurred to me. "And as part of the cover, I'll make sure her house is full of beautiful arrangements."

That may well end up bringing more business our way too, I thought. My mind raced ahead. If we did well, perhaps I'd be able to convince Grandfather to retire fully. He and Mother and Daisy could have a holiday – somewhere relaxing outside the city, with clean sea air, where he could get strong and healthy again... I wondered whether I might be able to drop them a small hint as to the truth of our good fortune.

"Your work at the Aviary must be kept secret, Marigold. You will not be able to reveal the truth to anyone else, not even your family," Mrs Finch said with that strange ability of hers to know just what I was thinking.

I twisted my hands in my lap. Here was the hardest part of the bargain. "I am not terribly good at lying," I admitted.

"You will learn," Sylla said, her words brooking no argument.

"I know it's necessary," I said quietly, "but lying to my family ... I've never really done that before."

Sylla propped her elbow on the arm of her chair and rested her chin in her hands. Her dark eyes were sharp on my face. "Really?" she asked softly. "You didn't pretend that you were pleased to be engaged to that fool, Simon Earnshaw? You haven't protected them from hard realities about the business? Made difficult choices alone to spare their feelings?"

"I – I—" I stammered over this. It seemed that Sylla knew it all. "Those things were small omissions, for their own good."

"I believe your honesty is an admirable quality." Sylla leaned back in the chair, watching me. "But the work we do here is vital. It is not hyperbole to suggest that the Aviary saves lives. In all things we must measure the cost against the reward – you should understand this – you are a businesswoman, after all. Keeping secrets from your family may be difficult." Here, something like pain flickered across her expression, though it passed quickly. "However, those secrets are for their safety, as much as the safety of those we work to protect. You will lie because it is the right thing to do."

"Is it worth it?" I asked, looking at the women in front of me.

"Yes," Maud said instantly.

"Yes." Winnie's hand pressed mine.

"Absolutely." Sylla spoke the word with utter conviction.

Mrs Finch was watching us all closely. "What is your next question, Marigold?" she asked.

I took a deep breath, met her eyes and saw the spark burning there. Something settled over me then, a curious feeling of calm.

"Where do we begin?" I asked.

PART TWO

London
Almost six months later

CHAPTER ELEVEN

I may have misjudged this, I thought as I shouldered the weight of the unconscious gentleman who was draped against me in the stairwell of the gambling den.

"Now, here's a fair prospect," the man slurred suddenly, briefly raising his head and gawping down the front of my gown. "Got a few coins to spend on a pretty thing like you. Show you a verrrry nice time." His watery blue eyes lifted to mine, and he scrunched them closed for a moment before opening them and looking at me expectantly.

"Are you ... trying to wink?" I huffed, adjusting his weight.

His meaty fingers reached for the lace-edged mask that was tied around my eyes, the kind that were worn by the female guests who came to gamble and enjoy themselves here at the Penny, and I glared at him. "Stop that right now."

"Is he awake again?" Maud asked, appearing beside me.

"Got a friend?" the man guffawed, delighted. "Two lovely ladies just for me. My lucky night. Told 'em all it was my lucky night, didn't I?"

"You mean before you lost almost a hundred pounds at cards?" Maud muttered. "Oh yes, very lucky."

Maud inserted herself under his other armpit, relieving some of the burden. Calvin Scrimshaw was not a light man. Nor was he a good one. As was becoming ever more apparent as his hand roamed across my backside. I twisted as best as I could, smacking it away.

"We need to get him up to Joe's office," Maud said in a low voice. "It's gone midnight. Sylla and Win are waiting."

A long, low snore escaped from Scrimshaw's lips, as

his body sagged into unconsciousness again, and Maud and I struggled to keep him upright, my feet sliding in my thin silk slippers as his head came to rest, pillowed on the ample cleavage revealed by my dress.

"Mari, love," a rough, amused voice came from behind us. "What are you doing in such an interesting predicament? Don't you know this is a respectable establishment?"

"Ash!" I panted, too relieved to bother coming up with a witty retort. "Give us a hand, will you? Sylla and Win are waiting upstairs, and I don't know how we're going to get him up there."

Ash was one of the owners of the Lucky Penny, the gambling den we were in. The man was a lovable rogue, a well-mannered scoundrel, and a friend to the Aviary. A couple of years older than me, with his overlong dark hair, square, unshaven jaw and gold earrings, he looked like a wickedly handsome pirate – and he drank and flirted like one too.

It was, I thought, a great skill, to flirt with every single person he met – male or female – and yet never to cross the line into unwanted over-familiarity. (*Wanted*

117

over-familiarity was a whole different story, of course. Tales of Ash's heartbroken lovers were legion.) It was a useful trait in his line of work, this ability to read people, to give them exactly what they wanted – he'd charmed more than one fortune out of his patrons over a cosy hand of cards.

With a theatrical sigh, Ash appeared in front of us, reaching out to grab Scrimshaw roughly by the shoulders and turn him round.

Allowing Scrimshaw to slump against him, Ash bent his knees and slung Scrimshaw over his shoulder, the man's arms dangling limply towards the ground.

"I thought he was supposed to be conscious for this bit," Ash puffed, climbing the stairs with a strength I had not suspected of his lean, wiry body.

"There might have been a small miscalculation in the dosage." I bit my lip. "I'm sure it will be fine, though."

Maud snorted. "Let's hope we can get some sense out of him."

Nerves writhed in my belly as I hurried up the stairs after Ash. I was close to finishing my training and this was our first big operation as a charm. I desperately wanted things to go well, but it looked as though I might have made a mess of things already.

We clattered unceremoniously into Joe's office – Joe was Ash's business partner, who was not currently on the premises – to find Sylla sitting behind his desk, impatience simmering in every line of her person. Her cool eyes went straight to Scrimshaw's prone body.

"Oh dear," Winnie said mildly, stepping forward while Ash deposited Scrimshaw in a chair. "It looks as though there may have been a problem with the dosage."

"What exactly did you give him?" Ash quirked an eyebrow.

"It's a compound made from several plants," I said. "It's harmless, really. Salvia, chamomile, a *touch* of opium…"

"Opium?" Ash kicked at Scrimshaw's foot, but the man didn't respond.

"Only a little bit," I said weakly.

"I told you this wasn't a good idea," said Sylla.

"It will be fine." Winnie waved her hand. "The science is sound. Mari and I allowed for a certain margin of error."

"Margin of error? Is the man even alive?" Sylla asked, rising to her feet.

Winnie pressed her fingers to his neck. "Yes," she replied. "I should think he'll revive momentarily."

"Let's hope so," Sylla said calmly. Too calmly.

"Well, I'll be off, then," Ash interrupted cheerily, having the sense to know when his particular brand of charm was about to encounter a brick wall. A good gambler knew when to fold, after all. "Lovely to see you as always, ladies. Give the bell in the corner a pull if you run into any problems." His eyes flicked to the drooling, unconscious form of the man in front of him. "Or if you need any help disposing of the body."

On that helpful note, he swaggered out of the door, sending me a mischievous wink over his shoulder as he left.

"Tell me what happened," Sylla demanded.

"Everything went exactly as planned," Maud said, as I slumped into a vacant armchair, rubbing my aching shoulders. "We sat down at the table beside Scrimshaw, flirted a little while he played, then Mari intercepted his drink, and I emptied the vial into it."

"About ten minutes later he seemed heavily intoxicated," I said, "and I convinced him to join me in the stairwell. Then ... he became a bit ... unconscious."

"But he woke up again," Maud put in quickly.

"Briefly," I admitted.

Sylla rubbed her temples with her fingers. "I see. May I remind you that the purpose of bringing him here was to question him? Do either of you have any suggestions as to how we are supposed to question an unconscious man?"

I could think of nothing. Disappointment and guilt seeped through me. My first proper investigation, and I had already made a potentially catastrophic mistake.

In the heavy silence, Win moved to the desk and poured herself a glass of water from a waiting jug. Then, without any further ado, she threw the contents into Scrimshaw's face.

"Wha—!" the man exclaimed, his eyes snapping open, his bleary gaze wheeling about the room.

A small gasp of relief passed my lips.

"Ah, good." Sylla came to stand in front of the desk, leaning her weight against it, her posture all business. "Mr Scrimshaw. We have some questions for you."

"Where...? What...? Who...?" Scrimshaw began. His eyes flicked to the corner of the room, and he let out a muffled shriek. "My God," he whimpered. "My God."

"Excellent." Winnie pulled out her pocket watch before noting the time down in the notebook on the desk. "The hallucinations have begun. That's interesting, Mari, isn't it? Sooner than I had anticipated."

"Now would be a good time to start asking questions," I said to Sylla in a low voice. "It's likely he'll only be coherent for a few minutes, but his inhibitions should be significantly lowered."

"Very well." Sylla straightened. "Mr Scrimshaw, I need to know the numbers of the safe deposit boxes that you and your associates have been using."

Scrimshaw's eyes darted between her and the corner of the room. "Can you see?" he croaked. "Can you see them?"

"Yes, of course I can." Sylla's voice was soothing. "And unless you answer my questions, I shall let them have you."

"The goats..." he whispered. "So many goats."

"Did he just say *goats*?" Maud asked.

"Capraphobia," Winnie murmured, nudging her spectacles up her nose. "Fascinating."

"The goats are here for you," Sylla said stonily. "Unless you give me the information I want. The numbers on the safe deposit boxes. Now."

"So many," Scrimshaw shrieked, curling back in his chair. "Not the horns!"

Maud choked on a giggle.

"Could you describe the goats?" Winnie asked, her pen poised. "For science!" she insisted when Sylla glared at her.

"Scrimshaw. The numbers," Sylla said again.

"Yes, yes, the numbers," Scrimshaw murmured, reaching out with a shaking hand for the pen that Sylla held towards him, casting nervous glances over his shoulder. "You'll keep them away?" he asked.

"As long as you cooperate."

When he had finished writing, Sylla picked up the paper, examined it with satisfaction, then folded it and tucked it into the neckline of her dress. She shook out her skirts.

"Well?" She lifted an eyebrow, looking between me and Scrimshaw. "What now?"

"Well, now he should—" I began, but I was cut off by Scrimshaw making a gurgling sound and slumping down in his chair. "Fall unconscious."

"Right on time," Winnie said, delighted, scribbling some more notes.

"And what if he hadn't given us the box numbers yet?" Sylla asked icily. "This whole operation has left far too much to chance."

"We got the numbers, didn't we?" Maud said. "I'll admit it hasn't gone *completely* smoothly—"

Sylla interrupted her with a snort.

"But for our first real job as a charm," Maud continued undaunted, "I'd say it was a success."

"We will discuss this later," Sylla said. "For now, Winnie and I need to leave out of the back before we are discovered, while you and Mari take care of *that*." She gestured disdainfully towards Scrimshaw, who had started snoring again. At least we hadn't killed him.

"I'll deliver the numbers to Mrs Finch, along with the key," Sylla continued. "You did get the key?"

I reached into the pocket of my low-cut ballgown – cherry red to match the rouge on my lips and cheeks – and pulled out the key I had lifted from Scrimshaw's associate earlier in the evening. He certainly hadn't minded my wandering hands. It had been a neat bit of pickpocketing – something I would never have expected to be a source of pride.

"Good," Sylla said, and it was ridiculous how widely this small, tepid bit of praise made me smile.

Sylla and Winnie departed, and Maud and I looked at one another for a moment.

"How do we get him back downstairs?" Maud asked.

"I think we can just sort of … roll him," I said.

"Not very dignified."

"Extorting all those poor widows out of their savings?" I shrugged. "It's the least he deserves."

Maud grinned. "Well, when you put it that way…"

With a lot of pushing and pulling, we succeeded in getting Scrimshaw back down the stairs. He remained dead to the world throughout, which was probably for the best.

When we reached the bottom, we managed to get him

up on to his feet again, supporting him enough to drag him, stumbling, across the crowded gaming floor.

Several of Scrimshaw's friends called out with lewd congratulations, one or two sent wolf whistles in our direction. Maud offered them a bawdy wink, while I subtly lifted Scrimshaw's arm as if he were bidding them all a jaunty goodnight.

We stuffed Scrimshaw unceremoniously into a hackney carriage and gave the driver his address. The driver did not so much as blink. I suppose he had seen it all before.

"You're sure he won't remember anything?" Maud asked as we watched the carriage drive away into the night.

"He'll have a tremendous hangover, and thanks to all his friends he'll assume he had the night of his life." I dusted off my hands. "He won't know a thing until it's too late."

"You did well, Mari." Maud nudged me. "I know Sylla is mean with her praise, but the tincture was a tidy way of getting the information – he likely won't realize there's been a breach for days; it gives us time we wouldn't otherwise have had. You and Win and your potions ... it's good work."

"It could have gone better." I sighed. "We cut it too close on the timings. Sylla was right: the formula isn't reliable enough yet..."

"We can make improvements," Maud said soothingly. "It takes time for everything to run like clockwork. The main thing is, thanks to us, all those innocent women get their money back. We helped people tonight – don't forget that."

Her words were like a warm blanket against the cool night air.

"You're right," I agreed, a smile spreading across my face. Now that we were out of the woods, relief swept through me. "My first big job done and we're all in one piece."

"Win didn't even blow anything up," Maud agreed with a laugh. "Cause for celebration. Come on, I think the newest member of the Aviary deserves a drink."

CHAPTER TWELVE

All in all, my first real outing with the Aviary had been relatively successful, which is why I was surprised the next day to find Sylla Banaji holding a gun to my head, attempting to murder me.

"Bang," she said flatly. "Dead again."

"I thought it was better this time," I managed.

Sylla sighed. "We can hardly mark this exercise on a scale. There is no better or worse. Dead is dead. Really, Mari," she said, her tone edged with displeasure. "I expected more from you."

I bit my tongue, already panting from several efforts to disarm her, which Sylla had deflected with embarrassing ease. Almost six months of training in this room and I still found hand-to-hand combat a challenge. Particularly against Sylla who seemed barely to exert herself at all. Each movement was economical, precise, and try as I might, I couldn't seem to get my own body to move in the same way.

Sylla held the gun out to me. "Let me show you again," she said.

Resigned, I stood, holding the barrel pressed lightly to her temple.

"First, I grab the gun like this," Sylla demonstrated. "Then I pull down in a sharp motion – this will break your assailant's finger. The snap it makes is really quite satisfying," she mused with a ghoulish smile. She pulled gently down on the gun, mimicking the movement. "Now, the crucial thing here is to get the gun as far away from you and with as much haste as possible, because there is every chance it will be discharged at some point. So, concentrate on swinging the arm away like so, and – if the opportunity presents itself – disarming your assailant completely. At this point you have several options. A well-placed elbow to the nose or stomach is wise. If your assailant is male, then the groin is, obviously, always a good choice. Nothing like watching a man writhe in agony to get the blood pumping."

"Writhing," I murmured. "Right."

My eyes strayed longingly to the wall where the cabinet of well-honed foils gleamed. "Can't we practise with swords today?" I asked wistfully. I may not be much use in a fist fight, but I had been delighted to discover an aptitude for fencing – something I would never, ever have found if I hadn't joined the Aviary, swordplay not being high on the list of priorities for a florist.

Sylla frowned. "We are not here to practise something in which you are already performing adequately."

I tried to disguise the way the word "adequately" made me feel ten feet tall.

"Besides," Sylla continued, "it is unlikely that you will find yourself in a sword fight on the streets of London. *Possible*, but unlikely."

"But it *is* likely I'll end up with a gun pressed to my head?"

Sylla shrugged, all nonchalance. "It happens," she said.

I tried not to think about that too much. I knew the work we did was potentially dangerous. There had been moments the night before when I had been almost stunned by the thought of how quickly and violently something could go wrong. I had kept my mind focused on the task in front of me, but sometimes it was overwhelming to think that these hours and hours of training weren't simply an exercise; they were necessary to keep me – and the rest of my team – safe.

"Fine," I said, swiping the damp curls away from my forehead. "Let's try it again."

Sylla's eyes narrowed. "First, let's discuss last night."

"What about last night?" I asked.

"How do you feel about it?"

I eyed her warily. "How do *I* feel about it?"

"Are you simply going to repeat what I say?"

"I only meant," I said, fighting down impatience, "that I thought you would rather share how *you* felt about it. I've been waiting all morning for you to give me some sort of assessment."

131

Sylla's head tilted thoughtfully to the side. The gun, which she still held loosely in one hand, tapped against her skirts. "Yes, I can see why you would think that was more important, but last night was your first time out in the field. It is one thing to train for it; it's quite another to put it into practice. When I ask how you feel about it, I am not being" – here, her lips thinned – "*sentimental*. I am asking because I wish to know, honestly, how you found the experience."

I blinked. Months after meeting her, Sylla was still an enigma to me, yet as a leader there was no one I respected more. I knew what it was to manage a team, to depend on others – though my work could hardly be said to be life or death as hers was.

"I found it…" I hesitated, sifting through my feelings. "Complicated."

"How so?"

"I felt nervous, anxious, even scared at times." I twisted my own skirt through my fingers. "I'm still not completely comfortable with the acting, the deception. I know things didn't go precisely to plan and it made me realize that the line between victory and defeat is terrifyingly fine. But..." I trailed away, then looked back up at Sylla's face and a smile tugged at my lips. "But I also felt powerful, competent, *daring*. I felt like I was part of something bigger, something I believe in. I liked that. I liked that very much."

Sylla didn't smile, but I was sure her mouth twitched briefly, before her expression cooled once more.

"That is all very well," she said briskly, "but you are quite right about that line. Our margin for error is slim at best. There is a reason all Finches have to undertake vigorous training. You" – she fixed me with a piercing look – "are not ready. Yet. Last night went well enough, but too much of that was thanks to luck rather than skill. You need more work, and you and Win need to be a lot more certain of your outcomes when it comes to your science experiments."

I tried not to bristle. I knew she was right. That was the worst of it, knowing that I still had so much to learn. "There are only a few weeks left of my six-month training period," I said, and I was embarrassed to hear a tremor in the words. "How will we make sure I am ready?"

Now, Sylla did smile, baring her teeth. "We will practise."

She lifted the gun to my head, pressed the cool barrel against my temple.

"Again," she said.

CHAPTER THIRTEEN

The next day I could not dedicate myself to practice. Instead, I had a very full shift planned at the shop. Since I'd started working at the Aviary, things at Bloom's had been busier than ever.

It hadn't been long before word got out about the new Duchess of Roxton hiring a personal florist, and as I suspected we found ourselves in great demand. Suddenly it wasn't enough to simply have one's personal maid arrange a few vases of flowers around the house – now anyone who was anyone wanted arrangements from Bloom's on display in their hallways, or flowers framing the front door, or spilling from fireplaces in a froth of colour. The designs became increasingly elaborate as society ladies tried to outdo one another in a frenzy the papers had dubbed "The War of the Roses".

I certainly wasn't about to complain.

These days, when a party was being hosted for the ton, there was simply nowhere to go but Bloom's.

Izzy was utterly baffled by this development, never having been considered a trendsetter before (in fact, according to her, before she became a duchess, no one seemed to notice she existed at all, though Max had vehemently protested this). But if there was one thing that talked in this city, it was power – and the Duchess of Roxton had plenty. The second thing that talked in London was money, and the Duchess of Roxton had plenty of that too.

With the payments from the Aviary, we were able to hire another pair of hands, and Daisy had insisted on spending more time on the shop floor as well. "Where the excitement happens," as she put it. Suzy has been training her, despite Grandfather's protestations.

"She's only fifteen!" he had exclaimed.

"I was working in the shop for some time before I was fifteen," I'd replied, trying not to be stung.

"Oh, but Daisy's just a *baby*," Grandfather had blustered. "She's not as grown up as you were at that age. An old soul, my Marigold."

It was fortunate that Daisy didn't overhear this, or he'd have had *two* disgruntled granddaughters on his hands. As it was, his answer made something inside me twist uncomfortably.

Still, Daisy did begin to work on the floor and was a quick learner. The business seemed to be running fairly smoothly, but the same could not be said of my garden, which was looking a little unkempt. I didn't like to ask Grandfather to grub around in the dirt, not when his knees sounded like hinges that needed oiling.

Help came from a surprising source in Scout, who had quickly demonstrated both a skill for anything garden-related, and – more importantly – a voracious interest in it. This was something of a double-edged sword: on the one hand, I was thrilled to have accidentally acquired an apprentice who cared so much about the garden; on the other, Scout was not yet capable enough to take over much of the work herself and training her actually took up more of my time.

I was beginning to feel like a doll being tugged in too many directions at once, by greedy, grabbing hands.

This morning, for example, rather than checking on the progress in my greenhouse, I was in the back room poring over the appointment book with Suzy.

"If you take the meeting with Mrs Hildegard at midday, then you should have time to make it to Lady Godalming at three," I said, scribbling notes as I went. "She loved the dinner setting you did last week and she's having guests again on Thursday who she's desperate to impress."

"Changed her mind four times at the last one." Suzy sighed. "Then settled on my first suggestion, once I managed to make it seem like her own idea. But she pays, doesn't she?"

"Oh, yes." I exhaled a little too loudly, looking at the list of figures neatly written alongside each name. "She certainly does. So..." I ran my finger down the list. "You'll take her and perhaps Lady Curtis..."

"Lady Curtis will want *you*," Suzy pointed out. "She caused a stink last time when you didn't come yourself. We want to keep her sweet. If you recall, she spent a fortune on shipping in all those orchids for her granddaughter's come out, and she's got the engagement party coming up."

"Yes, you're right," I said, rubbing my forehead. "But I don't think I'll have time... Perhaps Grandfather could go. He is the head of the family, after all. And he absolutely loves the Curtises' cook's vanilla sponge."

"And I reckon Lady Curtis has a soft spot for him," Suzy added with a gleam. "All right, I'll ask him."

"I've sent round the new order for Lady Stanhope," I said. "She asked for something dazzling so I went all out, but we should order some more of that pink ribbon she likes."

Izzy's mother was something of an invalid, not leaving her rooms in her lavish townhouse, but her daughter arranged for her space to be filled with flowers, and Lady Stanhope's delight was always so complete that I took pleasure in doing the arrangements myself as much as possible. If I had time I even delivered them, knowing I would be treated to an excellent gossip by the fire – Lady Stanhope seemed to know all the town news practically before it even happened. Izzy credited her with several of the Aviary's major breakthroughs.

"And you've already taken care of the three bouquet orders and laid out the day's buttonholes," Suzy said, consulting the list in her hand. "So that just leaves a visit to Mrs Evans and…"

"A note for you, Mari," Scout said, appearing at the door. She hopped over to the potting table and held out a familiar-looking envelope, slightly grubby at the edges, because Scout's fingers were always soil-stained these days.

Suzy groaned. "Her Grace is summoning you again." She rolled her eyes. "If I had a penny for every floral *emergency* that woman has had these past six months—"

"You *do* have a penny for them all, Suzy – we all do!" I grinned. It was an endless source of amusement to me that within the walls of Bloom's flower shop, Her Grace, Isobel Vane, Duchess of Roxton, was seen as the most ridiculous, demanding tyrant in London. When I told her that, she just laughed and said she was used to wearing many masks – one more didn't matter.

I opened the envelope and took out the note.

"I have to go," I said, skimming the contents. "I should think I'll be gone for a couple of hours at least. If you ask Grandfather about Lady Curtis, ask him about Mrs Evans too. Perhaps he can take Daisy with him – she's been begging to go on appointments."

"Will do," Suzy said. "Don't you worry – everything's in hand."

"And, Scout, there's just some weeding to do, and then if you could water the ferns…"

"And the Chamaedorea elegans," Scout finished for me, grinning broadly when Suzy's eyes widened. "That's the big, frilly palms," she explained proudly. "I know. Who'd 'ave thought I'd be here spoutin' Latin like I've been at one of them posh schools?"

"You're just where you should be," I said firmly, grabbing my hat from the nail on the wall and heading for the door.

After making my way through the busy shop, stopping every now and then to greet a customer, I stepped out into the dazzle of August sunshine.

The note had been from Mrs Finch, but rather than directing me to the Aviary as expected, instead I was instructed to make my way to Izzy's house as soon as possible. This was, I assumed, going to be a discussion of the events at the Lucky Penny. Hopefully, Mrs Finch would have already set about recovering the contents of the deposit boxes. I tried not to feel nervous, but thanks to my conversation with Sylla I was aware that the mission had not been marked down as an unprecedented success.

It was only a ten-minute walk to Izzy's home on Grosvener Square, and I took the opportunity to settle myself a bit. While I longed for it, the route didn't take me past any green space, but I was still able to appreciate the gentle rustle of the breeze through the trees dotted along Oxford Street. Soon, I knew those leaves would turn gold, but for now they hung on to the last warm dregs of summer, a mellow green, gorged on sunshine and almost ready to drop.

The day was warm, and I stomped along without my coat, feeling pleased with the violet gown I wore, trimmed with green silk that I had purchased from the

Aviary. My hat was a frothy confection to which I had pinned real dahlias, spiky, pink and outrageous in a crown along the brim.

Heads turned as I passed, but I didn't mind. Busy and scattered as I was, I still felt more like myself than I had in a long time.

Upon reaching Roxton House, I rang the bell and waited for Wheeler, the extremely dignified butler to open the door. It still felt wrong to be using the front door rather than the service entrance, but Izzy insisted. Though he had never said a word about it, I felt Wheeler's disapproval regarding this decision emanating from him in violent waves.

The ridiculously grand house might currently contain a duke, a duchess and a duke's sister, but it was Wheeler who left me feeling the most awe-struck.

"Miss Bloom," the man said now, with the briefest incline of his chin. "Her Grace is expecting you."

"Thank you, Wheeler," I said, with all the dignity I could muster.

He escorted me through to the entrance hall, where Max's seventeen-year-old sister, Felicity, appeared suddenly, barrelling down the staircase. She was dressed carelessly, her sleeves pushed up past her elbows, and her gleaming silver-blonde hair was pulled back in a plait, which fell over her shoulder. I noticed the end of it was blue and surmised that she had accidentally dipped it in her ink pot again.

"Ah, Wheeler," she puffed, as she straightened her spectacles. "I was wondering if you had seen my Norwegian dictionary? I'm trying to write a letter to Dr Lie and I keep getting lost conjugating the verbs."

"I believe the Norwegian dictionary was shelved last night in its proper place in the library," Wheeler said without inflection.

Felicity gave a rumble of frustration. "I told you, Wheeler, what you think of as mess is actually organized chaos."

Wheeler's silence on the subject spoke volumes.

"Oh! Hello, Mari." Felicity finally spotted me and danced down the final stairs. "What an excellent hat. I am a great appreciator of the radial symmetry of dahlias."

I grinned. "So am I, now that you mention it," I said. "I'll make sure we send over plenty this week; there have been some really lovely examples at the markets. You can have some for your study."

"I would love that." Felicity beamed. "I suppose you're here to see Izzy and her visitors. Secrets flying about all over the place. Well, I'll just grab my dictionary and get back to work. I really do think my life would have been easier if Mother had been more interested in having someone teach me Norwegian and less concerned about deportment." Felicity snorted. "I conquered walking when I was thirteen months old – I hardly think it required any further instruction."

With that, she whirled off in the direction of the library – an extremely graceful tempest – and I thought perhaps there was something to be said for deportment classes, after all.

Wheeler cleared his throat. "If you'll follow me to the drawing room, miss."

As we made our way down the hall, past various busts on plinths and pieces of priceless artwork, I found myself habitually taking stock of the flowers on show. I had sent over new arrangements only three days ago, so the elegant and sculptural designs of cloud-like blue hydrangeas spiked through with tall white delphiniums and fat, perfumed off-white roses still looked perfect. Perhaps something similar in shades of lilac would be nice next. Just because the displays were something of a ruse didn't mean I couldn't take pride in my work.

"Miss Bloom has arrived," Wheeler intoned, pushing open the door to the drawing room.

All heads turned in my direction, and I was surprised to see so many people here. Maud and Winnie were sitting on a straw-coloured silk sofa, happily examining the three-tier cake stand in front of them, which was laden with sweet treats. Izzy's husband, Max, already had his fingers wrapped round a delicious-looking petit four, the delicate little cake appearing even smaller in his massive hand. Sylla stood to one side with Mrs Finch and Izzy, clearly deep in conversation.

And standing by the fireplace, as tall and broodingly handsome as the last time we met, was Oliver Lockhart.

"It's you!" I exclaimed impulsively.

"Oh, good," Oliver said. "The weeping one is here. Lock up your library books."

CHAPTER FOURTEEN

"The weeping one?" Winnie looked confused. "Mari? She's the most cheerful person I know."

"Of course, you two already know each other," Izzy said. "I had actually forgotten that."

My eyes locked on to Oliver who was standing with one arm propped up against the top of the fireplace, as though he thought he was some sort of Austen hero. It was strange to see him in person again. I would be lying if I said I hadn't thought of him over the last six months, though I had almost convinced myself I had imagined just how dangerously handsome he was. Unfortunately, if anything, my memories didn't do him justice, and the sight of him now was creating a rush of peculiar feelings that I didn't have time to sort through.

His black suit, stark in its simplicity, was cut to perfection. In fact, everything about him was severe and buttoned up. Despite the warmth of the day, he wore his long, dark coat, which gave the impression he did not intend to stay and make himself comfortable. I felt an overwhelming and bizarre urge to mess up his necktie and tuck a daisy behind his ear.

"We haven't exactly been formally introduced," I said.

Izzy grinned. "Well, I can take care of that. Oliver Lockhart, please meet Miss Marigold Bloom. Mari, this is Oliver."

Oliver snorted. "Marigold Bloom? What a ridiculous name. It sounds made up."

There was a brief, awkward pause.

"I suppose all names are made up, really," I said cheerfully, and it was Maud's turn to choke on a laugh.

Something flashed in his eyes. "And what is Miss *Bloom*" – Oliver said my name as if he remained dubious of its authenticity – "doing here exactly? I thought you said whoever was on her way would be able to help me."

"Marigold is one of our newest recruits," Mrs Finch said matter-of-factly. "Indeed, it is thanks to your intervention that we found her, and I think we can all be grateful for that."

There was a murmur of agreement and Max appeared at my side, smiling down at me. I blinked, momentarily overwhelmed. Looking directly at Max was a bit like looking into the sun. I still wasn't used to his gleaming handsomeness. I had heard that in society he was considered something of a stiff, haughty figure, but around the members of the Aviary he always seemed utterly relaxed and his manners were flawless.

"Here, Mari, come and sit down and have a scone," he said, offering me his arm like the gentleman he was. "They're delicious."

"He'd know," Maud said with a sly grin. "He's had three already."

"Shall we get back to the matter at hand?" Sylla

asked, pouring herself a cup of tea. "Now that Mari is *finally* here."

"I only sent her the note half an hour ago," Izzy protested.

Sylla simply harrumphed as though the limits of time and space did not apply to her.

"Miss Bloom may be one of you," Oliver said grudgingly, "but I still don't understand why *he* is here." He gestured to Max.

"This is my house!" Max mumbled around his fourth scone.

"Oliver, I know it is one of your favourite hobbies, but don't be rude to Max," Izzy chided, coming over and standing next to her husband. "Or I shall write to Beth with several new and exotic seafood recipes."

"You wouldn't!" Oliver hissed. "That woman is a menace in the kitchen as it is."

"She absolutely would." Max grinned up at Izzy. "My wife is ruthless." The way they looked at one another made something ache in my chest.

"Oliver, Max is here in his governmental capacity. Once you lay out the whole story, then we will be able to decide if his help is required or if this is strictly an agency matter." Mrs Finch accepted the plate that Winnie brought over to her.

I felt my eyes widen at that. I knew that Max was involved at a high level with secret governmental business, but it was rare for his work to intersect with the Aviary's. I got the impression he and Izzy were careful to keep their jobs as separate as possible. I was also surprised to hear that Mrs Finch was considering taking on a case for a client like Oliver Lockhart – men of means tended to be able to solve their issues in far less covert ways than we typically offered.

"Everyone sit down and have some tea and something to eat," Izzy said, gesturing to the cluster of chairs arranged around the tea table, "then we can talk it all over."

"*Is* there anything left to eat?" Sylla lifted a brow. "Now that Vane has got his big bear paws on the cakes."

"I can always ring for more," Izzy said, cutting across whatever retort had sprung to Max's lips.

For a moment everyone settled in, and I was not displeased to find myself with my own plate laden with goodies. Izzy's cook really was excellent.

Reaching into my big leather bag, I pulled out a small box full of lavender shortbread, which I slid stealthily across the table to Max, who was sitting beside me. His eyes lit up as he palmed the box, slipping it into his pocket. Having discovered Max's sweet tooth when he visited the shop and devoured an entire tray of biscuits, it was an unspoken agreement that I brought a box whenever I visited.

"Marigold Bloom, if I wasn't already married..." he began, and Izzy elbowed him in the side.

Oliver made a noise that sounded suspiciously like a growl.

"So, Oliver," Mrs Finch said, drawing his attention back to her. "Why don't you tell everyone what you told me?"

I thought I saw a look of vulnerability cross Oliver's face, but it was gone in a flash.

He cleared his throat. "I asked to meet here because I wasn't sure if the Aviary would be interested in taking on my case. I know I am not exactly the typical client, and I don't wish to take advantage of our ... connection." The words were awkward, and he hesitated here, but no one spoke. Whatever the connection was that he was talking about, I assumed it was something to do with his relationship with Max and Izzy who seemed to know him fairly well.

"In fact," he continued gruffly, "I have done everything in my own power not to involve you in this mess for exactly that reason, but I have run out of places to go ... well, *people* to go to who I really trust." Again, there was the slightest faltering in his rigid posture.

"You're among friends here," Mrs Finch said, and I was surprised again by the softening of her voice. There were undercurrents here that I didn't understand. "You did the right thing by coming to us."

Oliver sighed, but some of the tightness left his expression. "I suppose I had better tell you the whole story from the beginning."

Shifting in his seat, his frown deepened for a moment, and he appeared to be choosing his words with care.

"Eleven years ago – when I myself was eleven – my mother and my younger sister died in a carriage accident." His words were clipped, devoid of emotion, but in his face there was a pain that he couldn't conceal.

"Being a child, I was never privy to the details of this accident and, honestly, I never had any reason to look more closely at it. Why should I? They were gone and my father and I remained." While his voice was steady, I could see that he was gripping the handle of his tea cup tightly enough that his knuckles whitened.

"My father passed away over three years ago. He and I did not have the best of relationships. He was a wealthy man and I have spent the time since his death trying to untangle much of the mess he left behind. Currently, I am attempting to remedy some of his more *questionable* business practices." Oliver placed his cup back on the table in front of him, flexing his fingers as though he wanted to shake the tension from them.

"Six months ago, I received a letter from one of my father's lawyers, referencing a trust that had been set up for my sister, one that she would be able to access on her twenty-first birthday – a date that was fast approaching. I was baffled by the existence of such a trust when my sister had been deceased for so long, and so I came to London to meet with him." Oliver's frown deepened. "The lawyer whom I met was an unfortunate blowhard with a tendency to waffle, but once he finally got to the point, he revealed that the trust remained in existence because my sister had never been declared legally dead."

"How can that be?" Izzy murmured.

"A pertinent question, Isobel." Oliver nodded. "And one that I asked myself."

"Much less politely, I'll wager." The words were out of my mouth before I could think better of it.

"Not a wager anyone would be wise to take," Mrs Finch said, with a small smile.

Oliver narrowed his eyes at me. "I was perhaps a touch … *uncivil*, but the man had taken me by surprise."

"And after your uncivil behaviour, did this lawyer finally get to his point?" Sylla asked, and it was clear Oliver was not the only one feeling impatient.

"Yes. He told me that after the accident only my mother's body was ever recovered. My sister was assumed to have also perished, but to have been washed away in a nearby river and therefore, without a body, could not be declared legally dead until seven years had passed. My father died just before we reached this deadline and I, of course, had no knowledge of any of this, so had not taken the appropriate steps to declare her dead myself."

"You had no idea your sister had never been found?" Maud asked.

Oliver shook his head. "We had a funeral for both of them. I did not know that we buried an empty coffin in Ellen's grave."

"How awful," Winnie murmured. "This must all have been such a shock."

Oliver's jaw tightened. "It was ... unsettling. Rather than sign the papers that the lawyer had waiting for me and closing the door on Ellen's life, I decided I needed to do some investigating of my own. I was left with too many unanswered questions and naturally the one that haunted me the most was simple: what if my sister was still alive somehow? It seemed strange to me that no sign of her had been found, and I could not discover if my father had organized a thorough search or not." Oliver's expression cooled even further. "He was not a careful man where his family was concerned. I went to the library to try to find any news articles relating to the accident. That is when I ran into Miss Bloom. Or rather when *she* ran into me."

His eyes flicked briefly to mine. "However, even after I had survived Miss Bloom's violent onslaught" – he ignored my huff of laughter – "I could find no information in the library records at all, and so I did what I thought at the time was best – I engaged a private investigator." At this, Oliver grimaced.

"Well, there's your first mistake." Sylla crossed her arms, expression smug.

"It seems to me to be a perfectly sensible course of action," Max said.

Sylla rolled her eyes. "Of course it would."

"Unfortunately, the investigator turned out to be a blockhead," Oliver continued, resigned.

Shocking, Sylla mouthed.

"But he did discover one useful piece of information. The accident hadn't taken place in England at all. It happened outside Paris."

"Paris?" Several voices piped up at once.

"Which is where I would have travelled next had it not

157

been for the actions of the aforementioned blockhead. It seems the investigator, a Mr Wylie…"

Here, not only Sylla but Mrs Finch, Izzy, Maud and Winnie all let out loud groans.

"I see his reputation precedes him." Oliver's lip curled. "To continue – in his infinite wisdom, Mr Wylie decided to put an advertisement in the paper."

"Let me guess." Sylla examined her fingernails. "The advertisement claimed you were looking for information on your long-lost sister because there was a fat inheritance with her name on it waiting in the wings?"

"Yes."

"Oh no," I murmured softly, my eyes widening in understanding.

"Oh yes." Oliver rubbed his temples. "I have been absolutely *inundated* with claims that my sister is alive and well and ready to collect her money." He reached into his pocket and pulled out a fat stack of envelopes tied together with a piece of string. "Here is a handful of the letters I have received. I thought perhaps you might like to go through them." His voice was tinged with weariness now as he threw the letters down on the table.

"Do you... Do you believe any of these letters are legitimate?" I asked hesitantly. "Do you believe your sister could be alive?"

A hush fell, something solemn lingering in the air.

Oliver looked down at his hands. "I don't know what to believe," he said finally. "Not now."

"Tell them the rest of it, Oliver," Mrs Finch said gently.

Oliver stood and stalked back towards the fireplace, as though he couldn't stand to be sitting around a tea table, looking at us. Instead, he stared into the grate – one that, as it was still so mild, I had filled myself with a playful spill of sunflowers, each petal like a lick of flame – his hands clasped behind his back as he spoke.

"A week ago a couple arrived on my doorstep in Yorkshire with a young woman in tow who they claim is my sister." He said the words quickly. "As you can imagine, it was not the first time this had happened since the advert was placed, but there are several key differences in this case."

He turned back to us, his fingers closing round the top of the back of his chair.

"This couple, a Mr and Mrs Lavigne, claim to have been living in France for the last twelve years. They arrived with a file full of papers, stamped by the British consulate, which confirmed the identities of them and their daughter, who they adopted eleven years ago. According to them, they rescued Ellen – who now goes by the name Helene – from the river after her accident, though the child had no memory of who she was or what had happened to her. Recently, however, they say this has changed."

"Hmmm," Sylla murmured. "Convenient."

"But possible," Winnie put in. "A head injury sustained during a carriage accident could lead to memory loss. There is much we don't yet understand about the human brain."

The earnest and deeply enthusiastic way she said it conjured unfortunate images of Winnie's lab full of jars of floating human brains. The haunted expressions on several of my colleagues' faces told me I wasn't the only one to picture the ghoulish scene.

"*Could* Helene be your sister?" Izzy asked, breaking the spell.

"My first thought was no. The Lavignes claimed to

know nothing of the advertisement, but I was struck by the timing, and while she is the right age and does resemble my sister, I felt no particular sense of recognition when I saw her."

"But if it has been eleven years…" Maud began.

"Would I recognize her?" Oliver finished. "I thought so, but … perhaps not."

"So you think Helene is another imposter?" I asked.

Oliver's grip on the chair tightened. "I don't know." The words sounded painful. "Sometimes she is like a stranger, not knowing her way around the house, or not remembering a particular anecdote. But there have been other things, things Helene has said, things I was sure only Ellen knew. Stories about our past…" He trailed off here for a moment. "And then, most importantly, there's the scar."

"What scar?" Sylla sat up straighter.

"My sister had a small crescent-shaped scar on her palm," Oliver said, gesturing to his own hand. "She got it during a childish mishap when we were playing together. Helene has not drawn attention to it, but I noticed it was there when she removed her gloves."

Max frowned. "Plenty of ways to affect a scar if one wants to use them as disguise."

Izzy snorted. "We once passed off Max as my deaf great-aunt thanks to Sylla's skill with theatrical make-up."

"No!" I exclaimed, temporarily diverted.

Max only smiled serenely.

"The issue is" – Oliver sat back down, leaning forward so that his elbows rested on his knees – "that Helene may or may not be Ellen. But if she's *not* Ellen, then how does she know the things she does? Stories about our childhood, nicknames, jokes we shared." He rubbed his forehead with his fingers. "Things no one else *could* know."

"She would have to know them from Ellen herself," I said, the realization dawning.

"So either Helene is Ellen, or the imposter met Ellen at some point?" Sylla summarized.

Oliver's jaw ticked again. "Precisely. As it stands, the Lavignes seem convincing enough to warrant further investigation. They have remained in my house in Yorkshire, where my staff are keeping an eye on them until I return. I did not want them anywhere near London while I came to consult with you, though they believe I am looking into their claim."

There was a long pause as this sank in.

Finally, Max broke it. "I can certainly dig around for some more information on the accident, but it seems to me that the Aviary will be best equipped to deal with this particular problem."

"Naturally," Sylla said. "I take it we will be sending someone to Yorkshire?"

"Yes," Mrs Finch said calmly. "We're going to send Mari."

My squeak of protest was drowned out by Oliver's horrified "You're going to send *who*?"

"Izzy's charm is busy with a separate case," Mrs Finch said. "And, besides, Mari is perfect for the part."

"What part?" I asked suspiciously.

Mrs Finch sipped her tea serenely. "The part of Oliver's fiancée, of course."

CHAPTER FIFTEEN

"My *what*?" Oliver was on his feet again in an instant, outrage written large on his face.

I had been temporarily stunned into silence. Max leaned over and slipped another scone on to my plate in a welcome display of support.

"It's simple," Mrs Finch continued, unruffled. "We need to infiltrate Oliver's home and be able to ask lots of impertinent questions and poke around the house, searching the Lavignes' rooms. Oliver's intended bride would have every reason to be extremely interested in both the house and his family. Mari is well placed to go, and with her skill at talking to people, at reading them, she is the perfect plant. Sylla, Winnie and Maud will collect whatever information they can about the Lavignes' history, and the accident itself."

Sylla nodded. "I see. Perhaps a trip to Paris is in order. I have been meaning to make a visit to Worth for some gowns."

"Win and I can hold down the fort here," Maud said. "And follow up on whatever information Max digs up."

"I haven't even finished my probationary period!" I protested weakly. "And what about the shop? I can't just *leave* and go to the middle of *nowhere* and pretend I'm getting *married*." I started panic-eating the scone.

"This will be an important part of your training, and Sylla said you did well the other night." Mrs Finch smiled.

"I said her work showed potential," Sylla was quick to correct her, lest I ended up getting an inflated sense of my own skills.

"And you won't be going alone," Mrs Finch continued.

"I will go as your chaperone. Your godmother, perhaps. You do have one, I suppose?"

"Yes, of course," I murmured, dazed. "But how would I possibly explain this to my family?" I managed thickly. Six months later, the lies I had to tell them still sat heavy in my stomach, no matter how important I knew it was to keep my secrets.

Sylla waved a hand. "Oh, that part is easy. You will simply tell them that Oliver Lockhart has declared his intentions and that you've been invited to a house party so that you can get to know one another better in a chaperoned environment before you agree to an engagement."

Thankfully, I had already swallowed my scone as my mouth dropped open at this. "You want me to tell them I am *being courted*? By *him*?" My voice was shrill as I gestured wildly at Oliver, who now looked offended.

"What's wrong with me?" he demanded.

"We have to tell your family a story that is as close to your cover as possible, in case the Lavignes send someone to check you out," Sylla said, her tone practical. "When you return, you simply tell them you found the two of you didn't suit, but that you had a lovely time in the lap of luxury. And besides" – she lifted her eyebrows – "if you explain that a very wealthy man has declared his honourable intentions and wants to whisk you off on a tour of his castle, don't you think they'll all be delighted to help take care of the shop while you're gone?"

"Well, yes, I suppose," I said, knowing that my family would probably want to throw a parade, especially after the whole Simon debacle.

"It's not a castle," Oliver murmured sulkily.

"It *is* sort of a castle," Izzy put in.

"This is what agents of the Aviary do," Sylla told me. "We haven't spent all this time training you for our own amusement."

"If it helps, Max and I had to do something similar last year," Izzy piped up.

"And that worked out perfectly," Max said quietly.

I darted a glance at Oliver, who was looking at the lovestruck couple with such obvious disgust that it was almost funny. Still, Sylla was right. Working with the

Aviary wasn't a game, and I couldn't quake at the first big challenge they set me.

"All right," I said. "I suppose if it's just for a few days it should be fine. Although" – I cast a look at Oliver – "you do realize you'll have to meet them all?"

"What?" Oliver looked confused.

"My family," I clarified. "If I'm going to disappear with you to join this house party, it's going to look a bit strange if you haven't introduced yourself. You don't have to actually propose, but you need to..." I cleared my throat, the words coming haltingly. "You know... Appear to be making the effort to ... woo me."

Oliver's face had turned a sickly shade of green. "No," he said firmly.

"You asked for our help," Mrs Finch reminded him. "This is the most efficient way to get answers."

"Why can't you just come as guests?" Oliver said desperately. "Why do we have to be" – he eyed me resentfully – "*engaged*?"

"Give me another good reason why you – a bachelor – have invited a young, unmarried florist and her godmother to stay in your house and dine with you and your family and wander around the house asking a lot of questions," Mrs Finch said.

"I – I—" Oliver stuttered. "Perhaps I want her to … arrange some flowers for me."

The look Sylla gave him was withering. "It is of absolutely no surprise to me that you desperately need our help."

"Developing a sudden interest in flower arranging may be stretching it a bit." Max pressed his lips together as though trying not to laugh, and Oliver skewered him with a glare.

"And let me ask you this." Mrs Finch leaned forward, a knowing glint in her eyes, "What possible reason have you given the Lavignes for haring off to London and leaving them kicking their heels in Yorkshire?"

"I told them I needed to speak with the lawyer," Oliver said stiffly. "To look into the information they gave me."

"So their guard will be up," Mrs Finch said. "Whereas we want them to relax. Let them feel like you believe them, so they let something slip."

"Yes, it's much better if you rushed down to London to propose to the love of your life," Maud said. "And what could be more natural than to bring her home to meet your long-lost sister?"

"So romantic," Winnie murmured.

Oliver made a strangled sound.

"Don't worry, Mr Lockhart." I managed a smile, my spirits perversely buoyed by his obvious discomfort. "I'm sure my family will love you."

The queasy look on Oliver's face deepened.

"Good." Mrs Finch stood, shaking out her skirts. "So Oliver will call round to Bloom's tomorrow afternoon and declare his intentions to court Mari, then we'll all set off for Yorkshire."

She said it as though she was talking about stopping in at the grocer's.

"Time to put you out in the field, Mari." The smile Sylla gave me was sharp. "And we'll see just what you're made of."

CHAPTER SIXTEEN

The next day I found myself in the fraught position of explaining a romance I'd never mentioned with a man they had never heard of to my (understandably) bewildered family.

"But, Mari, what on earth do you *mean* you're thinking of marrying this Mr Lockhart?" Mother asked, pacing the room as I tried to look calm. "Who is he?"

"I told you: he's a factory owner from Yorkshire." I said, fussing with the vase of violets I had placed in the middle of the dining table and trying to avoid eye contact with my entire family.

"But where did *you* meet a factory owner from Yorkshire?" Grandfather's face was scrunched in a frown.

"At the library," I replied promptly, delighted to be able to tell the truth for once. "Around six months ago."

"Six months!" Mother said faintly. "And you've been keeping it from us all this time?"

"I wasn't sure of his feelings," I said, sticking to the story I had devised with Mrs Finch. "We began writing to one another and it was only recently that I learned he returned my affections." I didn't have to feign the flush on my cheeks that accompanied this particular piece of fantasy.

"Well, I think it's *deeply* romantic," Daisy said, dropping into a chair and clutching at her heart. "To think he took such a fancy to you that for six months he's been wooing you with love letters. I can't *believe* you won't let me read them." She pouted. "Me! Your only sister and a burgeoning romantic heroine at heart. And now he wants to whisk you off to his big house and show you all that could be yours. It's like something from a novel!"

I cleared my throat. "It is certainly like a work of fiction," I agreed.

"This just seems so sudden," Mother said, wringing her hands.

When we had been sitting in Izzy's sitting room yesterday, this part of the plan had seemed like an awkward necessity, but suddenly faced with the very real prospect of breaking the news to my family, I was realizing the various pitfalls.

"But does this mean you plan to move to Yorkshire?" Grandfather asked.

Pitfalls like that.

"We haven't discussed the details," I said as airily as I could manage. "But we will. I'll be back in a week, and we can talk it over then."

"It all seems most irregular." Grandfather's frown deepened. "But at least the man is coming to introduce himself – that's something."

"And you say his godmother is coming to call as well?" Mother asked.

"Yes, Mrs Finch. She wanted to make sure you knew the whole trip was going to be well chaperoned. I think Mr Lockhart wants to…" I hesitated here, remembering the words Mrs Finch had advised me to use, though they made me cringe. "Impress me with his suit." I could just picture Oliver's reaction to this, which was actually quite helpful because I felt a smile flicker on my lips.

Mother's face softened at this. "That's to his credit, then. And you say he's … a man of some means?"

I cleared my throat. "I understand he has a very comfortable life."

"Mari, you are such a dark horse," Daisy squeaked, absolutely thrilled by this whole turn of events. "Keeping a secret lover, and a fabulously wealthy one too; I had no idea you had it in you!"

"Nor did I," I said dryly. "Who knows if anything will come of it? No one understands better than me that engagements can be broken. Perhaps after spending more time in my company, Mr Lockhart will realize we don't suit."

I was quite pleased with this little speech, which I felt paved the way for the inevitable demise of my pretend relationship very neatly, but all three of them stared at me with barely concealed horror.

"Mari!" Mother stood, gripping my hand. "You are a gem, and any man would be lucky to have you!"

"He should be kissing the ground you walk on!" Grandfather expounded.

"Writing you love sonnets!" Daisy chimed in. "*Does* he write you love sonnets?"

I choked on a laugh at the thought of Oliver Lockhart penning love poetry. "Well, not exactly…" I murmured.

"In fact, it speaks extremely well of him," Grandfather said hotly, "that he has formed such an accurate picture of you on so snatched an acquaintance. Some men have the good sense to know a diamond when they see one!"

"Yes, yes!" Mother was getting riled up now too. "I don't know why any of us were surprised that a handsome man would wish to whisk you away, Mari. If anything, we should have been *expecting* something like this."

Oh, God. My family of hopeless romantics were quickly tipping too far in the other direction. The appearance of self-doubt had been a misstep on my part, because now, in buoying me up, they were talking themselves into the idea that Oliver and I were part of some grand Shakespearean love story.

"I didn't say he was handsome," I managed.

"Oh," Daisy said, crestfallen. "Is he not handsome? But then in many ways that's better, isn't it? Because really it's about two *souls* recognizing one another..."

"Err..." I made a doubtful noise.

"When I think of what you went through..." Mother began. "If anyone deserves a happy ending, it's you."

"If only your grandmother was still alive to see this!" Grandfather groaned, plucking a handkerchief from his waistcoat pocket and loudly blowing his nose.

"No, no, don't – you'll turn me into a watering pot!" Mother began blinking rapidly, fumbling for her own lace handkerchief.

"We just want you to be happy," Daisy wailed.

The sound of the doorbell being rung exploded through the air.

Perfect.

I eyed my weeping family with apprehension. "I'll go and get that, shall I?"

Leaving them to compose themselves, I headed out of the dining room, along the hallway, and then down the stairs that led to the front door at the side of the shop.

When I opened it, I found Oliver and Mrs Finch standing outside. I felt a wave of relief at the sight of Mrs Finch's steady countenance. She looked utterly calm, treating me to that small half-smile of hers.

Oliver, on the other hand, was pale and miserably clutching a small bouquet of flowers, which he thrust at me.

"Let's get this sham over with," he said, stomping past me into the hallway.

"It was nice of you to bring flowers," I said as I closed the door behind them and moved ahead of him.

My arm brushed against his as I did so, and I felt a strange, electric tingling running the way down into my fingertips. All at once, I was very aware of how big he was, how much taller than me. And how nice he smelled, like sandalwood and green, open spaces. The air disappeared from the hallway, just for a moment.

Oliver looked down at me with a frown. "Mrs Finch brought them," he said gruffly.

"No, I didn't," she whispered in my ear, when he turned to examine the small entry hall.

I felt something light bubble in my chest at that.

"Um, I think I'd probably better warn you," I said as I climbed the stairs ahead of them. "My family are quite ... excited."

"I'm sure Oliver will have no problem with playing the doting suitor," Mrs Finch said tranquilly. "Will you, Oliver?"

His only response was a low growl.

"Very well," I said, taking a deep breath as I opened the door to my home. "I suppose this is really happening, then."

The moment the door swung on its hinges, they were on him like a pack of rabid dogs. I watched in mute amusement as my mother wept into Oliver's neck while Grandfather pumped his hand up and down.

"Delighted to meet you at last, we've been looking forward to it for so long," boomed my grandfather, a man who had learned of Oliver's existence approximately fifteen minutes ago.

"Welcome to the family!" my mother exclaimed.

"Thank you," Oliver croaked.

"Marigold, I thought you said he wasn't handsome?" Daisy exclaimed with devastating clarity.

CHAPTER SEVENTEEN

"You said I wasn't handsome?" Oliver sounded offended.

"I said that I didn't say you *were* handsome," I corrected.

He scowled, considering this. "I think that's the same thing."

"What is wrong with you?" My sister hissed in my ear. "That's the most handsome man I've ever seen!"

As the tips of Oliver's ears turned pink at this, I don't think Daisy was being as subtle as she intended.

"I'm sure we can all agree my godson is a handsome

devil," Mrs Finch chimed in with a winning smile. "Though I suppose I am biased."

"You must be Mrs Finch." My mother disengaged herself and came over to shake her hand.

"Mrs Bloom, you have a lovely home." It was bizarre to see the head of the Aviary calmly chatting with my mother. In fact, this whole farce was extremely strange, and I was no professional actress. I kept a wide smile pinned to my face, but from the concerned look Daisy gave me, it was edging dangerously towards a grimace.

"Please, won't you come in and sit down?" Mother showed our guests through while I went and placed the flowers Oliver had brought in a vase. I thought with a smile that he had accidentally landed on a choice that would do more to convince my family of our ruse than anything else: deep crimson roses.

Rose. *Rosa*. Meaning: passionate love.

By the time I returned to the sitting room, Oliver was sitting stiffly in a chair, being treated like an honoured guest.

"Ah, here she is now," Grandfather exclaimed jovially.

"Tell me, Mr Lockhart, what were your first impressions of our Marigold? Was it love at first sight?"

"Yes, tell us, Oliver," Mrs Finch said, all smiles.

Oliver's eyes flicked to mine, and I thought there was a slight flush on his cheeks. "I thought she was…"

I waited with interest to see how he would finish this sentence.

"Quite strange," he said, and then, possibly remembering himself at Daisy's giggle, he added in a lower voice, "and quite lovely."

Goosebumps erupted over my skin, and I mentally reminded my body that he was simply playing a part.

"Oh," Mother exhaled.

"And after this meeting you began a correspondence?" Grandfather asked, allowing a little disapproval to slip in.

"Err … yes?" Oliver said, and the word sounded like a question.

"My godson always was shy," Mrs Finch said, twinkling. "I know because he confided in me that while he understood that writing to Miss Bloom was technically a breach of etiquette, he simply couldn't *help* himself – he was so struck by her."

"Oh yes, she certainly struck me," Oliver said darkly. "Knocked me clean off my feet."

Here I let out a curious wheezing sound, which thankfully my family seemed to interpret as a display of emotion.

"So, you want to show Mari around your castle like in a fairy tale?" Daisy asked, practically bouncing in her seat.

"It's not a castle," Oliver said.

"Doesn't it have turrets?" Mrs Finch asked sweetly.

"Yes," Oliver replied grudgingly.

"And a drawbridge?" She clasped her hands in her lap.

"A small one," Oliver admitted.

"And aren't there gargoyles?"

Oliver looked put out. "There are ... several historical *carvings*."

"Sounds like a castle to me," Daisy whispered, looking delighted. "To think, our Marigold, living in a castle."

"I'm not going to be living in a castle," I said hastily. Honestly, trying to manage everyone's expectations was giving me a headache. "We have things to discuss, but there's no need to worry about me leaving you and the business behind. As it is, I'm not sure how we'll manage even for a week."

I hadn't meant to say that aloud, but I suppose it was fair enough to have some anxiety over the matter, however much I was enjoying watching Oliver Lockhart squirm.

"We'll be *fine*, won't we, Mother?" Daisy said.

"Of course we will," my mother replied, though her tone was doubtful.

Grandfather was looking between us, his expression hard to read.

"Honestly, Mari, I think it's exciting," Daisy insisted. "You deserve to get away from work for a bit, and we'll see how we get on without you. I mean it's not as if you're going to be here for ever, is it?"

Her words and the easy way she uttered them made me start. I knew she was only saying them because she thought there was a chance I might be marrying and moving away – prior to this, I wondered if my family had ever entertained the idea that I might leave one day. I certainly hadn't, but the idea suddenly struck me forcefully. It hadn't been something to consider with Simon – an arrangement that had been made precisely so everything would stay exactly the same.

But things were different now, weren't they? I wasn't marrying Simon, so what *were* my plans? After my engagement was broken off, I hadn't even considered leaving, hadn't thought about anything changing. But what if I didn't stay? Could I really do something else? Did I *want* to? The questions left me breathless, as if the ground in front of me had sharply dropped away, the safe path to the future vanished.

Perhaps joining the Aviary had been the first step into the unknown. I hadn't thought about it at the time, but in signing up, hadn't I started a journey of my own – one that had nothing to do with my family, with the business? Had I joined because I *wanted* something else?

The questions flew through my brain, so rapidly, so overwhelming that I felt my legs tremble.

"The last thing I would want to do is come between Miss Bloom and her family, or your business," Oliver said suddenly and with startling sincerity. "I greatly admire what you have built here."

"Your father was in factories, I understand?" Grandfather asked.

"He was." Oliver's brow crinkled. "Though he and I had very different priorities when it came to the wellbeing of our employees."

Grandfather's gaze sharpened at this. "I have heard stories about the working conditions in some of those factories that were deeply upsetting."

"That is putting it politely." Oliver smiled tightly. "I believe I have a responsibility to drastically improve the conditions beyond the threadbare legal requirements. Everyone has a right to safety and dignity in work. And I owe our workers a debt – without them, there would be no business." He hesitated here. "My godmother speaks very highly of Bloom's; she told me a little about some of the women you employ."

I lifted my eyes in surprise at this.

"We are proud to have many talented women working for us," Grandfather said easily. "As you say, without them, Bloom's would not be what it is."

"Still," I said, thinking suddenly of those women, remembering that it wasn't only my family who depended on me, "do you really think you'll be able to manage this week? I have gone over things with Suzy and Scout and I've written detailed instructions but perhaps…"

"We'll manage," Grandfather said, with a steel I hadn't heard in his voice for a long time.

"Let's have some tea, shall we?" Mother asked brightly. "We're all desperate to get to know Mari's young man."

"Wonderful," Mrs Finch said. I hoped I was the only one who saw the small kick she aimed at Oliver's ankle.

"Wonderful," he repeated mechanically, his teeth bared in something I thought was supposed to resemble a smile, but only made him look like he had indigestion.

"Gosh, he really is *so* handsome," Daisy murmured dreamily.

"Why don't you invite Mari for a walk in the park?" Mrs Finch asked some time later, after Oliver had been subjected to my family's inquisition and had made passable efforts at answering their questions politely.

"Yes!" he gasped, seizing on the opportunity with

more enthusiasm than I had previously seen him exhibit. "Miss Bloom? Would you walk with me?"

"Of course," I said, getting to my feet. "If that's all right with you, Mother?"

"Yes, yes," Mother agreed at once. "It's a lovely day. You young people should enjoy yourselves."

"I shall be just behind you," Mrs Finch said, playing the mindful chaperone. "After I take my leave of your family, Miss Bloom." Here she and my mother shared a conspiratorial twinkle at allowing the two young lovers some privacy to whisper sweet nothings to one another.

Oliver leaped to his feet and strode for the door with an urgency that I hoped everyone put down to ardour.

"Don't do anything I wouldn't do," Daisy said to me with a wink.

When we reached the street, Oliver took a breath that sounded like a drowning man coming up for air.

"My God," he said weakly.

"You did well." I smiled, reaching out to lay my hand on his arm.

It was a thoughtless gesture, but as the moment stretched out between us, I felt colour rush to my cheeks.

He looked down at my fingers, and just as I was about to pull them away, he covered them with his own, pulling my hand through to the crook of his elbow.

Without another word, we set off in the direction of the park, and I tried to ignore how nice it felt to stand so close to him, to feel the hard muscle of his forearm under my hand. After all, I reasoned, my family might glance out of the window and it wouldn't do for the two of us to look like strangers.

"I don't know how we are possibly going to keep this act up for several days," Oliver huffed.

"It won't be as bad in Yorkshire," I said. "My family know me so well; it's much harder to lie, and they're very … invested."

"Yes, I certainly got that impression," Oliver said dryly. "I thought your sister was about to ask me for my suit measurements at one point."

"She absolutely was," I confirmed, "but I stepped on her foot very hard."

I thought perhaps there was a hint of a smile in Oliver's eyes, but he only said, "Ah, that would explain the strange groaning sound, then." He hesitated for a moment. "I thought it was … nice, actually. The way they all care about you. I only wish they didn't care quite so *loudly*." He winced. "I suppose real families are noisy things."

There was something quiet and sad about him that made me want to have strong words with his dead father.

"The point is, the worst is behind us," I said airily, moving us away from the subject of family. "We'll have every advantage when we're in Yorkshire."

"Are you always this relentlessly cheerful?" Oliver growled. "It's giving me a stomach ache."

I was about to reply, when another couple stepped out on to the pavement in front of us.

"Oh. Miss Bloom," Simon Earnshaw said, full of false cheer. "How nice to bump into you."

His eyes ran over me from top to toe, a brisk inventory that lingered on my sunny yellow gown, the curls that had slipped their pins, the peek of my red silk shoes, and his mouth thinned, making it clear just how much he found me wanting. My stomach swooped, the shame I was so sure I had left behind, washing over me.

"Mr Earnshaw," I said, my voice small in my own ears. I didn't even sound like me and I hated it.

"I don't believe you've been properly introduced to my wife, Mrs Earnshaw?" he continued, and I met the timid gaze of Sarah Hardison-now-Earnshaw, who was just as pretty and sweet-looking as I remembered. "We were married last week."

"Congratulations," I managed, wondering why – after all that had happened in the last six months, when I knew I could knock Simon Earnshaw clean off his feet in one move if I wanted to – *why* did I still feel so miserably self-aware in his presence?

"Thank you," Sarah said, her voice shy. "It's nice to see you, Miss Bloom. I must compliment you on your hat."

"Miss Bloom always did have *singular* taste," Simon said, with a smile that felt like a knife slipping between my ribs.

Under my hand I felt Oliver's arm stiffen. Honestly, I had almost forgotten he was there.

"I'm sorry," I said, flustered. "I'm being rude. May I introduce Mr Lockhart?"

"Miss Bloom's fiancée." Oliver's deep voice cut in smoothly, and I saw Simon's eyes widen, saw the same measuring look he'd given me now running over Oliver Lockhart, and I couldn't help but enjoy the frown this produced.

Oliver held out his hand and Simon took it, failing to hide a wince, that made me believe Oliver's grip was rather … forceful.

"Mari, you're getting married?" Simon's casual use of my name was clearly deliberate, and Oliver seemed to loom taller at my side. "I had no idea."

"It hasn't been officially announced yet." My voice was pitched a little high.

"But it will be soon," Oliver said, treating Simon to a dismissive glance. "After all, only a *complete* fool would let Marigold Bloom slip away."

At this point, I think my grip on his arm was the only thing keeping me upright, because I could have fallen down in shock, and not only at the neat insult directed at Simon – no, my name on Oliver Lockhart's lips was doing strange things to my insides.

"I mean," Oliver continued, "you'd have to be a *buffoon* of the highest order, an empty-headed, witless dunderhead of dazzling proportions, wouldn't you?"

As if this wasn't enough, he looked down at me and smiled.

That smile.

It burst through me like a shot of strong liquor, leaving my heart pounding, my limbs tingling. If I had thought Oliver Lockhart was handsome when he scowled, then his smile – soft, full lips, a glint of white teeth, a crinkling of warm, dark eyes – made him simply staggering. I could do nothing but gape, mindlessly, at his perfect face, so perfect that it didn't make sense, so perfect that my brain struggled to understand what I was actually seeing.

When I finally tore my eyes away, it was to see a wide-eyed Sarah appearing similarly glazed. Simon looked like he'd been presented with a glass of sour milk.

"Yes, well," Simon sneered. "Good luck with that."

Instantly the smile dropped from Oliver's face, replaced with an icy contempt. "And the same to you." He directed the comment at Sarah, and Simon's face reddened.

With that, Oliver swept past them, tugging me along with him on shaking legs.

"I take it that was the fool you were engaged to," he said in a low voice once we were out of earshot.

"Yes," I managed.

"Fortunate that you managed to dodge that particular bullet, then."

"How did you know it was him?"

Oliver glanced down at me, his expression hard to read. "You went all … strange. And I didn't like the way he looked at you."

"Oh," I said. "Well, thank you for that. It was nice to see him put in his place like that."

"It was my pleasure."

"Of course," I said with a sigh, "once we break off our pretend romance, everyone will think I've let another man slip through my fingers. I'm sure Simon will be delighted by that."

Oliver seemed struck by this. "We'll just have to make sure everyone knows that ending our relationship was your choice," he said finally. "Plenty of people will be more than happy to tell you I'd be impossible to live with anyway."

The words were gruff, and they drew a smile from

me as we entered the park. "But, Mr Lockhart, only a *complete fool* would let me slip away. What will Simon Earnshaw think of you then?"

Oliver snorted. "I couldn't care less what that chucklehead thinks of me. His opinion is not worth a brass farthing." He came to a stop next to a bed full of phlox in bloom. Their playful pink petals were splashed magenta in the middle.

"You know," he said, suddenly awkward, "I am grateful" – here he touched his tie, cleared his throat – "to the Aviary, I mean, for helping me. I will do whatever I can to make sure this ridiculous false engagement plan doesn't hurt you or your reputation."

"Thank you," I said, surprisingly touched.

His eyes flicked to mine. "Yes, well. Don't start getting all misty-eyed again; we've got enough to deal with, without you and all your *feelings*."

"Quite right," I agreed primly.

He cast me a suspicious glance.

"Though, of course, you're going to have to pretend *you* have feelings for me in front of the Lavignes," I added. "If we are to be convincing. So frustrating, all these *emotions*. I do hope you're a good actor, Mr Lockhart."

Oliver's jaw was set, a muscle twitching. "I suppose we will find out, Miss Bloom." He cast his eyes to the heavens, before muttering under his breath, "What have I got myself into?"

I hid my smile as we turned and made our way back to Mrs Finch, but his question rang in my ears. What *had* we got ourselves into? And were we going to be able to come out the other side unscathed?

PART THREE

Yorkshire
August, 1898

CHAPTER EIGHTEEN

The next day we were in Yorkshire. It seemed a miracle to me, that it was as simple as getting on a train, and that only hours later I could be hundreds of miles from the city in which I had spent my whole life.

As the distance sped past, and we left the sprawl of the city behind, I felt no shame in pressing my face to the windows of our fancy first-class carriage. I had only travelled by train once before, and it certainly hadn't been in the sort of luxury that Oliver Lockhart seemed to take for granted. Mrs Finch, too, seemed as unflappable as ever, sitting quietly in the corner with her book.

As we moved further and further from London, it was as if a weight was being lifted from my chest, and I didn't understand why. Daisy's question of the day before rang in my ears. *It's not as if you're going to be here for ever, is it?*

Would I only stay at Bloom's if I didn't marry – or if I married someone who wanted me to continue working? Presumably such an arrangement would mean that the man in question would take over the shop. And did I even want to get married at all? My heart had been badly bruised by Simon, and the man was objectively a buffoon. Surely, it was better not to risk it, not to make myself vulnerable again.

After what had happened six months ago, such thoughts had been sealed away tightly in a box, but now that box had sprung open. I was forced to admit to myself that one day I wanted a family, and hard as it was to imagine, when I saw Izzy and Max together, I knew that if I ever *did* marry, then I wanted what they had – a true partnership between equals. But was such a thing even possible? Their relationship was nothing like mine had been with Simon.

As the questions tumbled noisily over one another in my mind, I goggled at the countryside unfolding outside the train: the neat handkerchief squares of green and yellow and amber, separated from me by the thin sheet of glass that felt cold under my fingertips.

The train moved so fast, and we shed the distance effortlessly, miles piling up behind us like a line of casually discarded clothes dropped on the way to bed. The world was, after all, so much bigger than London, and it had been – in the end – almost laughably easy to leave. I didn't think my life was small; it was busy and full of good work and good people, triumphs and the occasional catastrophe, and it was *mine*.

But.

That word lingered. But perhaps there could be more. It seemed more obvious here, setting out on this wild caper... There *was* more. If I wanted it.

I was giving myself a headache.

We changed trains at Peterborough for York, and it seemed only moments before we were arriving, spilling out on to the platform with the other passengers. Two hundred miles further from home than I had ever been.

"Barker should have brought the carriage to meet us," Oliver said, scanning the crowded station, as we made our way through the scrum. "I wrote to Beth, to tell her about our plans."

Catching my look of curiosity, he added, "Barker is my aide-de-campe, and Beth – his daughter – is my housekeeper."

"Aide-de-campe?" My brows lifted.

"It's Oliver's fancy way of saying he doesn't want to hire any other servants," Mrs Finch said. "Barker runs his household."

"Don't let Beth hear you say that," Oliver muttered. "Ah!" He straightened up. "There he is now."

With a flick of his wrist to the stewards who were carrying our bags, Oliver strode towards a carriage that was – as Daisy would say – bang up to the mark. Enormous, gleaming, gilded to within an inch of its life, with prancing gold unicorns painted on the doors.

I eyed it with alarm.

"Hideous, isn't it?" Oliver said sourly. "I told Barker to replace the last one – after your colleagues reduced it to tinder, actually – and when he kept coming to me with talk of springs and axels and seat cushions, I told him in no uncertain terms that I didn't care, didn't want to hear another word about it and to just buy whatever the hell he wanted. I believe this was his revenge."

Oliver looked at the fairy-tale carriage, suitable for Cinderella herself, like it was a mouldy old pumpkin.

"Here you are!" The man who must have been Barker stepped forward, all smiles. I'd place him somewhere in his fifties, and his accent was pure Yorkshire. "And this young lady must be your future bride!" His smile widened and he winked at me. I smiled back, knowing that Oliver's servants were in on the ruse.

"That's enough, Barker," Oliver growled.

"Just happy to see you taking steps towards settling down, young Oliver," Barker continued to tease him. Clearly used to this, Oliver only rolled his eyes, yanking the door to the carriage open.

"Barker, this is Miss Bloom and Mrs Finch," he said gesturing between us. "Mrs Finch, Miss Bloom – this is

Barker. Feel free to ignore every word that comes out of his mouth. Now, get in."

"Oliver." Mrs Finch's tone was without emotion, and she said only that, uttering his name calmly while she treated him to a long look.

There was a pause.

"Apologies." Oliver's chin dipped. "I meant to say, would you care to get in?"

"Lovely." Mrs Finch reached out her hand, and Oliver automatically lifted his to help her into the carriage.

"Miss Bloom?" He quirked a brow.

"Thank you, Mr Lockhart," I said, sweetly slipping my fingers into his and allowing him to help me inside too. I got the impression that Oliver wasn't used to performing such social niceties, and this impression was confirmed by Barker's choke of laughter.

Swinging into the seat beside me, Oliver closed the door and stuck his head out of the window. "Can we get going now, please?"

Still chuckling to himself, Barker climbed up on to the box, and soon we lurched away, through the twisting streets and away from the middle of town.

The carriage was like nothing I had ever travelled in before. The seats were plush, soft velvet the colour of bluebells, and instead of the noisy rattle of a hackney over cobbles, the ride was smooth as glass.

Oliver lapsed into silence, and across from me, Mrs Finch pulled out her book once more. I returned to my new favourite pastime: staring out of the window. The view was hypnotizing – ever changing – and I watched avidly as we moved out of the city, and the scenery and the light altered in front of me like a magic trick.

"Oh!" I couldn't help the breathy exclamation that fell from my lips when we eventually emerged on to the moors. *"Please,"* I managed, turning to Oliver. "Please can we stop? Just for a moment?"

He looked at me, his dark eyes inscrutable, then he reached up and knocked on the roof of the carriage. We came to an abrupt stop, and sending disjointed thanks over my shoulder, I yanked the door open and spilled out on to the road, almost falling to my knees in my hurry.

Green.

I had never seen such green. I was in the middle of the tumbling landscape, a lush covering of ferns and starry, purple heathers punctuated with rugged trees, the unmoving guardians of centuries. Peaks rose and fell, the scene undulating under the endless blue sky, and I could see for miles. Everywhere I looked was wild, untamed.

I only stood, utterly still, as if I could grow roots myself, as if – if I willed it hard enough – I could become a part of it all.

It was a dream. It was *literally* the stuff of my dreams, making me feel as though I knew this place, as though I had been here before. I felt my lips part, my eyes filled with unexpected tears.

A presence appeared at my elbow, and I blinked up at Oliver. Without a word, he handed me his handkerchief.

Ruefully, I wiped at my cheeks where the tears spilled over. "I really don't cry all the time," I quavered.

He gave a huff of disbelief. "All evidence to the contrary, Bloom."

I started at the casual use of my last name, without the "Miss" attached. It felt right coming from him – gruff and not quite polite. Not precisely warm but almost … friendly.

"It's so beautiful," I managed, steadying my voice and

holding out the handkerchief. "I've never seen anywhere so beautiful before."

"Keep it," Oliver said. "You seem to need one often enough."

"Thank you," I said, tucking it into the sleeve of my dress.

"Are you ready to go?" he asked.

Reluctantly, I nodded, and he helped me back into the carriage. As we drove away, I skimmed my fingers along the end of my sleeve, brushing the edge of his handkerchief, curiously thrilled by the knowledge it was there.

We continued for another hour or so, perhaps longer; I couldn't tell you exactly, because I was too busy gorging on the scenery. It was a landscape you would never tire of – and it went on for *miles*.

"We're almost there," Oliver said finally, his voice breaking the quiet. Leaning over me, he pointed up to where the road climbed to the right. As we rounded a bend, I gasped again.

"That ... that's your *house*?" I choked.

Oliver tugged at his collar, eyes flashing. "Yes," he said shortly.

I lifted my brows at him. "I thought you said it wasn't a castle?"

"It's not a castle," Oliver said stubbornly. "It's a hall. Lockhart Hall."

"Lockhart," I leaned towards him, close enough that I could see the almost black rim around his dark irises, and I pointed out of the window. "*That* is a castle."

And it was. Perched high on a jutting stone cliff that tumbled dramatically away on one side, it looked like the sort of castle that a demon king might inhabit. There were turrets twisting into the sky, for goodness' sake! And a thousand windows cut into the dark stone. It looked as though it should have banners flying, men in suits of armour stomping around, perhaps a dragon or two breathing fire to ward off inquisitive villagers.

I had thought Mrs Finch was exaggerating about the drawbridge, but there really was one of those too. It was lowered over a stream that ran a steep drop below the front gate. I supposed that when the drawbridge was raised, the house was an island to itself, completely isolated. From what I knew of Oliver Lockhart's character, that was probably just how he liked it.

We clattered across the drawbridge, and through the gate in the surrounding high stone wall that led to a small courtyard.

"These walls," I said, looking up at them. "This place was some sort of fortress?"

Oliver made a hum of agreement. "Those narrow cuts in the stone are arrow slits; archers could stand behind them and shoot at unwanted guests."

"How often have you used them on *your* unwanted guests?" I asked with a smirk.

"I haven't yet. But I have certainly been tempted."

"Speaking of whom," Mrs Finch murmured, and I realized that she was not distracted by the Gothic monstrosity in which we found ourselves – she had her eyes firmly on the three people stepping out of the shadowed doorway instead.

In an instant, I felt myself on edge. I was reminded, forcibly, of the reason we were here.

"Are you ready?" Oliver asked me, his mouth set in a grim line.

"Yes," I replied, fixing a sunny smile on my face. "Time to meet the family."

CHAPTER NINETEEN

"Mr Lockhart, you're home!" A woman broke from the small group and rushed forward to greet us. Though her accent was English, it was touched by a musical lilt that I assumed was a French influence. "And you've brought guests," she added, as Oliver helped Mrs Finch and me down to the ground. There was just a hint of over-familiarity in her voice that struck me as strange. It felt as if she was the one welcoming us to her home.

"I have," Oliver said abruptly. "May I present Miss Bloom, my ... *fiancée*." The word came out slightly strangled, but Oliver pressed on. "And her godmother, Mrs Finch."

He turned to us as the other two people stepped forward. "Miss Bloom, Mrs Finch – my sister, Helene, and her parents, the Lavignes."

I dropped into a curtsey and regarded the three strangers in front of us.

Mrs Lavigne was a handsome woman in her forties, dark-haired and elegant. She was dressed in a simple gown of dusky lilac that looked well made and expensive, and she stared at me with eyes round with astonishment.

"Your fiancée?" she managed. "But you never mentioned…"

Mr Lavigne interrupted, recovering faster than his wife. "What a happy occasion!" he boomed, reaching out to shake my hand in an energetic pumping motion. "Mr Lockhart has kept you a surprise, my dear!"

He was a slight man, several inches shorter than his wife, but an animated energy seemed to ripple over him. That and the enormous dark moustache that graced his top lip, carefully curled up at the ends with wax, made him seem larger somehow. Unlike his wife, his clothes were not at all tasteful or elegant; his orange waistcoat, clashing wildly with his forest-green suit, was loud and eye-catching. I thought I saw him send an approving glance towards my own gown, which was, I would admit, quite a vibrant shade of pink.

"Yes, Mr Lockhart," Mrs Lavigne said, rallying swiftly. "What a sly fellow you are!"

"It's all quite new," I said, casting my eyes down and aiming for demure shyness.

"I couldn't be sure Miss Bloom returned my feelings and would accept my suit," Oliver said with the stiff quality of someone reading from a script – precisely because Mrs Finch had scripted this for him.

"Mr Lockhart is too modest." Mrs Finch stepped forward, instantly at ease in her role as the doting godmother, well pleased with her charge's success on the marriage mart. "It was clear to me from the first that he and my goddaughter were meant for one another. I have never seen two young people so in love." She lifted a handkerchief to her eye and dabbed, her voice quivering with emotion.

Oliver frowned down at me, his brow deeply furrowed. He looked less like he was in love with me, and more like he had never before perceived a human woman. His eyes flicked to the back of my hand, which had come to rest lightly on his arm. He swallowed. "In love. Yes." The words were a croak.

It would have to do I supposed, resisting the urge to pinch him.

"And he couldn't wait to bring his future bride home with him to meet his long-lost sister!" Mrs Finch said. "Such a romantic tale, and so moving. It's like something from a novel!"

"Yes, yes," Mrs Lavigne said hastily, and I felt the weight of her gaze lingering on me. "Helene, darling, come and meet your future sister-in-law. It seems there is much to celebrate."

At this, Mrs Lavigne dragged her daughter forward, and I found myself face-to-face with Oliver's possibly-sister.

The first thing that struck me was that she didn't look very much like her brother. Where his skin was the warm gold of wet sand, hers was milk pale. Her hair was brown, and so were her eyes, but they were not so dark as Oliver's, nor did she possess his dark brows or enviably long lashes. There was, perhaps, some resemblance in the high cheekbones, the tilt of the chin, but it was not pronounced.

Helene was eyeing me with apprehension, and I had the impression at once of someone who was painfully shy.

"How do you do," she said softly. She did not hold out her hand, and I noticed she was wearing pretty lace gloves so there was no opportunity to examine the scar Oliver had mentioned.

"I'm very happy to meet you, Miss Lavigne," I hesitated. "I'm sorry, or do you prefer Miss Lockhart?"

A flush lit Helene's cheeks. "I ... we haven't—" She cast a look at her mother. "I think perhaps Miss Lavigne?" she said finally.

"We still haven't got used to it." Mrs Lavigne smiled warmly at her daughter. "But even now that Helene is happily returned to the bosom of her family, *we* will *always* be her parents."

She spoke firmly and sincerely. For Helene's sake, I was glad of it. Whatever was truly happening here, it seemed she had parents who cared for her.

"Although, if you are really to be sisters, surely Helene will suffice?" Mr Lavigne broke in. "And that way we neatly dodge all this confusion." He beamed, clearly pleased with his solution, and I couldn't help smiling back.

"How right you are," I agreed. "I hope you will call me Marigold," I said to Helene. "Or Mari, if you prefer. That is what my sister calls me, after all."

"I have never had a sister before." Helene smiled tremulously and held out her hand, which I took. "But I always wanted one."

"Then it's settled," I said.

"And we should get your guests inside and show them to their rooms," Mrs Lavigne said, again with that touch of condescension I didn't like. She certainly seemed very at home at Lockhart Hall.

If Oliver felt anything was amiss, he didn't show it. "Yes, thank you. Barker," he called over his shoulder. "I will show the ladies in, if you could take care of the luggage and arrange with Beth for some refreshments?"

"Right you are," Barker replied easily, already leading the horses away.

Mrs Lavigne's nostrils flared, and I guessed she wasn't too keen on the informality of the household. I had to admit, I was surprised by it myself. Mr Lavigne did not seem similarly troubled, only smiling wider at us all.

Without another word, Oliver strode ahead and through a front door that seemed fifty feet tall and built to withstand battering rams. Inside the entry hall, it became clear at once that this strange house was going to live up to its Gothic promises. The entrance was enormous, with high ceilings and – yes – a suit of armour hunched rather sulkily in one corner. For such a big space, it did not benefit from much natural sunlight, and as a result it felt dark, almost oppressive. The air was significantly cooler in here, the contrast sending a shiver dancing across my skin.

"Welcome to the mausoleum," Oliver muttered.

"It's certainly very … atmospheric," I said, eyeing the enormous and very ancient-looking chandelier still lit by candles.

Oliver snorted. "Oh yes, we've got plenty of atmosphere. Beth! BETH!" he yelled.

A woman appeared, wiping her hands on her apron.

She was around thirty, with dark curls and wide green eyes. This must be Barker's daughter because the resemblance between them was striking, her laughing expression so similar to his that I liked her at once.

"What did I say about shrieking like that, Oliver?" she chided. Her eyes slid to mine. "Er ... Mr Lockhart, I mean."

"Beth, the Lavignes are well aware of how informal we are." Oliver grunted. "There's no need to go putting on airs for my ... *betrothed*." He looked slightly less queasy this time, but I noticed Beth press her lips together.

"I am Beth Barker," she said, stepping towards me. "You'll forgive Oliver's poor manners, I'm sure. You must be Miss Bloom."

"I am," I said. "And I'm very happy to renounce ceremony too; Mari will suit me perfectly. And this is my godmother, Mrs Finch." I gestured to her.

Mrs Finch only smiled serenely, offering no one her first name. Personally, I thought this was because she didn't actually have one. I wasn't even convinced that Mrs Finch was her real name at all, and no one at the Aviary seemed to know very much about the woman, though Izzy had once told me that there was a Mr Finch somewhere.

"Perhaps you could show Miss Bloom and Mrs Finch to their rooms," Mrs Lavigne said, directing her words to Beth, while her gaze barely flicked in her direction. "And then we may all take tea in the drawing room."

I couldn't help the way my eyebrows flew up at this, and when I met Beth's eye, the glimmer I saw there made me think this was not the first time she had experienced Mrs Lavigne's high-handedness.

Oliver, on the other hand, seemed again not to notice. "I'm going to the library," was all he said, as he turned and stalked away. "Let me know when you want me. And tea had better involve something to eat because I'm starving."

"Believe it or not, that was Oliver on his best behaviour," Beth murmured to me in a low voice as she led the way up the staircase. The Lavignes headed off – presumably in the direction of the drawing room.

"Really?" I asked.

"Oh yes." A smile pulled at Beth's lips. "I've never known him to actually agree to sit down to tea before. Then again, we don't usually have visitors."

By this point we had reached the top of the staircase and Beth turned left, leading Mrs Finch and me down a long corridor. The scale of the building was almost absurd, and we passed a number of doors and made several turns before coming to a stop.

"Your rooms are down here," she said. "The Lavignes and Helene are staying at the other end of the house."

"A map would probably be most helpful when the time comes to search for them," Mrs Finch said. "If you could draw one up?"

"Of course." Beth nodded, reaching out to open the door in front of her.

"Never mind finding the Lavignes' rooms," I said. "We'll need a map to find our own!"

Beth gave a chuckle at this. "You soon get used to it," she promised. "Besides, almost all the rooms are shut up, so you can't go too wrong."

"Shut up?" I repeated as we stepped through to a bedroom that was large and just as gloomy as the rest of the house so far.

"Usually it's only us and Oliver who are here," Beth said. "But there are over a hundred rooms in the house.

Most of them are left closed. In fact, this is the most people we've had in Lockhart Hall since Mrs Lockhart was alive." She gestured around the room. "I hope this is all right for you, Mari? Mrs Finch, your room connects through the door here." Beth opened the door in question revealing another room, the mirror image of my own.

"It's lovely, thank you," I said, because though it was dark, and though the giant furniture felt heavy and old-fashioned, I hadn't neglected to notice that the room smelled pleasantly of beeswax and clean linens, or that on the enormous dressing table there was a vase of slender grasses tipped with elegant tufts of pale lavender.

"These are pretty," I said, touching my finger to one.

"Yorkshire Fog," Beth said, sounding suddenly shy. "It's just grass, I know, but Oliver said you had a liking for flowers, and we don't have much to choose from around here, as you can see." She waved her hand towards the window, and I moved over, pushing the heavy curtains to one side.

"What is that?" I managed.

"It *was* the garden," Beth snorted derisively. "Though that's not what I'd call it now. Mrs Lockhart had it kept beautiful, but after she died..." She trailed off here, but I had to admit I was barely paying attention; I was so enthralled by the view.

We were higher up than I thought, and clearly at the side of the building now. Sprawled in front of me was a tangle of weeds and unkempt garden – huge in scale, like the rest of the house. I could just make out the shape of the overgrown footpaths that cut through what must have once been a lawn but was now a waist-high spread of grasses, gently bobbing in the breeze. There were hints of flower beds, stone walls, crumbling and tumbled over with ivy. And the elevated position meant that all around it, the view of the moors spread out like water, green and restless.

As I looked at it, my heart started beating faster and one word rang in my mind, clear as a bell.

Mine.

I jumped back from the window as if it had shocked me. *Mine?* What sort of a reaction was that? A wildly inappropriate, demonstrably false one. Flustered, my eyes darted to Mrs Finch, who was watching me with an impassable look.

"Perhaps, Beth, you could give us your impressions of the Lavignes while we are alone," she said.

My hand pressed against my chest, where my heart still thumped too hard, too loud. Yes. The Lavignes. *Stop being distracted, Mari*, I chided myself. *There is work to do.*

"They are all right, I suppose," Beth said grudgingly. "Polite, not too demanding, careful with Oliver when he's around."

"But?" Mrs Finch prompted.

"I can't put my finger on it exactly. They're too comfortable here. It's as if they think the place belongs to them now. As if they have a … claim on it. Which I suppose they might…"

"Do you think Helene could be Oliver's sister?" I asked when Beth left this thought unfinished.

Beth's head tipped to the side. "If that isn't the question I've been asking myself every minute of this last week…" She sighed. "I don't know. I've been here my whole life so I knew Miss Ellen up until the day she and the mistress disappeared, and the truth is that Helene *could* be her. She has the look of her, and she certainly seems to know a lot about her, remembers things that I don't see how she could know otherwise. Miss Ellen, though, she was a real bright light – full of questions, forever getting in scrapes."

"That doesn't sound like the woman we just met," I murmured.

"No," Beth agreed, "but a lot can change in eleven years."

"Particularly if Helene's story is true," Mrs Finch mused. "Such a tumultuous experience would leave its mark."

"So it remains a mystery," I said.

"Not for much longer." Mrs Finch's smile was sharp. "We're here now."

CHAPTER TWENTY

Tea was predictably uncomfortable. Fully recovered from the shock of our arrival, Mrs Lavigne seemed all too happy to fling herself into the role of hostess, peppering Oliver with questions about me and our engagement while his answers got shorter and shorter.

"But do tell us, Mr Lockhart," she pressed, as she carefully poured herself a second cup of tea. "For how long has this romance been going on?"

"Six months," Oliver replied curtly.

"Six months!" Mrs Lavigne exclaimed. "And to think you never said a word! I assure you, Miss Bloom, not a single word!"

"I can believe it, Mrs Lavigne!" I laughed. "At first even I had no idea about Mr Lockhart's feelings for me." Here I peeped at him from under my lashes. One of us, I reasoned, should at least be playing the part.

Oliver looked back at me, his expression stony.

"It has been such a whirlwind," I continued breathlessly, enjoying his discomfort far too much. "We began writing to one another once a week, but soon the letters flew back and forth, and Mr Lockhart is such a *poet*. His way with words is truly moving."

Oliver choked on his tea.

"Really?" Mrs Lavigne tried and failed to conceal her surprise.

"Oh yes," I said. "My favourite letters were the ones stained with the tears he shed as he composed his beautiful odes to all my virtues."

"You do have so *many* virtues," Oliver agreed, and I knew that he meant something quite different.

I didn't know why teasing Oliver Lockhart brought

me such pleasure, but it did, and if it coincided with the goals of the Aviary, then so much the better.

"Goodness me," Mrs Lavigne said. "How lovely, Mr Lockhart. How did you and Miss Bloom meet?"

"We met at the library," Oliver said shortly, reaching for a biscuit, which he crammed in his mouth, presumably to prevent future questions.

"Ah!" Mr Lavigne twinkled at me. "Charming. A fellow novel reader, I presume?"

I shook my head. "I'm afraid my sister is the great novel reader in the family. I was actually in the horticulture section."

"Horticulture?" Mrs Lavigne's eyebrows lifted, as she eyed me over the top of her tea cup. "You have an interest in gardening, Miss Bloom?"

"More than an interest," I said. "I am a florist by trade. My family own a flower shop in London."

"A *florist*?" Somehow Mrs Lavigne managed to inject the word with enough horror that you'd have thought I told them I ate children for a living. "Forgive me, Miss Bloom," she said. "I hadn't realized that your family were … in trade."

At this, Oliver seemed to show some sign of life. "Why should that be a surprise, Mrs Lavigne? As you know, I am *in trade* myself." His words were dangerously calm, but I saw the flash of temper in his eyes.

"Oh, well, that is quite different," Mrs Lavigne began, as though it was obvious.

Mr Lavigne reached across and put his hand over his wife's for an instant. "Forgive my wife," he said jovially. "In France, people are much more comfortable talking openly about such matters. We have all of us perhaps forgotten our English manners."

Although he said the words lightly, something uneasy filled the room. Across from me, Helene shifted in her seat.

"Of course you are right," Mrs Lavigne said brightly. "Please forgive me. The England I remember was so rigid and set in its ways. It is charming to find that in these modern times, true love triumphs over social expectation."

"I don't know about that," I said carefully, "but certainly in the case of Mr Lockhart and myself, we both inherit businesses from our grandfathers before us.

I don't think there is really anything to scandalize society about our marriage."

"And Miss Bloom is the only one of us who actually inherits anything of true value," Oliver put in unexpectedly. "The business she has helped to build is something remarkable, while I am left trying to untangle a poorly run, morally bankrupt mess."

"Oh, but, Mr Lockhart, how can you say such a thing?" Mrs Lavigne laughed. "When you have all this." She gestured at the room in which we sat – though dreary and uncomfortable, it was undeniably *grand*.

Oliver only scoffed into his teacup.

"Are you not pleased with your future home, Miss Bloom?" Mrs Lavigne asked me sweetly.

"Very pleased," I responded calmly. "Though I must confess, it is the garden that holds the greatest promise for me."

Mrs Lavigne wrinkled her nose. "I myself cannot stand getting my hands dirty, but I suppose that is what gardeners are for."

"And you, Helene," I asked quickly, determined to draw her out. "What are your interests?"

"Oh, our Helene is accomplished at so many things!" Mrs Lavigne broke in. "She embroiders like a dream and sings like an angel. Well, we should have known, with the way she takes to such things that she was born in a place like this, with every advantage given to her."

"Funny, I don't remember my sister being able to carry a tune," Oliver said almost idly, though there was a keen look in his eye.

Before Mrs Lavigne could leap in again, Helene smiled, the expression almost fond. "No," she said in her soft voice. "I was a dreadful disappointment to my singing master at first, but I did improve eventually." She looked down at her hands. "I remember singing here once – at Christmas. Father said at least it drove all the guests away."

Oliver looked stricken for a moment, then nodded.

"It is wonderful what a good teacher can do, isn't it?" Mrs Finch said, unravelling the tension that filled the room once more with her calm tone. "My goddaughter knows that only too well." The smile she gave me then was glimmering with mischief only I would see. The instruction I had had recently was very different to the accomplishments Mrs Lavigne spoke of – I doubted Helene's teachers taught lock picking.

"I do," I said, smiling back. "Did you go to school in Paris, Helene?"

"Just outside the city," Helene said.

"And did you—"

"I must say these biscuits are delicious," Mr Lavigne broke in. "Beth truly has a way in the kitchen."

Oliver hummed, the sound dubious. In truth, the biscuits were quite dry and strangely … salty.

"Yes, they are positively dangerous for the waistline," Mrs Lavigne agreed. "Though, I'm sure Miss Bloom will manage one or two more." She held the plate towards me, and in her eyes I saw a small spiteful look that I had seen many times before. Her gaze lingered on my body for only a split second, but I felt the intended barb wrapped in her light words, the way a cat might scratch: sharp, fleeting and deadly accurate. It was depressing how often such a thing happened, often enough that the jab barely registered as a surprise.

"I'm sure I will," I replied amiably, taking another biscuit and biting into it with every sign of enjoyment.

I understood exactly how much it irritated women like Mrs Lavigne to see me living my life, fat and happy and unapologetic. As expected, her smile dimmed.

"Perhaps now would be a good time for Mr Lockhart to give you a tour of the house, Marigold?" Mrs Finch purred, and I knew from the way she said it that she had noticed Mrs Lavigne's little dig as well.

"Yes," Oliver said at once, jumping to his feet. "What a good idea."

"And I shall have a chance for a comfortable coze with the Lavignes. I'm fascinated to hear all about you," Mrs Finch continued.

"But … surely" – Mrs Lavigne's eyes flashed between Oliver and myself – "the young couple should have a chaperone?"

"Mrs Lavigne!" Mrs Finch sounded shocked. "I hope you are not impugning Mr Lockhart's honour? Surely, here in his own home, with so many people in the house, he can be trusted to show his future wife the grounds unchaperoned?"

"Of – of course." Mrs Lavigne looked flustered. "I only meant… I would never suggest such a thing. I—"

"I think we'll be off, shall we?" Oliver interrupted smoothly as he stood, holding out his hand to me. When I slipped my fingers into his, he squeezed them a touch too hard, enough to let me know how he felt about all the teasing that had been taking place.

Without any further conversation, we left the room, my arm through his. I put a little extra sway in my step for Mrs Lavigne's benefit. One thing was certain: she may hide it behind polite smiles, but the woman didn't like me. I turned everything that had happened since we arrived over in my mind and came to the conclusion that I had put a spoke in the wheel of Mrs Lavigne's plans. Whether that was because she was an imposter, or because she resented the interference of another woman in the home she wished to claim for her daughter, was a question to which I didn't know the answer. Yet.

"So, that went well," I said in a low voice, once we were safely out of earshot.

"Beautiful odes?" Oliver said icily. "The *tears I shed*?"

"I thought it was a nice touch," I replied, as we

walked down a long hallway and then through several connected rooms. The house was colder here, the furniture covered in dust sheets. Light slanted in through half-shut curtains, dust motes wheeling in a sleepy dance.

"And *you* are doing very little to convince these people that we are happily engaged," I pointed out.

"I'm sorry we can't all be such accomplished actors," Oliver grumbled.

"Actually," I admitted, "I'm not good at acting. I hate telling lies – it makes my skin itch."

"You seem to be doing a good job to me."

"For some reason it's easier when I know it will irritate you."

"Bloom." Oliver exhaled deeply, shaking his head. "You could test the patience of a saint."

The laughter died on my lips as he pushed through a set of wide French doors, and suddenly we found ourselves outside.

Still arm in arm, we stood on a wide stone platform that ran the length of this side of the house. It had once been, I supposed, a terrace. A sun trap, warm under the early evening sun. Now the stone was rough, crumbling in places. There was a rotted pergola sagging against the wall at one end, the skeleton of some long-dead climbing plant still clinging in parts.

We walked down a short flight of stone stairs until we reached the lawn I had seen from my bedroom. The paving stones were unsteady, and Oliver held my arm a bit tighter. As I had thought, the grass here grew almost to my waist.

I held out my free hand, my fingers gently brushing against the tall fronds.

Neither of us said anything, only stood, looking over the wreck of what must once have been a beautiful garden. I could feel the warmth from his body against my side, could smell the sandalwood on his skin. He kept hold of my arm, even though no one could see us now.

"I never come out here," Oliver said finally. "It's much worse than I remember."

I turned to look at him, but he kept his eyes firmly planted on the horizon. His face was blank, except for that tell-tale tightening about his jaw.

"All I see is potential," I replied.

He gave that almost-smile. "Ever the optimist," he said.

"This is my job, Lockhart. You may safely defer to my expertise. This is no lost cause: only a place that needs a little time and care."

"Where would you start?"

"First?" I smiled. "I'd probably mow the lawn. I hear they even have machines for that these days."

We fell quiet again, and I took a moment just to feel the sun on my skin, to absorb once again the pleasure of so much space. It was quiet here, the kind of quiet that never fell over the city. The kind that was broken only by the cheerful trilling of a robin, who sounded pleased not only with himself but with the whole world.

"Why did you bring me straight out to the garden?" I asked.

"You said you were most interested in the garden," he replied nonchalantly. "I hadn't thought about it in a long time. Most of the time I make myself forget it's even here. It was … my mother's favourite place."

He doesn't say any more, and I don't ask him to. The

pain in his voice is well hidden, but I hear it all the same, the jagged edges to the words.

"Even like this," I said finally, "it's still beautiful. Nature makes no mistakes."

Oliver's hand came up to cover mine, only briefly. It was barely a touch, but I felt it down to my toes.

"Sounds like something an optimist would say to me," he said gruffly. Then, shaking his head, Oliver turned, pulling me with him and back towards the house. "Anyway, let's go. Might as well show you the rest of this old wreck."

CHAPTER TWENTY-ONE

Oliver dragged me through several rooms, all of which had that same ghostly feeling of abandonment, and he casually reeled off phrases like: "This is the saloon." "This is the smoking room." "This is the pink room."

"You have a room just for ... being pink?" I asked.

He looked around the room as if seeing it for the first time, and shrugged. "It was a sort of sitting room. The walls are pink."

"I see."

"And through here is the gallery."

We walked through to a long room bristling with oil paintings that covered the walls almost from floor to ceiling. It was … overwhelming. Particularly as many of the portraits in their heavy (and dusty) gold frames managed to make their subjects seem rather unsavoury.

"Horrid bunch, aren't they?" Oliver nodded towards the paintings of many, many men who looked pleased with themselves, in various stages of historical dress. "Not a decent one among them. Made their money off other people's misery – all to make this house bigger and bigger with the profits. I keep trying to find better ways to use the money. Improving conditions in the factory and the workers' cottages has been a start, and of course there are various charities, but something sickening happens to very rich men after a certain point. They don't need to do anything; their money only keeps making more money. More than anyone could need in a hundred lifetimes, but still less than most of the people who sit on it feel entitled to. I have seen greed that you couldn't imagine."

We stopped in front of a picture of a man, silver-haired

and elegant, with hard, cold blue eyes that sent a shiver down my spine.

"My great-grandfather, for example," Oliver murmured. "An extremely bad man. Very vocal in his opposition to abolishing slavery. Ironic, really."

"Ironic?" I asked over the leaden feeling in my stomach.

"My mother's grandmother was a slave in part of the Spanish colonies," Oliver said, moving towards the end of the room, where a painting was hung, low on the wall, tucked away from the rest. "Which means his great-grandson who inherited the lot, including his precious house, is directly descended from slaves."

This painting was different – not only because of the warmth it carried, the splash of colour in this horrible, gloomy room, but because of the subject matter: a woman and two young children.

I recognized Oliver at once. He was about eight years old and already frowning as if he held the artist – or, really, the rest of the world – in weary contempt. Beside him, her hand resting on his shoulder, was a woman who could only be described as dazzling. Here were Oliver's features: the bold, dark eyes, the dangerous cheekbones, the dark, tumbling hair and golden skin. Unlike Oliver, however, there was a light about this woman, a smile in her eyes, a spark of mischief.

"My mother, Violante," Oliver murmured.

"She was beautiful," I said, and the words came out almost in a whisper.

"Incredibly so," Oliver said, his posture rigid as he looked at the painting. "I imagine that even my father, cold-hearted bastard that he was, must have thought so when he met her in Spain and whisked her away to England. Enough that he married her despite the 'blight' of her heritage, as he so frequently called it later on, presumably when the spell wore off and he realized he wasn't a man capable of love at all."

The words were said coolly, but each one sliced like a keen-edged blade. So much pain delivered so calmly, so brutally, that I felt winded.

"That ... that's terrible," I managed.

"Terrible for everyone involved," Oliver agreed, and now he just sounded weary. "Terrible for my mother, terrible for my great-grandmother, terrible for the millions like her, and the legacy that lives within each of us now. That lives within *me*." Unthinking, he had pressed a hand to his heart. "Here, in a house built on all that pain." He looked about him. "Sometimes, I think I should just burn the place to the ground and be done with it." The words were quiet, as if he were speaking to himself.

I shivered again. How easy it was in my own life to imagine these things so far away, so distant. It had been less than seventy years since slavery was abolished in this country, and everyone knew that finally passing a bill in Parliament was a long way from dismantling a brutal and ongoing reality faced by many, no matter how pleased we liked to feel about ourselves.

After a long moment of heavy silence, Oliver cleared his throat. "And, of course, this is Ellen." He gestured to the girl in the picture, and I stepped forward to look more closely.

"It could be her," I said softly, taking in the small girl, with her light brown hair and wide eyes. There was an energy about her, a glint of mischief in her gaze. "She doesn't look anything like you or your mother."

"Ellen was adopted as a baby," Oliver said. "She was the result of one of my father's affairs, and when her mother left the baby on our doorstep, I think Father would have shipped her off to some horrible institution if my mother hadn't stepped in. She wouldn't hear of it. As far as she was concerned, from that first moment, Ellen was hers." Oliver smiled, a small, soft smile that made my toes curl up in my pretty pink shoes. "I was only one at the time, so we were brought up together – at least until I was shipped off to school."

"And your father didn't mind such an arrangement?" I asked carefully.

Oliver gave a short laugh, every ounce of softness leaving his face. "Mind it? He didn't seem to care much either way. He had very little to do with me, but he barely acknowledged Ellen at all."

"And yet he left her money in his will," I said.

"Mother presented Ellen to the world as her daughter. Ellen might not have looked like my mother, but she certainly looked like our father. Anything he left her was for appearance's sake alone, believe me. And though it is a lot of money, in truth it represents an almost insultingly small fraction of his fortune. Something I intend to remedy."

I took a moment to digest that, and what exactly it meant about Oliver's own circumstances. Perhaps Mrs Lavigne's shock at our connection was more warranted than I wanted to admit. It was also interesting that Oliver planned to settle more money on his sister. I wondered if the Lavignes knew about that.

"I take it that the story Helene told about singing at Christmas was true?" I said.

Oliver reached up, rubbed his brow. "It was. There have been so many things like that, things only Ellen would know. And the scar..." He looked at me. "Why can't I simply accept that she is Ellen? When all the evidence points that way. I feel as if I am going mad, swaying wildly from one conclusion to another."

"Perhaps you are just scared to believe it," I said gently.

We were interrupted then by the sound of the door opening. Swinging round, I found Helene herself approaching us, somewhat tentatively.

"Mother said I should come and find you, Mr Lockhart," she said timidly. "She wondered if you had any special instructions for dinner."

"Why should I have any special instructions?" Oliver asked. "Beth will do just as she usually does. Cook the life out of whatever lump of meat she chooses to serve."

I stifled a giggle at this, while Helene only looked at him, round-eyed.

"I'm sure Beth has it in hand," I said, more diplomatically.

Helene, however, had been distracted by the painting we were standing in front of.

"Oh!" she exclaimed, lifting her hand to her cheek, which was flooded with colour. Emotion washed over her features. "It's her," she murmured.

"It is a good likeness of Mother, isn't it?" Oliver said, his voice more gentle than I had heard it before.

Helene's eyes flew to him. "Y-yes," she said. "A very good likeness." Her gaze moved to the image of a young Oliver. "You hated that suit," she said. "She had to bribe you with cinnamon biscuits to get you to wear it."

"That's right." Oliver exhaled. "I had forgotten."

Helene continued to stare at the painting, the expression on her face strange, almost wistful.

I exchanged a glance with Oliver, and in his eyes I saw nothing but unanswered questions. My heart hurt for them both.

"We should return to the rest of your company," I said. "It must be time to dress for dinner."

"*Dress* for *dinner*?" That seemed to break through Oliver's fog of uncertainty. He sounded disgusted.

"Yes, it's what people generally do in polite society," I replied evenly.

"*People*," Oliver grunted. "This is precisely why people are dreadful. And why I choose to have as little to do with them as possible."

"Well, *we* are people, and now you have our delightful company for dinner," I said, casting a smile at Helene, who returned it tentatively.

"But why must I change what I'm wearing, only to sit down with the same people I have spent all day with?" he whined.

"Perhaps" – Helene smiled shyly – "we had better ask Beth to make you some cinnamon biscuits."

Oliver gave a surprised bark of laughter. "Good God, don't do that!" he exclaimed. "Let's not ruin that beloved childhood memory with her dire attempts at baking."

And with that, he offered one arm to me and one to Helene, and the three of us made our way back to the doorway.

Before we left, I cast one last glance over my shoulder at the painting of Violante and her children. *What happened?* I wanted to ask her. *Where is your daughter now?*

Those dark eyes only looked steadily back at me, and a moment later we were gone, leaving her behind in the shadows.

CHAPTER TWENTY-TWO

Despite Oliver's protests, he arrived for dinner dressed in an immaculate dark suit, and he looked so handsome that pretending to be desperately in love with him seemed suddenly all too easy.

"Blame Barker," he muttered when I commented on how nice he looked. "Seems to have taken advantage of my absence and ordered me a whole new wardrobe from the tailor, now that we're *entertaining*." He tugged at his necktie in annoyance.

"I think that sounds very enterprising," I said, sipping

the glass of wine that Barker had poured for me when we sat down at the table. "You're fortunate to have him."

"Should have known you'd be on his side," Oliver grumbled, leaning back in his chair at the head of the table. His gaze raked over me for a moment before he added, "Your hair is different."

I lifted a hand to my hair, which Beth had carefully plaited and pinned so that for once my unruly curls were swept into an elegant chignon, only a couple of tendrils left loose to frame my face. The lemon-yellow dress into which I'd changed was one of my best, and the wide neckline left my shoulders bare, the loose strands of hair brushing them gently.

"Thanks to Beth's interventions." I grinned. "She's a marvel too."

"I must say," Mrs Lavigne interrupted, clearly overhearing this part from where she sat across the table between her husband and her daughter. "That style suits you very well, Miss Bloom. And what a *bold* dress too. You cut quite the figure. I feel almost dowdy by comparison." Her laugh was musical.

"You could never be dowdy," I said lightly, trying hard

to ignore the familiar prickle of her honeyed words, the same Simon would have used in her place, I'm sure. "You and Helene carry everything off with such elegance."

And this was not a lie; both women looked very well in different shades of pale blue, pretty and demure.

"I think we gentlemen may consider ourselves fortunate to be in the company of so many lovely ladies." Mr Lavigne beamed, his fingers stroking his luxuriant moustache.

"Extremely fortunate," Mrs Finch agreed serenely. Her own dress, a beautiful deep crimson silk had reduced me to a puddle of envy when I first saw her this evening.

"My dressmaker is a genius," she had said to me with a small, pleased smile. "I will introduce you, if you like."

"Yes, please," I had replied vehemently – finding a dressmaker who knew how to dress bigger bodies with such flair was rare indeed.

"What do you think, Mr Lockhart?" Mrs Lavigne pressed now, dragging my attention back to the moment.

"About what?" Oliver asked, glaring down at the plate that Barker placed in front of him. As much as I liked Beth, it was hard to disagree with Oliver's assessment of her culinary skills as I peered at the piece of brown meat (beef?) dressed with some sort of brown sauce and various limp accompaniments.

"About the ladies' gowns, of course!" Mrs Lavigne laughed teasingly. "Do you think Miss Bloom puts us quite in the shade?"

"What the devil should I kn—" Oliver began, but I kicked him in the ankle, and he flinched, turning to me with accusing eyes.

I used my own to try to remind him that we were supposed to be *deeply in love*.

Oliver sighed. Then he looked at me again. This time the look lingered, ran along the lines of my gown, skimming from my exposed shoulders up to my face, and I felt a jolt of unexpected heat rush through me.

"I think Miss Bloom sets everyone in the shade," he said finally with awkward gallantry. "She looks like..." Here he hesitated, looking at me as if for guidance. "A lemon drop," he finished with an air of desperation.

I laughed. "A lemon drop?"

"Yes," Oliver said more firmly now. "Lemon drops are my favourite. And they're pretty. Like you."

Something peculiar seemed to be happening in my chest.

"Well," Mrs Lavigne tittered, "I suppose now we can all see the poetic side of Mr Lockhart's character."

Oliver returned to scowling down at his food, colour touching his cheeks, and I resisted the urge to fling my fork at Mrs Lavigne.

Instead, I took a deep breath, toying with a carrot – at least I thought it was a carrot – on my plate. Mrs Finch had managed to get very little out of the Lavignes in mine and Oliver's absence, and we had both agreed that dinner presented the perfect opportunity for a politely veiled interrogation. After all, idle chatter was one of my particular skills.

"I hope you won't mind my asking," I said, looking over the table and past the warm flicker of candlelight to the Lavignes, "but I must admit I'm absolutely desperate to hear the story of how Helene and Mr Lockhart came to be reunited. As you can imagine" – I fluttered my lashes at Oliver – "Mr Lockhart has been rather scant on the details, and it is such a romantic tale."

"Miss Bloom." Mr Lavigne chuckled. "And here I thought it was your sister who was the novel reader."

"I think anyone would find it hard to resist being swept up in a story like this, and one with such a happy ending." I picked up my wine glass and sipped casually. "I understand the accident was in Paris, Helene? Do you know why you and your mother were there?"

Helene cleared her throat. "No, I don't. There is much that I still don't remember about that part – only pieces of the journey. We were on a boat, and Mother was very sick."

"She always did suffer from terrible seasickness," Oliver put in. "She couldn't even go out in a rowing boat on the lake without turning pea green." It was another fact to add to the tally of what Helene knew.

Helene nodded. "The accident itself is nothing but a blur. Only the image of the inside of the carriage, a sharp noise, I think, loud and frightening. Then everything goes ... blank."

"For which I think we can all be extremely grateful," Mr Lavigne said firmly.

"Yes." Mrs Lavigne covered her daughter's hand with

her own and squeezed. "I'll always be glad that part of the experience is lost to you."

"It must have been awful," I said gently. "You were so young. Your parents are quite right that missing that particular memory can only be a blessing."

Mrs Lavigne's face softened at this. "From what we have been able to piece together, Helene's accident took place in an area called Le Pecq, just outside Paris."

"It's a place where the river loops round," Mr Lavigne continued, gesturing with his hand to indicate the serpentine path of the water. "It seems that during the accident Helene was thrown quite some distance from the carriage and ended up in the water. She had suffered a nasty head injury and travelled down river some way, before being washed up on the banks somewhere to the north. From there, she wandered, disorientated, towards the village of Herblay, where we were living at the time."

"I remember none of this," Helene said. Oliver was watching with an expression that was impossible to read.

"When she was found, a ten-year-old child, bleeding from her head" – Mrs Lavigne's face contorted with emotion – "she answered questions in French, but didn't seem to remember anything but her name – Ellen, which the people who found her took to be *Helene*."

"You must understand," Mr Lavigne said earnestly, leaning forward, "that we tried to find out where Helene had come from, but it didn't occur to anyone that she would be connected to an accident that happened over ten miles away, involving a Spanish woman who was presumed at the time to be travelling alone."

"From what I have been able to discover," Oliver added, "the authorities were under the impression that my mother had travelled to Paris by herself. By the time they realized Ellen had been in the carriage, it was easy to assume her body had been washed away, and my father was perfectly happy to accept this explanation."

My opinion of Oliver's father continued to sink lower and lower.

"We were unable to have children of our own," Mrs Lavigne said with a tremble in her voice. "When Helene appeared, she seemed like a gift from God. She was alone in the world, and we took her in, raised her as our own. For months we spoke only French, and we tried to piece together information about her past, but Helene remembered nothing."

"It was all … a blank space," Helene said quietly.

"We didn't even realize she spoke English at first," Mrs Lavigne said, eyes wide. "And, if I'm truly honest, after a while we stopped asking questions. We couldn't stand the thought of finding anything out that would mean Helene was taken from us." She lifted her napkin to her face and dabbed her eyes. "I'm sorry," she said tearfully. "It has been hard." Here, her husband's hand came down on her shoulder, while she clung to Helene's fingers.

They made an affecting picture, the three of them holding on to one another. I felt my own throat tighten.

"About two months ago, Helene had another accident." Mr Lavigne picked up the thread of the story. "A silly domestic scene involving a basket of apples and a loose floorboard. Helene hit her head, and although she was soon perfectly well, she began having these strange … visions, like waking dreams."

"The first thing was a room with a rocking horse in," Helene said. "It was old and missing one of its eyes, so I used to comb its mane over to cover it. Threaded my ribbons through the hair to make it pretty. I could remember it so clearly; hear the sound it made as it moved, a sort of soft creak."

"My rocking horse," Oliver said, his gaze frozen on Helene's face.

She smiled tremulously. "Yes, that was why I wouldn't let anyone get rid of it, even though we were too old to ride it any more. You said the eye was lost in battle."

"That's right." A smile flickered on Oliver's lips now.

"It took a while for us to realize these images were memories," Mr Lavigne said. "Memories of her life here." He looked around the dining room.

"Is such a thing really possible?" I murmured, caught up in the story they were weaving.

"The doctor we consulted in London certainly seemed to think so." Mr Lavigne shrugged ruefully. "When we realized what was going on – that what she was seeing was not a strange dream or hallucination, but rather memories that had been somehow unlocked; we wanted to consult with an expert before turning up and upending the life of Mr Lockhart."

Quiet fell over the table as everyone absorbed these words, and Beth appeared, clearing the plates in front of us, while accepting our murmured thanks for the meal she had prepared.

"But let us turn to more pleasant things," Mrs Finch encouraged.

"Yes." I sent a friendly smile across the table towards Helene. "Do tell us about your life in France. It is clear it has been a happy one."

"Oh yes," Helene said, returning my smile shyly. "Very happy."

"We have not been able to give Helene the life she might have had here, of course," Mrs Lavigne said, a defensive note in her voice. I couldn't help feeling frustrated. I was certain I could get Helene to open up more, but her parents seemed always to want to speak over her. I couldn't work out if it was because they liked the sound of their own voices, or because they were trying to keep Helene from saying too much.

"But we did our best," Mrs Lavigne continued. "We lived a quiet life; my husband had several investments that paid well, and we could afford to send Helene to a very good boarding school. His work as a merchant meant that we travelled a lot, and it was good for Helene to have that stability. Especially after what she had been through."

"Oh? Which school was that?" Mrs Finch asked. "I have a niece who attends Lycée Fénelon."

"Lycée Sainte-Geneviève is not actually in Paris." Mrs Lavigne sat taller in her chair. "But it is a very respected school for young ladies just outside the city."

"Of course." Mrs Finch smiled, as Barker and Beth laid out delicate plates that held a mess of cream and fruit, and a crumbly substance that might have been sponge cake. "After all, they have a walking advertisement in the form of Helene here. Anyone can see she is a well-brought-up, educated young lady of refinement."

Mrs Lavigne seemed placated by this, visibly relaxing under the compliment.

"Well, I for one am glad that such a difficult story has such a happy ending," I said, lifting my glass in a toast. "And that we can all be here together sharing this lovely meal."

"Hear, hear," Mr Lavigne echoed vehemently.

We raised our glasses and then tucked into our desserts, which were surprisingly tasty. It seemed that adding a good deal of sugar to things made them much more palatable.

"I wonder, Miss Bloom, if—" Mrs Lavigne began, and I found I was steeling myself for what would come next, but nothing did because Oliver stood abruptly from the table, his face a mask of panic.

"Stop!" he yelled.

CHAPTER TWENTY-THREE

We all stared at him for a moment, words still dying on Mrs Lavigne's lips, cutlery suspended in the air.

"Are you quite well?" Oliver cried, running to Helene's side. She cringed back, eyes wide. "Beth, get in here!"

Beth appeared in the doorway, breathless. "Whatever is the matter?" she asked.

"Does this have strawberries in it?" Oliver demanded, gesturing at the table.

"Strawberries?" Beth looked blank and then her own

face paled. "Oh, goodness, yes, I didn't think. I..." Her eyes darted to Helene.

In an instant, Oliver had Helene on her feet. "Did you eat this?" he demanded, still holding her by her arm.

"Y-yes," she murmured, clearly frightened. Her eyes moved to her father, her mother, then to me.

"Mr Lockhart," I said gently, rounding the table. "What is it? What's wrong?"

His gaze swung to mine, and I saw nothing but blind panic there. "We must call the doctor," he croaked.

"Why?" Mrs Lavigne demanded, her voice high. "What has happened?"

Helene made a sound of realization, her eyes widening. "Strawberries," she whispered. "S-strawberries made me ill."

"What?" Mr Lavigne snapped, clearly riled.

"Eating strawberries makes Ellen very unwell," Oliver snapped, equally sharp. "Last time, her throat swelled up so much she could hardly breathe. The doctor said..."

There was a beat then, a moment when everyone absorbed these words. A moment when all eyes turned to Helene who – apart from looking shaken by Oliver's outburst – showed no signs of ill effect at all.

"Helene has not had a reaction to strawberries for many years," Mr Lavigne said quietly, breaking the silence.

"She outgrew it," Mrs Lavigne added quickly. "It happens often with children."

Oliver seemed to realize he was still gripping Helene's arm. "I apologize," he said stiffly, taking a step back, and then another. "I didn't mean to... I only thought..."

"An understandable moment of concern for your sister," Mrs Finch said soothingly.

"Commendable, really," Mrs Lavigne said, though her face was still pale, and she regarded Oliver warily.

"Yes, well." Oliver's eyes wandered over the rest of us. His hand went to his necktie, and he tugged at it as though it was strangling him. "I think that's enough excitement for one night. If you'll excuse me."

And with that, he gave us a curt nod, swung on his heel and strode from the room before anyone could say a word.

"Well," Mrs Lavigne said, after another frozen

moment in which we all stood perfectly still. "I suppose we should all retire for the evening. It has been a long day of travelling for Miss Bloom and Mrs Finch."

"Yes, yes." Mr Lavigne exhaled loudly, his rigid posture finally relaxing. "We have been thoughtless indeed, making demands on your company. It is no wonder emotions are running high."

Helene stood, watching the door where Oliver had left, gripping the back of the chair with her hand, and I saw that her knuckles were raised and white.

After we had said our goodnights, I sought out Beth and she took me to find Oliver. In the vast warren of this house, I had no idea where he might be, but I knew I would not be able to sleep until I had seen him.

"He'll be in here," Beth murmured, coming to a stop outside the door. She gave me a long searching look. "I am glad you came," she said finally. "It is time Oliver had someone else on his side."

Before I could respond, she disappeared back in the direction we had just come from. I stood for a moment, gathering myself.

I was in a part of the house that Oliver and I hadn't reached during our tour, and I had no idea what stood on the other side of the door. Given the sheer number of rooms I had already encountered, it could be anything – there were plenty of colours left for a green room or a yellow room, or perhaps it was a room for smoking meats, or shooting poor people.

It turned out it was none of those things. When I knocked lightly and pushed the door open, I found myself standing on the threshold of a library.

The walls were heaving with books, carelessly disordered, but clearly well read – no handsome tomes for appearance's sake here. There was a large desk, piled high with papers. Worn rugs that must once have been vibrantly colourful were strewn across the floor, making the space feel softer.

A huge fireplace stood on the wall in front of me, a fire crackling that sent warm orange light flickering over the scene. It felt comfortable, homey, like someone *lived* here. This, I thought, was what this house could be with some care. It didn't have to be cold and impersonal. It could be a home.

Arranged in front of the fire with its back to me was a single high-backed armchair, and I could just see the arm of the man sitting in it, a glass of amber liquid clasped loosely in his fingers.

"Not now, Beth," came Oliver's voice, a weary edge to it. "I don't want company; I want to get horribly drunk and scowl into the fire."

I moved into the room, stepping forward until I was level with the chair. Oliver sprawled there, his jacket and tie discarded in an untidy heap on the floor beside him. His collar was undone, his sleeves rolled back to his elbows revealing strong, muscled forearms. His fingers, wrapped round the glass, were long and elegant. He wore a gold signet ring on the smallest one.

Curled up in his lap was an enormous orange cat, and the hand not holding on to the glass of brandy was gently stroking the purring creature.

"Why can't you have company while you do those things?" I asked.

Oliver's head swung to the side, his eyes lifting to meet mine.

"Bloom!" he exclaimed with enough energy to displace the cat, who gave a hiss of displeasure. "What are you doing here?"

I moved towards the fire, holding my hands out in front of me, enjoying the warmth that melted over my fingers and keeping my back to him so that he wouldn't see too much of the concern in my face.

"I came to check on you, of course."

"I don't need anyone to check on me." Oliver's words were clipped. "*Especially* not you."

I swung round at that. "What do you mean especially not me?" I asked, stung.

"It's not appropriate," Oliver said stiffly. "I have been … imbibing."

"Imbibing?" I quirked a brow. "Oh, you mean you've been drinking. How can you have when we've only been apart for five minutes?"

"I think you'll find that a man can get a lot done in five minutes if he is focused on his goal," Oliver said, and for some reason the way he spoke the words sent a shiver across my skin. I stepped closer to the fire, hoping to chase away the chill.

"If you've decided to sit here and get drunk, don't let me stop you," I said. "Though I hope you don't make a habit of it."

I looked back at him over my shoulder, and he scowled. "Of course I don't make a habit of it. If I did, it would take a lot more than five minutes of knocking back brandy to have me in my cups, wouldn't it?"

"Then why did you decide you needed a drink now?" I asked, cautiously pressing my luck.

There was a moment where I didn't think he would answer. He looked into the fire, his brows tipped down as the light kissed his profile with its golden touch.

"I have been alone for a long time," he said finally. "If Ellen came back ... if I found my sister, and then something happened to her ... *again* ... I don't know what I would do." The words were soft, a confession, and I didn't know how much of this honesty was owed to the brandy, but I was glad to hear him say them anyway, even as I felt the hurt there.

"That makes sense," I said, dropping to the floor, and arranging my skirts around me as I sat with my back to the fire, my eyes on him. "I should think such an idea would be terrifying. If anything happened to Daisy, I don't know what I would do either."

He looked down into his glass. "I must be starting to believe them," he said. "That she is Ellen, I mean. In the moment, I simply reacted as if she was. That must mean I believe."

"Perhaps," I agreed. "Or perhaps you *want* to believe."

He made a noise that could have been agreement. "The damned rocking horse. Even I had forgotten about that. Every detail ... even down to the sound it made." He sighed, a sound of frustration. "Do you think people really can grow out of a reaction to food like that?"

"I don't know," I said honestly, "but Winnie will. We'll write to her tonight. We have the name of the school in France for Sylla, and you have the name of the doctor the Lavignes consulted in London. Maud will look into him." I smiled. "You're not in this alone. We will untangle it all. We'll find the truth."

His head fell back against the chair, and he looked at me through half-closed eyes. "I almost believe it when you say it."

"As you should."

I was distracted then by the cat who approached me, butting at my hand, and twining around me in a clear demand for attention. I was happy to oblige, stroking it as it lolled to the floor in front of the fire beside me, purring like a steam engine.

"I didn't know you had a pet," I said.

Oliver snorted. "He isn't a *pet*." He eyed the cat sourly. "He's here to catch mice. Bloody old ruin is full of them. If anything, he's a member of the staff."

As the member of staff in question was wearing a smart leather collar with a silver disc hanging from it, carefully engraved with the name Marmalade, I took this description with a pinch of salt, but I said nothing more on the subject, restricting myself to a small, knowing smile.

"If you're going to sit here and drink brandy, do you think you might share?" I asked instead.

Oliver leaned forward, holding the glass out towards me. "I only have one glass," he said. The words sounded like a dare.

I took the glass from him, our fingers brushing as

I did so. The dark curls of his hair had fallen across his forehead and the open top buttons of his shirt revealed a triangle of golden skin. I thought how much I liked him like this – loose-limbed and dishevelled.

And then I remembered I had no business thinking about liking him at all, so I buried my face in the glass, taking a long gulp of the amber liquid. It burned down my throat and I spluttered.

To his credit, Oliver didn't say anything, only smirked as I handed the glass back to him.

"One glass," I said, when the burning subsided, and I could talk again. "One chair."

Oliver's eyebrow lifted. "I don't have many visitors."

"Why not?"

"Because I don't care for the company of other people."

"Oh," I said.

"No need to look like a kicked puppy, Bloom." Oliver sighed deeply. "*You're* not other people."

"I'm not?"

His eyes met mine, and in that moment I could hear my heart beating so loudly I was surprised he didn't remark upon it, enquire whether I needed medical attention.

"No," he said quietly. "You're … something else altogether." He took another sip from his glass. "Anyway, why is it always you interrogating me? Perhaps I have some questions of my own."

"Such as?" I asked.

"Such as why did you agree to marry that awful toad we met in the street?"

I shifted, surprised. "It seemed like a good idea at the time. Simon's father owns the building Bloom's is in. It made sense as a business opportunity."

"Simon's father…" Oliver trailed off, a distant look in his eyes. "You mean the man who propositioned you?"

The outrage on his face warmed my heart. "Yes, but the Aviary took care of that. Thanks to you."

"I hope they bloody castrated him," Oliver muttered darkly into his glass.

"I believe Sylla handled the matter, so I wouldn't put it past her."

"So your family were willing to let you marry the toad for the sake of the business?"

I stretched out my legs, wiggling my toes to stop them from falling asleep. "They didn't know it was only for business. I told them I liked Simon. I *did* like Simon … I think. He was very sweet to me, at least in the beginning."

"What does that mean?" Oliver asked.

I shrugged. "When he courted me at first, it was all gifts and sweet words. When our relationship … *progressed*, things changed." I glanced at Oliver here, preparing myself for any judgement I might see on his face, but there was none – he only watched me steadily. "He started making a lot of comments," I continued. "Little things. Things about the way I looked, the way I dressed, the way I behaved. He told me I was *too much*. Not wife material, I suppose."

I kept the words light, but Oliver's expression grew increasingly furious.

"He belittled you," he said roughly. "Made you feel small, ashamed."

My eyes flashed to his. "Yes."

He must have seen the surprise in my face because this time when he smiled there was no warmth to it at all; this smile was a parody of the real thing, something bitter and sad.

"I watched my father do the same thing to my mother for eleven years. Men like that, they're the ones who are small. They imagine inadequacies in others to make themselves feel better. Believe me, it is a very good thing you didn't marry him." The look he fixed me with then was solemn. "He would have dimmed your light, Marigold Bloom. And that would have been a damn tragedy, because you blaze brighter than anyone I have ever met."

His words spread through me, slow and searing like the brandy that I could still taste on my tongue. I felt my mouth open, but no words came out. In the glittering light from the fire, Oliver's eyes were almost black.

Suddenly he exhaled, falling back into the chair again. He lifted the glass to his lips and drained it. "This is precisely why I shouldn't drink. Or speak to people. I don't even know what I'm saying. You should go. We wouldn't want Mrs Lavigne getting the wrong impression."

"That you were trying to seduce your fiancée?" I

said, but the joke fell flat, the words loud and awkward between us.

Oliver's eyes turned away from me, towards the fire.

"Goodnight, Miss Bloom."

CHAPTER TWENTY-FOUR

When I woke the next morning, I was groggy from lack of sleep. Unsurprisingly, I had spent much of the night tossing and turning, agonizing over the events of the day in my mind.

While I knew it should have been the encounters with Helene and the Lavignes that occupied my thoughts, I'd be lying if I said I hadn't spent more time picturing a pair of dark, flashing eyes, if I hadn't heard the words "you blaze brighter than anyone I have ever met" playing over and over in my mind. I wondered if I had imagined the heavy, drugging sensation of that moment as it stretched between us, the way the air thickened, my heartbeat a wild staccato that I could feel everywhere.

The quiet didn't help. I had never known anything like the thick blanket of silence that fell over the world at night out here on the moors. London *never* slept, and to me the symphony of rattling hackneys, leary drunks and street sweepers was as soothing as a lullaby.

Here, the absence of sound felt unnatural, broken only by the occasional mournful wail of the wind or a jagged screech, which I eventually attributed to an owl, after first reassuring myself that no one was being murdered directly outside my window.

All in all, it was in a slightly worn and definitely agitated state that I approached the table in the breakfast room (a different dining room from the one we had eaten dinner in, because apparently one needed a separate room for every meal).

Only Helene and Mrs Finch were in there, and Helene looked more relaxed than I had seen before thanks to Mrs Finch's animated chatter.

"Good morning, Marigold." Mrs Finch smiled up at

me over her coffee cup. "Beth has laid out tea and coffee, and she said she'll be back shortly with the food. I was just regaling Helene with tales of my grandmother and her brush with spiritualism."

For a split second I wondered if I was so tired that I was imagining things, but then my training kicked in. "Oh, yes," I said, sitting down across from the pair of them. "Those stories were always very … entertaining." My eyes flicked to Mrs Finch, looking for a clue, but she only drank her coffee with an unruffled calm.

"Yes, indeed," Helene agreed, nodding her head so that the curls arranged around her face bobbed. "Mrs Finch told me that for a brief time, her grandmother actually performed seances!"

"Mmm," I replied non-committally, reaching for the silver coffee pot on the table and wondering what on earth Mrs Finch was up to now.

"Once, in Paris I went to see a spiritualist perform, an American lady," Helene continued, and there was some colour in her cheeks. "She was marvellous. There was one point where the table we were sitting round levitated clear off the ground."

"I should think that would have been terrifying," I said, lifting the coffee pot in offer of refilling her cup.

"No thank you." Helene shook her head. "I can't stand coffee – my French friends found me a sore disappointment; it was far too English of me to prefer tea." She smiled, and I chuckled.

"But to return to the levitating table..." Mrs Finch nudged.

"Oh, yes!" Helene tilted her head to the side. "It wasn't terrifying precisely. More thrilling. I was fourteen and my friend and I had sneaked away from our lessons to attend." Her smile dimmed.

"Well, I can't blame you for that," I said, wanting to encourage her to keep talking. "I'm sure I would have done the very same thing myself."

"And I," Mrs Finch agreed. "But then, thanks to my grandmother, I was fascinated by it all. In fact" – here, Mrs Finch sat back in her seat and I knew whatever this bizarre fiction had been in aid of was about to become clear – "Grandmother always said that I, too, had the gift."

"Really?" Helene shivered, nothing but innocent

delight in her face. I felt a pang of warmth towards her. I had been watching her so closely, and yet I was struggling to determine if she was telling the truth or perpetrating a ruse. Most of the time, I was certain that she was precisely the sweet, diffident young woman she appeared to be, but sometimes ... sometimes there was something ... *off*. Just a little out of balance, a tiny flicker across her face. A look that was almost pain or fear that had me questioning her.

Mrs Finch nodded solemnly. "Perhaps you would like a demonstration?"

"A demonstration?" A flash of uncertainty lit Helene's eyes.

"Surely you're not going to make the breakfast table levitate?" I grinned. "If I'm not mistaken, these teacups are antiques."

Mrs Finch laughed. "Nothing so dramatic, I'm afraid." She turned to Helene. "Do you know anything about palmistry?"

I could hardly suppress my laugh of surprise. The woman was a genius.

"Oh, yes," I said eagerly, leaning forward in my chair.

"Do show Helene." I nodded encouragingly at the young woman. "It is simply fascinating, I promise you."

"You want to read my palm?" Helene said cautiously, but I could feel her interest.

Mrs Finch shrugged. "I do not promise to be able to tell you much, but it is always interesting to try to get a glimpse into the future, is it not?"

"The future," Helene murmured thoughtfully. "Yes, of course." Then she laughed, embarrassed. "What do we need to do?"

"Why nothing at all," Mrs Finch replied. "I will only examine at your palm, if I may? The right hand is best."

"Certainly," Helene said, holding out her right hand. Mrs Finch took it and gently turned it over.

"Fascinating," Mrs Finch said. "Marigold, come here and look – I know you will be interested too."

I got to my feet, carrying my coffee cup with me and made my way round the table to peer at Helene's hand, which was cradled in Mrs Finch's.

At once I saw the scar that Oliver had mentioned: a small crescent shape below her little finger. It looked absolutely real to me.

"Now this line here," Mrs Finch said, pointing at the crease that ran down Helene's hand from beside her thumb, "is your lifeline. And I'm glad to say that it is long indeed. I believe you will outlive us all, Helene!"

Helene chuckled. "Well, that is nice to know."

"Hmmm..." Mrs Finch frowned. "This line is your heart line. Unfortunately it has been slightly disrupted by the scar you have here."

"Oh, yes," Helene said, and as she looked at the scar, an expression of such desolation passed over her face that I couldn't imagine what she must be thinking of. Then she blinked and smiled shakily. "A silly childhood accident. Oliver climbed a tree and I did not care to be left behind. When I cut my hand on a jagged branch, it bled so much I almost fainted and would have fallen. He was furious that I had followed him when he told me not to, shouted at me the whole time, but he rescued me, carried me down on his back."

I smiled softly. "Yes, that sounds like him." It sounded *so* much like him that I knew at once the story was true.

Helene cleared her throat, looked down at her hand once more.

"Hmmm." Mrs Finch ran her finger gently over the scar. "Well, it makes it harder to read of course, but it is another long, well-curved line and so I think it is safe to say there is another happy ending in your future. You will find love, Helene, and it will be a great love that lasts many years."

"Oh!" Helene flushed with colour. "Do you think so? I—"

"My goodness, and what is going on here?" Mrs Lavigne's arch voice shattered the moment, and I turned to find her entering the room with Oliver on her heels.

"Good morning," I managed, and he gave no outward sign of any discomfort beyond his usually surly demeanour.

"Mrs Finch was telling me about her grandmother," Helene said, and I couldn't help noticing that much of her stiff unease had returned with Oliver's presence. "She was a spiritualist, and Mrs Finch was reading my palm."

Helene had snatched her hand away, and now had them both neatly folded in her lap.

I saw Oliver's eyebrows twitch ever so slightly.

"It is only a game, really," Mrs Finch said lightly. "Sadly, I do not have the same power that my grandmother possessed, but I do enjoy the practice of palmistry, so intriguing what one can divine. It's why I was so unsurprised when Mr Lockhart declared his intentions towards my goddaughter. It was clear to me from the beginning that the two of them were destined." She leaned forward, tapping her nose knowingly. "Matching heart lines."

"How interesting," Mrs Lavigne said. "I had no idea. And did I overhear something about Helene's romantic future?"

"Bright indeed, Mrs Lavigne," Mrs Finch replied, while Helene blushed again.

"I do hope so." Mrs Lavigne smiled. "My greatest wish for my daughter is the same happiness that I have found with her father. In France we were not really in a position to bring Helene out into society, but I expect that will change soon."

Oliver looked startled and shifted in his seat uncomfortably. "Oh. Yes." It appeared he had only just realized he might have some responsibility in presenting his unmarried sister to the rest of the world. A responsibility that would certainly involve *other people*.

Mr Lavigne bustled through the door at that moment. "I see I am a lazy oaf this morning." He beamed. "My apologies."

"Not at all, my dear," Mrs Lavigne said. "It seems you have beaten the cook to breakfast, after all. Poor Beth seems rather *overworked*." She smiled sweetly at Oliver, who only scowled back.

"If Beth wants any help, she only has to ask," he said shortly. "She has the running of the house well in hand and has for many years."

"Of course," Mrs Lavigne acquiesced, condescension in every word, "when one has been a bachelor for so long, I suppose that is the way these things happen, but soon Lockhart Hall will have a new mistress." She treated me to one of those long looks that felt like honey over steel. "I'm sure Miss Bloom will make *many* changes."

As Oliver's frown deepened at this, I could only assume that Mrs Lavigne was attempting to remind him that marriage would disrupt the running of his house in ways he might not like.

I opened my mouth to reply, but Oliver surprised me by jumping in first.

"Miss Bloom, of course, will have whatever she wants."

I felt colour burning in my cheeks.

"Can I pour anyone some more coffee?" Oliver asked, seemingly untroubled.

"Not for me, thank you," Helene said when he held the pot over her cup. "I was just telling Miss Bloom that I never outgrew my dislike of it, despite being practically a Frenchwoman."

"That's right," Oliver said easily. "I had forgotten." I knew it for a lie, could read it in his face, though I doubted anyone else could. He had been gently testing her again. And she had passed. Again.

At that moment, Beth and Barker appeared, carrying in silver chafing dishes that they lined up on the side table against the wall.

After two more trips, they lifted the lids from the dishes revealing piles of bacon, sausages, cold meats, kedgeree, grilled tomatoes, devilled kidneys and fluffy scrambled eggs.

My stomach gave a growl of appreciation. It seemed that breakfast was the meal at which Beth shone, and from the pleased look on her pink face, she knew it too.

We descended on the spread with enthusiasm, and when I sat back down it was with a plate piled high.

"Forgive me, Beth." Mrs Lavigne held up her hand, and I realized she hadn't partaken of any of the food on offer. "Would it be possible to get just some thin porridge and perhaps a plate of fruit?" She cast a smile around the table. "A lady must sadly sacrifice to maintain her figure."

"Of course," Beth said politely, heading back towards the kitchen.

"You know, Miss Bloom," Mrs Lavigne said, picking up her teacup, "I discovered the most wonderful reducing diet in France."

"Oh, really?" I said, as I tucked into my bacon.

"Yes, it involves drinking vinegar, which is unpleasant of course, but one cannot argue with the results. I believe Lord Byron used the method himself." She poured a cup of coffee from the pot.

"I'm sure you're right," I replied when it seemed

some response was necessary. "His poetry was quite melancholic, wasn't it? The poor man must have been dreadfully hungry."

Helene choked on a giggle at this, and her mother sent her a sharp look.

"Yes, well, better to be hungry than a glutton," Mrs Lavigne said snippily. "We ladies must suffer for the sake of beauty, mustn't we?"

"Must we?" I echoed.

"One doesn't want to be…" Mrs Lavigne trailed off as though tactfully reaching for the right words, while her nose crinkled in distaste. "Overly *large*."

"Nonsense," Oliver snapped, and all attention swung to him.

"I'm sorry?" Mrs Lavigne looked flustered.

"I said, *nonsense*." Oliver carved into a piece of ham with unnecessary violence. "It seems to me that women have quite enough suffering to do without adding drinking vinegar into the mix."

"Ah, but Miss Bloom understands my meaning, I'm *sure*," Mrs Lavigne rushed in, shooting me a sly glance. "It is such a struggle for some of us to remain thin, but it is important, too. The desire to be pleasing in our appearance is in our nature! We women want to be *petite*. Delicate and dainty, what is beautiful, what is most appealing…"

"I understand your meaning perfectly, Mrs Lavigne," I said as evenly as I could manage.

"Miss Bloom is perfectly appealing as she is," Oliver said shortly.

There was an awkward pause then, and once again I felt something warm unfurl inside me. Helene's eyes darted between Oliver and myself, something like surprise in them. If I had to guess, I would say she hadn't imagined he would defend me.

"It is curious, isn't it?" Mrs Finch said softly. "That society seems determined to make women smaller and smaller. It is almost as though the world is frightened of us, of what we may be if we were … unrestrained."

"Goodness!" Mr Lavigne chuckled. "This is as good as having that Fawcett woman to breakfast, isn't it?"

"What a charming compliment," Mrs Finch said, her smile showing her teeth.

After another awkward pause, Oliver cleared his

throat. "I hoped today that the Lavignes and Helene might join me on a journey into York," he said, abruptly changing the subject and introducing the plan we had agreed upon the day before.

Mr and Mrs Lavigne exchanged a look of confusion.

"You know we are at your disposal, sir," Mr Lavigne said cautiously. "Is there any particular reason for the journey?"

"I feel we are overdue a visit to my lawyers there," Oliver said. "They handle my day-to-day business and are consulting with the legal team in London to deal with the matter of Helene's inheritance and any other claims on the estate. They require further information in order to draw up the appropriate papers."

"Of course, of course." Mr Lavigne nodded. "These lawyers do seem to enjoy tying things in knots."

"Well, I will be delighted to see York," Mrs Lavigne said happily. "Perhaps Helene and I can attend to some shopping. No doubt there will be many social occasions on the horizon for which we must look the part. It would hardly do for us to show Mr Lockhart up!"

Oliver stretched his mouth into something that I

suppose he thought approximated a smile, but it was clear that he was condemning Mrs Finch and her plan to Hades.

"Mrs Finch and Miss Bloom, I hope that you will be able to entertain yourselves in our absence," Oliver replied dryly.

"Oh, I'm sure we'll find something to do," Mrs Finch purred. "Don't you worry about us."

CHAPTER TWENTY-FIVE

"We must search both rooms systematically," Mrs Finch said a couple of hours later when we stood inside the doorway to the Lavignes' bedroom. "What are the rules?"

"Quick, efficient, undetectable," I replied, repeating the words that had been drummed into me throughout my training, though this was my first opportunity to put them into practice.

"Thankfully the Lavignes are tidy sorts," Mrs Finch said, looking around. "This should be relatively straightforward."

The room was similar in layout to my own, and while Mrs Finch moved towards the two large trunks that stood at the foot of the bed, I headed for the armoire, where both Mr and Mrs Lavigne's clothes hung.

"The scar on Helene's hand was real," I said, feeling carefully along all the seams in the first of Mrs Lavigne's gowns.

Mrs Finch nodded, tapping inside the empty trunks, in search of any hidden compartments. "Yes," she said. "And old too. I'm no expert but it must be at least several years for the skin to have paled as it has."

"Which would imply she *is* Ellen," I whispered, moving on to the next dress.

"So it would seem." Mrs Finch's lips pressed together.

"But you're not convinced."

She hesitated. "I can't like the Lavignes," she admitted. "And there is something about Helene that I can't put my finger on..." She sighed. "I don't know. It is like a tickle at the back of my brain."

"You are very good at reading people yourself, Mrs Finch," I said.

She smiled. "Well, Mari, you and I have much in common, don't we? I'd say we're both clever, successful businesswomen. We both have a sense of when something is, shall we say ... off kilter."

I nodded, pleased. "Exactly. That is how I have felt too. I'm not sure Helene is lying precisely, but sometimes ... there is something..."

"Yes," Mrs Finch agreed. "*Something.* Of course, there are the strawberries to consider as well."

"Is it possible she outgrew her reaction to them?" I asked, moving further down the rail.

"Possible?" Mrs Finch shrugged. "I suppose so, but the intensity of the attacks she used to suffer as Oliver described them make it seem unlikely to me. I had Barker telegraph Winnie first thing this morning, as well as sending messages to Sylla and Izzy."

"Sylla is in Paris now?" I asked.

"Yes, and I have directed her to visit this Lycée Sainte-Geneviève, to see if the story there matches up with what the Lavignes have told us."

I moved on to searching Mr Lavigne's clothes – a more time-consuming job, thanks to the incredible number of pockets men seem entitled to. I wondered not for the first time why women are not afforded the same luxury.

"I'm not sure what it would take for Oliver to feel reassured that it is her," I mused.

"Whatever he needs he shall have it," Mrs Finch said. "After all that Oliver has done for the Aviary, it is the least he deserves from us."

"After all he's done for the Aviary?" I repeated. "What do you mean?"

Mrs Finch only treated me to a long look. "That is for Oliver to tell you, I think. Have you found anything?"

"Some tobacco, ticket stubs, nothing important," I admitted. "You?"

"There are hidden compartments in both the trunks," Mrs Finch said thoughtfully. She tipped the case so that I could see the small drawer in the false bottom. "They are empty, but it does beg the question why the Lavignes needed them."

"Wait." I felt my hands fold round a piece of paper and pulled it from one of Mr Lavigne's pockets. "It's the advert!" I exclaimed, smoothing it out. "The one Oliver's private investigator placed."

Mrs Finch came to look over my shoulder. "The one they claimed they hadn't seen," she said thoughtfully.

"So they lied," I murmured. "They knew that Ellen had money waiting for her. It was no coincidence that they turned up now at all."

Mrs Finch pursed her lips. "It is certainly interesting. Although it doesn't prove anything. Helene may be the real Ellen, and her parents didn't previously think there was a strong enough incentive to return her to her home in England – perhaps they avoided doing so if they feared they might be parted from their daughter before she came of age. She is turned twenty-one now, and free to do as she chooses."

"I find it hard to imagine Mrs Lavigne wouldn't have been on the first boat over, if she thought there was a chance of installing her daughter here. She's certainly made herself very at home, hasn't she?" I said.

Mrs Finch nodded. "It is clear that woman is particularly displeased by your presence, Mari. I imagine she thought she would be running the house on her daughter's behalf before the year was out."

"She's ambitious," I said.

"Perhaps we may use that to our advantage."

We swiftly completed the rest of the search, turning up no further helpful clues or pieces of information. Aside from the advertisement in Mr Lavigne's pockets, their belongings supported the story they had told us – they were middle-class British citizens who had lived in France for many years.

The labels in their clothes and shoes were French – some of them appearing several years old and neatly repaired. They had paperwork in English, including a letter from the doctor they had seen in London – a Dr Wright – who wrote to confirm that, while he believed Helene's second accident had resulted in no further injury to her brain, it was perfectly possible it might have recovered memories that were previously lost. There were also travel papers for the three of them and Helene's official adoption papers, carefully kept, and I remembered Oliver saying that he had already seen these.

There were French face lotions, French perfume, but English shaving cream, which Mr Lavigne must have picked up when they were in town.

Helene's room was similarly unhelpful. She had

brought a lot less with her, and unlike the Lavignes'
room, I found myself feeling guilty and uncomfortable
about pawing through her meagre possessions.

A handful of gowns with nothing hidden in the
seams, shoes, a few hair ribbons. There was hardly
anything personal at all, only a Bible bound in pale blue
leather slipped under her pillow.

Inscribed inside the cover in beautiful, faded
calligraphy was the name of the school Helene told us
she'd attended: *Lycée Sainte-Geneviève*. Tucked between
the pages was a piece of embroidery that I supposed
Helene had done herself when she was younger. The
stitches, large and unruly, formed a wobbly heart with
her initials, HL, inside.

Mrs Finch frowned over this for a moment, running
her finger over the thread, before tucking it neatly back
in place.

I sighed. "Nothing."

"We shall have to wait and see what news the post
brings," Mrs Finch said, with none of the frustration
I was feeling. When she caught sight of my face, she
laughed. "This is often the way of it, Mari. Investigations

take time; it is a matter of fitting many small pieces together until you have a complete picture. It is likely that we learned more today than you think."

"Such as?" I asked, curious.

"Such as, that for all their talk of what they sacrifice for their daughter, Mr and Mrs Lavigne don't seem to prioritize Helene when it comes to shopping – she has less than half the number of gowns Mrs Lavigne has brought with her." Mrs Finch said. "Such as, the fact that not one of them has travelled with anything personal." Here she held up a finger. "Now, you see that as a lack of clues, but in itself it is strange. Which of us would travel abroad, on a journey of unspecified length, without so much as a letter from a loved one, a diary, an appointment book, or any number of other trivial little things we think nothing of carrying with us?"

"Only someone who was hiding something," I said slowly. "Someone who wanted to be as anonymous as possible."

"And in that context Helene's Bible stands out." Mrs Finch shook out her skirts as she glanced around the room, checking not a thing was out of place. "It is a sentimental object. She brought it with her when the entire family have eschewed anything else of the sort. Why?"

"Perhaps she is particularly pious?" I said.

"Perhaps," Mrs Finch said, "though I have not observed anything else to make me think so."

"And she keeps it under her pillow," I said slowly. "To hide it from her parents?"

"Another possibility," Mrs Finch agreed. "Now, I have some correspondence to attend to. Take some time to yourself; I am sure it will be a while before Oliver returns."

I couldn't remember the last time I had been left to my own devices with nothing pressing to do with my time. While Mrs Finch returned to her room, my feet took me, almost without thought, to the garden.

Pushing my way through the lawn, I bent over the rough sections that I assumed had once been flower beds, bordering the space, taking in the size and shape of them, looking out for what survived. There were weeds, lots of them, and I couldn't resist kneeling and pulling some of them out with my bare hands, unearthing as I did so, a patch of cheerful asters: pale, delicate purple with their sunny golden centres. The sight of them made me smile, holding on so stubbornly beneath all this neglect. There was no one to appreciate them, and yet they bloomed anyway.

Aster. *Symphyotrichum*. Meaning: Daintiness.

I looked down at the small patch I had cleared. It hadn't been a lie, what I told Oliver – there was still life here, that it was still beautiful if you knew how to look.

Getting to my feet, I brushed absently at my skirts. They would be in York for some hours yet, I supposed. Perhaps I might use the time to practise honing my observation skills.

Before I could talk myself out of it, I headed back to the house and through to Oliver's library. I hesitated before the door for a moment, and then pushed it open.

The room was just as warm and cheerful in the light of day, even without the homey crackle of the fire, and the air had the same wonderful, papery scent as Mudie's did, delivering an instant sensory hit of comfort. It was,

I thought, the single room in this house where a person *wanted* to spend their time.

Marmalade was in situ too, and as he stalked over to me, I half expected him to start hissing, warning me away from his master's domain. Instead, he weaved around my legs, as if inviting me in.

Stepping over the threshold felt strangely forbidden, but I reminded myself that Oliver had never said that I couldn't be in here.

And I wanted to practise.

I wasn't going to go through his things, or invade his privacy – well, not any more than I already was by being in a place that was so clearly *his*. But I wanted to *look*. I wanted to see what I could find out if I was careful, meticulous. I wanted to know more about Oliver Lockhart, the strange, bad-tempered man who had started occupying too many of my thoughts. To discover what his connection was to the Aviary and how he had done them a service.

For a moment, I stood in the middle of the room. The fact that it was so different from the rest of the house was significant, I realized. He didn't like Lockhart Hall, or what it represented, but he *wanted* a home – a place of ordinary pleasures: books and brandy and a fat orange cat purring in his lap.

The single chair, the single glass sitting beside the brandy decanter made something in my chest ache. Oliver might claim that he didn't care for company, but I thought about what Beth had said the evening before, just outside this room. That Oliver needed someone on his side. Was he lonely?

I moved to his desk, which was enormously untidy, trailing my fingers along the edge. There were stacks of papers, and I deliberately didn't look at them. This wasn't a search, like it had been in the Lavignes' rooms. I didn't know *what* this was, really, but certainly the rules were different.

Still, I saw opened boxes of charcoal, a scattering of chewed pencils. An artist? I wondered. Did he draw?

I made my way to the bookshelves, eyeing the titles, which covered an enormous variety of subjects, from natural history to Elizabethan theatre, to an entire section on jewellery design and something called "gemology". There was also a huge number of well-thumbed novels, which I knew Daisy and Mother had devoured. I smiled at that. Oliver Lockhart was a secret romantic, after all.

If I hadn't been looking so carefully, I would never have noticed it, but somewhere on that long, long wall of books was one that was different to the rest. It was a slim volume, and it had been handled so much that the title on the spine had worn away completely. All that I could see was an embossed design that looked like a foxglove.

Foxglove. *Digitalis*. Meaning: riddles and secrets.

I reached out and pulled the book from the shelf, only it didn't come away in my hand. Instead, the top of the book moved, but the bottom remained stubbornly in place. Puzzled, I pulled again, harder, and then a strange, mechanical whirring sound filled the air.

I jumped back with a gasp as an entire section of the bookcase lurched towards me.

Raising a hand to my pounding heart, it took me a moment to understand what I was seeing. It was a door.

Tentatively, I gripped the edge, and pulled it towards me. It swung open easily, on silent hinges, and beyond the opening it created I saw a steep flight of stairs, leading down into darkness.

Naturally, I went down them.

However, as I got further down the stairs, it got darker and darker, the only light filtering in from the open door I had walked through. I stopped on one of the steps, waiting for my eyes to adjust, and in the gloom I realized I had just about reached the bottom, and that beyond the stairs was a single, large room filled with dark, bulky shapes.

There must be lights in here, I reasoned, as I stepped gingerly forward. Candles somewhere, perhaps? I began feeling around in search of them.

"Oof!" I exhaled, as I crashed into something. I put my hands out. It was some sort of table, and as my fingers moved across it they closed over something cold and hard.

"What are you doing in here?" a voice demanded from behind me, and suddenly the room was filled with light.

I whipped round to find Oliver frowning at me.

In my hand I held the biggest diamond I had ever seen.

CHAPTER TWENTY-SIX

"I – what? You're ... back?" I babbled. "Is this ... a *diamond*?"

Oliver folded his arms across his chest. "It is. Indulging in a spot of jewel thievery, Bloom?"

"No!" I exclaimed, practically hurling the jewel at him in my sudden panic. "Of course not!"

He caught the diamond in his hand as casually as if it were a tennis ball and placed it on the workbench beside him.

"Then might I ask again... What you are doing down

here?" His voice was mild, and I couldn't decide if he was angry or not.

"I was in the library," I began, and then I trailed off.

"I am following the story so far." Oliver nodded.

"And I pulled a book off the shelf," I continued slowly.

"Mm-hmm." He motioned with his hand that I should go on.

"And then a door opened in the wall and there were stairs, leading into the dark."

"So naturally you went down them."

I looked at him in bewilderment. "Of course I went down them," I said. "There was a *door* in the *wall*. A secret door. In a library!"

"The library part is important, is it?" Oliver asked.

Now it was my turn to narrow my eyes at him. "You are being deliberately obtuse," I said, "but I know you would have done the same because *you* are a secret reader of Gothic novels!" I hurled the words at him in accusation.

His mouth dropped open. "I am *not*!"

"Yes you are," I insisted. "I saw them on your shelves."

There was a moment of silence. "Those are Beth's," he

said finally, and I scoffed, letting him know that I wasn't falling for that one.

"My reading habits are neither here nor there," Oliver said a touch too quickly. "The question remains: what are you doing *here*?"

I had finally calmed down enough to take in where *here* was.

It was a large square room, with white walls and, unlike the library, it was immaculately tidy. Two long workbenches stretched the width of the room, separated into separate work areas, with vices clamped to the sides and dozens of small, intricate tools laid out on strips of scarlet fabric. There was also a giant furnace built into the end of the wall, though it was currently unlit.

And the diamond was not the only jewel in here. No, scattered across the benches were gems of all different shapes and sizes and colours. Some of them were loose stones, but others were set in pieces of jewellery in various stages of completion.

If you had asked me what Oliver Lockhart was keeping in a secret room below his house, I might have suggested expensive bottles of wine or barrels of brandy, or even the remains of visitors who had irritated him. This certainly wouldn't have been on the list. I didn't even know what *this* was.

I blinked back to him. He was watching me with an expression on his face that I couldn't read, but that I thought might be something close to nervous. Which made no sense at all.

Glancing up to the ceiling, I saw the lights he had turned on. "Are those *electric* lights?" I asked.

Oliver's eyes followed mine. "I need good light when I work," he said.

"When you work," I repeated, and I looked again at the tables around us. "You're a … jeweller?"

"Well, I'm not using all these diamonds to bake a cake, am I?" Oliver said, but there was still that look about him, the wary one that I didn't understand.

"You made these?" I moved down the table, looking at the pieces he was working on. They were beautiful. Delicate and lovely, each one a work of art.

"Yes."

"You *made* these," I uttered again, drinking in the sight of them.

I stopped in front of a pair of bracelets, almost identical. There were, I noticed several pieces that had a duplicate next to them.

"Why are there all these doubles?" I asked.

He shifted. "Those are..." He hesitated. "Part of the work I do for the Aviary."

"For the Aviary?" I murmured. "What does the Aviary need you to make jewellery for?"

Oliver looked down at his jacket, brushing an invisible bit of dirt from his jacket sleeve. "Sometimes there are women who need the financial security that a piece of jewellery provides," he said briskly. "Like everything else, however, their jewellery is not their own. It belongs to their husbands or their fathers, and those men may dispose of these pieces however the whim takes them. If I make ... an *alternative* piece – a convincing counterfeit – then the Aviary's clients can hide the originals somewhere safe, in case they should ever need them."

I took a moment to absorb that information. Oliver finally met my eyes.

"Don't look at me like that," he muttered.

"Like what?" I managed.

"Like I'm going to lose another handkerchief to you," he said sharply. "It's not anything worth getting emotional over. I find the work interesting. It's no hardship for me to do it."

"I don't think that's the whole story," I said softly, thinking about everything he had told me in the gallery yesterday. "I'm working on my deductive reasoning, and I think you want to help these women because they remind you of your mother."

I almost couldn't believe I had said the words aloud. Oliver looked stricken for a moment.

He cleared his throat. "Yes," he said shortly. "They do. Her marriage was an unhappy one. An abusive one, that left her with little autonomy. She had no one to turn to, no safe place to run. I believe that she was leaving my father when she died, returning to Spain. That's why she and Ellen were in France."

I stared, beginning to understand. When Oliver had found out the accident was in Paris rather than London, he had also found out that his mother had run away. Without him.

"Where were you?" I asked, the words barely more than a whisper.

"I was away at school," he said roughly, then quickly in the same breath he added. "I don't blame her. I am glad she was leaving him. I wanted her to do it. I just..."

"You wanted her to take you too," I finished.

Again, we were quiet.

"Why did you choose the book?" he asked finally.

"What?"

"The book to open the door. Why did you pull on it?"

"Oh," I said, fidgeting. "Something about it looked different, I suppose. And then it had a flower on it, a foxglove."

"Foxglove for secrets," Oliver said, and he clearly noticed my surprise. "My mother's little joke. This was her room originally, though it looked different then, a sanctuary of sorts, I suppose."

"How did you even learn to do all this?" I asked, reaching out towards a dazzling ruby necklace, but stopping short of actually touching it. I had never seen anything like the creations on display down here, didn't come from a world of rubies and diamonds.

Oliver reached over and picked up the necklace, then he gently took my hand by the wrist, pouring the gemstones into my palm, where they sat, cool and heavy, the vibrant scarlet of spilled blood.

"After the accident, I came back for the funeral, but my father swiftly sent me back to school in London. I was angry, grieving, and I started slipping out of the place whenever I could, looking for trouble." He gave me a rueful look. "One day I got into a fight with a group of boys in a – let's say less than reputable – part of town, and despite my high opinion of myself I did not come out the winner."

"What happened?" I asked, setting the necklace carefully back down.

"I tried to drag myself back to school, but I only got as far as Clerkenwell. I don't precisely remember, but apparently I lost consciousness on the doorstep of one of the jewellers there." Now his smile turned fond. "Mr Peets owned the place, and when he found me – a scrubby little schoolboy with a bloody nose, he took me in and cleaned me up. He was gruff and no-nonsense, but kind in his way. I don't know why, but the whole story spilled out of me – about Mother and Ellen and school and my father. It was probably disjointed nonsense, but he listened, and afterwards he showed me around his workshop. I was fascinated."

"He taught you?"

Oliver nodded. "Over several years, when I kept turning up at his place like a bad penny. Clerkenwell is teeming with craftsmen, so he introduced me around, encouraged my interest, and I had the opportunity to study different techniques." Amusement threaded through his voice. "Not the education my father thought he was paying for, though I did just well enough in school to keep out of trouble."

He spoke with more animation than I had seen before, and I felt a strange kinship with him – I understood at once that the way he felt about his work was the way I felt about my garden.

"When I left school and came home, I began creating this room. Mr Peets had put me in touch with Mrs Finch and she and I started up a correspondence. I was interested in finding a way to use my skills and my resources to do something … better."

"What did your father think about all this?" I asked, puzzled.

Oliver gave a short laugh. "He didn't think a damn thing about it. Richard Lockhart never had the slightest interest in me or anything I did, beyond the fact that he had a son to whom he could leave his business and this home, just as his father had and his father's father. *There have been Lockharts at Lockhart Hall for five hundred years.*" These last words were uttered in a scathing tone, presumably an impression of the man himself.

"He was a fool," I said coldly.

"Excuse me?"

"Worse than a fool," I amended. "In many, many ways, but a fool in this. That he didn't try to know you, that he didn't see your talent for himself."

Silence fell. Oliver stared at me, his eyes wide. I could see the pulse leaping in his throat.

He took a sudden step towards me. Another step, crowding me back against the workbench. My own breath was coming fast and my whole body felt … *hectic*, tingling wildly.

He lifted his hand then, his fingers coming to cup my face. His thumb traced a line across my cheekbone, and his gaze dropped to my mouth before rising to meet my own.

My lips parted on a soft exhale.

"Why," he said softly, "are you covered in dirt?"

"I..." I tried to think, to formulate words. "What?" I managed.

His eyes roamed my face. "You have mud on your cheek, on your clothes."

I lifted my own fingers to my face, dimly aware that they were trembling. He caught my hand in his own. "I was gardening," I said unsteadily. "You have asters."

Oliver's eyes gleamed, even as he stepped back. He turned my palm over, and though I had washed my hands when I came in from the garden, there were stubborn crescents of dirt under my fingernails. For a moment I saw my hand through Oliver's eyes. It was not the delicate hand of a lady – it was rough in places, calloused – but he looked at it with that strange smile on his lips.

As the distance between us increased, I found I could

breathe again, though I swore I could still feel the ghost of his touch on my cheek. I pulled my fingers gently from his grip.

"I have asters, do I?" he said. "And what do asters mean?"

"Daintiness," I said, still flustered but trying to hide it. "Perfect for you."

He laughed.

Oliver Lockhart *laughed*, and I wanted to bottle the sound, to keep it for ever.

"Maybe you're right, Bloom. Perfect for me," he said. "Now, we'd better go and clean up. As I understand it here in polite society, we dress for dinner."

The next morning, I woke to a loud sound that I couldn't identify. *More of these peculiar country noises*, I thought, rushing over to the window and dragging the curtain aside.

Below me, three men with machines were mowing the lawn.

CHAPTER TWENTY-SEVEN

"I have been thinking, Mr Lockhart," Mrs Lavigne said the next day when the company was gathered in the drawing room, "about our visit to York."

Rain drummed against the windows, and we had all settled there with our own entertainments. Helene had her eyes down, focused on her embroidery. Meanwhile, Mrs Finch sat at a small table, dashing off several letters, and Mr Lavigne had embroiled Oliver in a game of chess that he didn't seem particularly invested in.

"What about it?" Oliver asked, carelessly moving one of his pawns and looking incredibly bored when Mr Lavigne chided him over the folly of the decision.

"Well..." Mrs Lavigne cast aside the periodical she was reading in favour of gifting him with the full weight of her attention. "We are all *excessively* grateful for your continued hospitality in allowing us to remain at Lockhart Hall..."

"This is my sister's home too," Oliver said shortly. "It is hardly hospitality on my part. She is as entitled as I am to be here." Helene's eyes lifted to his at this, and Oliver's face softened. "I would not want to lose her company a second time."

A look I was coming to recognize passed over Helene's face. It was as if she expected no kindness from Oliver at all; as if every time he offered it, she was taken aback.

"Of course, of course," Mrs Lavigne simpered, "and that is greatly to your credit. But I wondered if you had given any thought to Helene's future?"

"Mother," Helene murmured, but Mrs Lavigne ignored her, only keeping her attention fixed on Oliver.

"I suppose Helene's future is up to her," Oliver answered.

"What a *man* he is, Miss Bloom!" She laughed, drawing me into the conversation. "Mr Lockhart doesn't understand what I am hinting at, but I'm sure you do."

I set aside the letter from Daisy that I had been rereading for the third time, guilt crawling over me.

There have been one or two small problems, she wrote, *but nothing for you to worry about; I'm sure it will all be set right in no time. Mrs Payne did kick up quite a fuss about her delivery, but then how was I supposed to know that lilies are fatal to cats?? And we removed the flowers so quickly that the feline wasn't even in the same room as them, but the way she was carrying on, you would have thought I had been trying to murder the wretched animal.*

And naturally it is unfortunate that Robbie is laid up after his accident at the flower market on Thursday (it was hardly his fault that that silly man's horse decided to bolt in the middle of a crowd despite what that nosy flower seller had to say!).

However, Grandfather and I have taken to attending together and I must say I find the whole thing thrilling.

Scout asked me to send you a list of questions, which I enclose separately because half of them include Latin of which I can't make head nor tail. I'm afraid that Grandfather doesn't hold out great hopes for the newest of the hybrid roses, but perhaps you will be able to work your magic on them once you are home!

Tearing my attention away, I tried to focus on what Mrs Lavigne had said.

"I believe Mrs Lavigne means that you should consider introducing Helene into society," I managed.

"Society can go hang," Oliver said succinctly.

Mrs Lavigne's smile began to look a touch frozen. "But surely, sir, you can see that without your introduction it will be very hard for Helene to meet people her own age, to make friendships ... perhaps to form an attachment of her own."

"Mother," Helene said again, softly, and she and

Mrs Lavigne had one of those wordless exchanges that mother and daughter can share with only a glance.

"You know I only care for your happiness, dear," Mrs Lavigne insisted, and the words held a steel that had Helene's shoulders slumping with defeat.

"Mrs Lavigne is quite right," Mrs Finch piped up unexpectedly, and all eyes swung in her direction. She smiled at Oliver, and it was a smile full of schemes. "At the very least, you really do need to introduce Helene to the local gentry as soon as possible. You can't expect the poor girl to stay cooped up in this house indefinitely!"

"I'm sure Mr Lockhart has no intention of keeping Helene to himself for ever," Mr Lavigne chimed in.

"Exactly," Mrs Finch said, "so why rest on our laurels when there is so much to celebrate? You must throw a dinner to celebrate your engagement, Mr Lockhart, while we are still here to enjoy it!"

"I can't think that is necessary," he said, glaring daggers at Mrs Finch.

"Surely, there is not time..." Mrs Lavigne began, clearly not wanting the spotlight of their first social event to be on anyone but Helene. "I believe you said you were planning to stay for only a few more days?"

Mrs Finch waved her hand. "Oh, plenty of time for something informal. Dinner, dancing, just a handful of guests." Oliver's expression darkened with every word out of her mouth. "Why, I'm certain we could pull such an event together in a couple of days."

"A couple of days!" Mrs Lavigne exclaimed.

"Yes." Mrs Finch nodded, and like a magician pulling a white rabbit from her hat, she presented her trump card. "I have received a letter today, informing me that the Duke and Duchess of Roxton are passing through Yorkshire in two days' time, taking a tour of the north, and I know that they are close friends of yours, Mr Lockhart... What better opportunity to celebrate your engagement *and* introduce them to your lovely sister?"

A brief, dazzled silence followed this announcement.

"The Duke and Duchess of Roxton?" Mrs Lavigne uttered, once she had picked her jaw up from the floor. "I – I had no idea you were acquainted, Mr Lockhart."

Oliver cast another dark look at Mrs Finch. "Yes, we are acquainted, though I wouldn't say..."

"Roxton, Roxton," Mr Lavigne murmured, his tone thoughtful. "Now, didn't I read something about his marriage in the society papers recently?"

"Indeed you did!" Mrs Lavigne exclaimed with some agitation. "It was the social event of the decade! A double wedding, with the St Clairs, at St George's no less. Why, even the Prince of Wales attended!"

"It was a miserable crush," Oliver grumbled, and then reared back at Mrs Lavigne's high-pitched reaction to these words.

"*You* attended the wedding?" she screeched.

Before he could reply, Mrs Finch cut in. "I believe Mr Lockhart was part of the bridal party."

"Only because that damned fool Max—"

Oliver was stopped short here, by Mrs Lavigne murmuring "*Max*" in awed tones.

"From what *I* heard," Mrs Finch said sweetly, mischief in every word, "it was a beautiful service. Very emotional. Why, even the *hardest* heart might have been moved to shed a tear."

"The church was very dusty," Oliver said hotly.

"Well, well," Mrs Lavigne all but purred. "This does

put quite a different light on the matter. The Duke of Roxton! It seems Helene will be moving in very high circles indeed." The naked calculation on her face was hard to miss.

"Oh, but surely I am not—" Helene began, colour high on her cheeks. "We shouldn't put Mr Lockhart to such trouble. I couldn't ... that is ... a *duke*!" This last word was spoken in such distress that one would think Mrs Finch had suggested Oliver introduce Helene to Lucifer himself.

"Nonsense." Mrs Lavigne dismissed this outburst with barely a flicker of acknowledgment. "But can an appropriate event really be put together in so short a time?"

"I'm sure with Mr Lockhart's resources nothing is impossible," Mrs Finch said. "Marigold and I will speak to Beth."

Clearly understanding – as I did – that there was a reason Max and Izzy needed to descend on the house, Oliver was left with little choice but to concede.

"It seems it is all decided," he said sourly.

Mrs Lavigne stood, flustered. "Thank heavens we

went to York yesterday, for I have a whole new wardrobe on order, but I shall have to impress upon the dressmaker the urgency of my need!"

"Helene's too, I should imagine," Oliver said, his tone dry.

"Perhaps, Mr Lockhart, we may prevail upon you to borrow the carriage?" Mr Lavigne added smoothly, a knowing twinkle in his eye. "The women, you know, will have much to attend to!"

"Of course," Oliver agreed. "I shall have Barker bring it around."

With that, the Lavignes departed in a flutter of anticipation, Helene tugged along after them like a limp rag doll.

"What have you dragged me into now?" Oliver groaned, scrubbing his hand over his face. "Years I live an unencumbered, quiet life in this house. Three days in your company, and apparently I'm throwing a *party*?" He said the word "party" as if it left a bad taste in his mouth.

"It will be good for you," Mrs Finch said. "This place could do with a bit of cheer. And you won't have to invite too many – thirty or forty or so of the local types."

"Forty people!" Oliver's stricken expression deepened.

"Just enough to fill out the dance floor," Mrs Finch explained.

"*Dancing...*" Oliver shuddered, and it seemed there was a worse word than "party", after all. "*Why* does it have to be *dancing*?"

"More to the point, why does it have to be anything?" I interrupted here. "What has Izzy discovered?"

"All I know is that she has information and she deemed it necessary to deliver it in person," said Mrs Finch. "I suggested the house party as an appropriate ruse. It will also give her an opportunity to meet the Lavignes herself."

"And you think there is more that they're hiding?" Oliver said, his posture stiffening. "Because of the advertisement you found in their belongings yesterday?"

He had been quiet when we told him about that last night, troubled and withdrawn.

I myself was uncertain. Helene seemed utterly convincing. And yet ... and yet something worried at me. Something I couldn't put my finger on.

One thing *was* certain, however: it was getting easier

and easier to pretend to be part of a newly engaged couple.

Whenever I had looked at Oliver over dinner the night before, it was to find his eyes already on me; something in them had made my heart beat faster. I had to firmly remind myself of several important things: that this whole romantic relationship was a ruse; that I had an important job to do for the Aviary, an organization in which I believed wholeheartedly that had invested in my training and were depending on me to be focused and clear-headed; that Oliver Lockhart was – according to the evidence I had seen so far – one of the richest men in the country, and decidedly not for me; and finally that – whatever my family may have said in the heat of the moment – Daisy's letter made it clear that I was not in a position to abandon my responsibilities to them, even if the offer *did* present itself.

Which it wasn't going to. For all the perfectly sensible aforementioned reasons.

"The advertisement, among other things." Mrs Finch sighed now. "All I can say is that I suspect the Lavignes are hiding something."

"Do *you* think she is Ellen?" Oliver turned to me. It was the first time he had asked me the question directly, and there was tension in every line of his body as he waited for my answer.

"I think the evidence suggests that she is," I said carefully, "but until we know the full story, how can any of us be sure? Mrs Finch is right that the Lavignes are keeping secrets. At the very least, their interest in returning Helene home is not as altruistic as they have claimed. But whether their ambitions extend to fraud is another question. Having more of our people here under the guise of the party can only be a good thing."

"And naturally Mrs Lavigne was suitably awed by the presence of the duke and duchess," Mrs Finch mused. "In cases such as this one, introducing elements that will unsettle or distract the subjects may lead them to accidentally reveal more than they intend. Mrs Lavigne's attention will be on them. She wants an advantageous match for her daughter."

"You think she wants to marry Helene off?" Oliver said.

"*That* part of the arrangement is not in the least

suspicious," Mrs Finch said, her tone reproving. "With such limited opportunities open to women, I think you would find most mothers would want the same." She tilted her head. "But I do wonder..." She didn't finish the thought. "Let us suppose," she said finally, holding up a finger, "hypothetically of course, that Helene *is* an imposter, that the Lavignes are perpetrating a ruse of some kind. The possibility that they will get caught will increase dramatically the longer they are here. There would only be more opportunity for mistakes, for a lie to falter. But if Helene were established as your sister and then *married*, if they collected her inheritance and then left this house..."

"Then they would have the money without living in fear of discovery," Oliver said slowly.

"If you accept Helene as Ellen, she will have a fortune," I pointed out. "You have already made it very clear you intend to share your father's money with her – above and beyond what he left her himself. She is an heiress."

"Helene is a sweet, pretty young woman," Mrs Finch added. "A little old to be making her come out in society, but with all her advantages I think Mrs Lavigne can probably aim high. The Lavignes might not only get money out of such an arrangement – their daughter could gain a title. Their influence would grow."

Oliver looked miserable.

"We are making progress," I said with a confidence I didn't actually feel. "If we pull at enough threads, this whole thing will unravel soon enough." Unthinking, I rested my hand on his arm. "We don't know what information Izzy has already, nor what she and Max may observe that we might miss. If I have learned anything from the Aviary, it is that a charm of finches will always work better than any individual."

Oliver looked down to where my fingers gripped the soft fabric of his jacket.

"Then by all means," he said with a sigh, "let's throw a party."

CHAPTER TWENTY-EIGHT

The next two days passed in a blur of preparations. Despite Mrs Finch's airy confidence, throwing together a party for forty people at a moment's notice in a house ten miles from the nearest town was no small undertaking.

It helped that Oliver had money to throw at the problem. A lot of money. I tried not to react to the number of carts and carriages that began arriving from York, unloading everything from glassware to shellfish, table linens to crates of champagne.

Servants employed by the agency that Mrs Finch

had engaged descended in a mess of feather dusters and kitchen knives. Suddenly Beth was overseeing a kitchen staff of eleven and nine housemaids, while Barker found himself up to his elbows in footmen.

Oliver looked constantly as though someone was pinching him.

"There are people *everywhere*," he said to me on the morning of the party when we met in the hallway, his expression hunted. "I just found someone trying to bathe Marmalade."

I lifted my brows. "I imagine that went well."

"There was a lot of hissing."

"From you or the cat?"

"Very droll, Bloom," he said over his shoulder, already striding off towards his library, where I knew he would hide for the rest of the day. "With a wit like that, you're wasted on flowers."

In fact, flowers were precisely my focus. I had taken delivery of those myself at the crack of dawn. I knew perfectly well just how much they must have cost, almost down to the stem, and it was more than even my most spendthrift clients in London would have laid out.

Oliver had ordered so many that it was going to take me hours to arrange them all. Not that I was complaining. Not after Beth showed me to the flower room.

Unlike most of the house, it was light and airy – thanks to the tall windows that overlooked the lawn, and which had been given a scrub by the enterprising new maids. Long workbenches ran all the way along two of the walls, and mounted above them were hooks and pegs and empty wooden spindles for holding twine and ribbon. There was lots of clever built-in storage, too, and when I opened the cupboards I found dozens of beautiful antique vases and urns, thick with dust.

Though the room was mostly empty, the florist sent over enough trimmings to fill it out a little. Dozens of silver pails held the flowers, and even with my high standards I had to admit that the quality was exceptional. Barker appeared with brand-new secateurs and floristry wire, and when I thanked him for thinking of them, he told me with a knowing wink that Oliver had sent for the items himself.

All in all, Oliver's flower room was easily four times the size of the space we had at Bloom's for carrying out this kind of work, and I propped the door open, letting in the cool air and the smell of freshly mown grass, humming as I got to work.

I had been in there for hours, filling all the vases, making centrepieces for the tables, creating buttonholes for the gentlemen and corsages for the ladies out of sprigs of the soft, purple heather gathered from the moors at my request, when Oliver finally reappeared, sticking his head round the door.

"Izzy and Max are due to arrive shortly," he said, wandering over to my workbench where I was putting the finishing touch to the final arrangement.

I wiped my hands down the front of my apron. "Is it that time already?"

"You were enjoying yourself," he said, reaching out to touch the delicate white petals of an anemone.

I nodded. "I've missed this." I gave an embarrassed laugh. "Silly to say after only a few days."

"Not at all." Oliver leaned back against the bench, his long legs stretched in front of him. "I understand. Flowers are your passion."

"Yes," I said, reaching up to straighten one of the

stems. "I love the whole process – growing them, tending them, arranging them. Making something ... beautiful." I raised my eyes to his, then smiled and gestured to the gorgeous bouquet in front of us. "Not bad for something that started as no more than seeds and dirt."

"No, not bad at all," he said, his eyes searching my face. "Bloom's must be very important to you," he said slowly.

"It is," I agreed. "I love the shop, our customers, the way that the flowers we sell become part of the fabric of their lives." I hesitated, thinking about all the secrets that Oliver had shared with me. "Recently, though, I have been wondering..." I trailed off.

"What?" he asked.

"I don't know." I fiddled with the hem of my apron. "I'm proud of Bloom's, and my grandfather built that beautiful, special place from nothing. It's extraordinary – it's his legacy and it's going from strength to strength."

"But?" Oliver prompted gently. I looked into his face and saw no judgement there, only an attentive interest in what I was saying.

"But..." I exhaled. "I wonder if it's ... enough." Saying

the words aloud felt like a betrayal and I winced. "It feels as if there's a limit to what I can achieve there – with the space, with the business, and perhaps I've reached that. I think that's why I joined the Aviary, because the work they do is so … *big*. It helps so many people and I love that. And I love *this*." I gestured to the flowers in front of us. "If only I could use my work to make a difference."

Oliver nodded, as though it made perfect sense. "If that's what you want, then I'm certain you will find a way to do it."

"How can I?" The words came out small. "I'm already stretched so thin between the Aviary and the shop. My family needs me. I'm being selfish, ungrateful."

"Ungrateful?" Oliver snapped, the familiar scowl dropping into place. "What nonsense, Bloom. You have worked incredibly hard to help your family business reach its full potential and now, when you have achieved that goal – no small feat, by the way – you want a new challenge, a bigger challenge. It's not selfish; it's called *ambition*."

I reeled back, as though physically struck. "Ambition," I repeated blankly. I felt the shape of the word settle over me, and it felt ... right. A name to that gnawing feeling that I had tried to ignore for so long.

Perhaps realizing that I was feeling overwhelmed, Oliver changed the subject. "Do all these flowers have their own secret meaning too? I only know about the foxglove because of Mother."

"They do." I gathered myself and pointed at the anemone he had touched. "Anemones mean forsaken love. It comes from Greek mythology. After the jealous gods killed Adonis, Aphrodite wept and anemones sprung up from the ground." I pointed to the apricot-coloured dahlia, with the perfect symmetry that had so appealed to Max's sister. "Dahlias mean eternal love or commitment. I use them a lot in wedding flowers, or pair them with tulips for an engagement."

"What do tulips mean?" Oliver asked.

"I declare my love for you," I said unthinkingly, and the words hung heavy between us. I cleared my throat. "We always sell plenty of these in spring when love is in the air."

"What about these ones?" Oliver pointed to a perfect pink camellia.

I swallowed a groan. "Camellia – they mean, um ... *longing for you*."

Oliver made a humming sound in the back of his throat. "Very romantic, the language of flowers."

"Yes, I suppose," I said, "though not always. There are plenty of plants that can be used to send a very different message. Marigold actually means grief, which my grandfather was up in arms about when he found out what my parents had named me, but Mother dug her heels in. She said that she thought marigolds were lovely, very cheerful flowers." I smiled, ticking more examples off on my fingers. "Columbine means foolishness, tansy is hostility, petunia is anger or resentment." I brushed the cloudy white head of a lacy hydrangea. "Hydrangea means boastfulness or heartlessness."

"Not always so innocent as they seem, then," Oliver said lightly, and I felt relieved that we'd navigated our way back to steadier waters.

"Not at all." I grinned. "They're not just messages either. For as long as there have been people, they've been using plants to heal or to do harm. There's plenty in here that could do either."

"Really?" Oliver looked intrigued.

"Mmm," I said. "These frilly hydrangeas, for example, contain small amounts of cyanide."

"*Cyanide?*" Oliver glanced at the flower in alarm.

I laughed. "Yes, very small amounts." I nodded my head towards the window. "What's growing out there is worse. The leaves on buttercups can cause terrible blisters, lobelia will make you vomit, hellebore will do that too, but much worse beside. There are records of a man dying within eight hours of drinking even one ounce of water in which the roots have been soaked. Deadly nightshade – well, that speaks for itself..."

"Stop, stop!" Oliver laughed. "Or I shall be too frightened to ever leave the house."

I grinned at him. "I'm sorry, I've been doing a lot of research for the Finches. Winnie and I have been working on creating holistic remedies, as well as certain compounds that might ... help with the work the Aviary does."

Oliver shivered, leaning back once more against the table and eyeing me warily. "You might as well be a hydrangea yourself. Pretty as a picture and deadly as any weapon."

"I think that's the nicest thing anyone has ever said to me," I replied, trying to decide what my body was going to do when his words made me want to laugh delightedly and burst into tears at the same time.

Apparently, I was going to do neither of those things, however, because what I did instead was lean forward to press my lips to his cheek.

When I pulled back, Oliver's eyes had darkened. He reached towards me, looping his finger through the waistband of my apron, tugging me closer to where he still leaned negligently back against the bench.

I was hypnotized by the heat in his gaze, my pulse drumming wildly as our faces inched closer and closer together. I could feel the warm touch of his breath coasting over my own lips, and my stomach leaped, even as my eyelids fluttered closed.

Oliver's fingers reached up and brushed my cheek, the same movement he'd made yesterday, and this time I knew it wasn't to rub away any smudge. This time it felt as though electric sparks flew beneath his fingertips.

"*Bloom*," he breathed, the distance between us closing even further.

"Oliver?" a voice called, shattering the moment, and my eyes snapped open.

Oliver lurched to his feet as I staggered back, away from him. My hands were curled into fists to hide their trembling. I stared down at the floor, too overwhelmed to meet his eye.

"There you are!" Beth appeared in the doorway, her eyes darting between the two of us. "I – I hope I'm not interrupting?" I couldn't be certain, but I thought there were traces of amusement in her voice.

"Of course you're interrupting," Oliver said with startling honesty. "What do you want?"

Beth was unmoved by his sour tone. "I wanted to let you know that your guests have arrived," she said, smiling so that a dimple popped in her cheek. "But perhaps you'd rather just ignore them."

"Don't be ridiculous, Beth," Oliver muttered, trailing after us as she and I hurried back into the hall. "Of *course* I'd rather just ignore them."

CHAPTER TWENTY-NINE

Making our way through a hive of activity, we found the rest of the household in the entrance hall, waiting to greet the new arrivals, who were climbing down from their carriage in the driveway.

Max and Izzy strolled through the door, arm in arm. Izzy's smile was broad as her gaze landed on Oliver.

"Oliver!" she exclaimed, extracting herself from Max's arm and kissing Oliver soundly on the cheek. Oliver withstood this with a stoic expression. However, I heard Mrs Lavigne's breath catch beside me, startled by the familiarity.

"Lockhart, my old friend," Max boomed, taking his own turn pumping Oliver's hand up and down with an enthusiasm that had Oliver wincing. Max's smile only widened as Oliver glowered at him.

"It's so kind of you to invite us to stay," said Izzy.

"Not at all," Oliver replied stiffly. "May I present my fiancée, Miss Bloom, and her godmother, Mrs Finch?"

Izzy and Max exchanged polite if distant greetings with us, though I saw Izzy's eyes sparkling beneath her hat as we shook hands.

"And this is my sister, Helene," Oliver said. "And her adoptive parents, the Lavignes."

"Your Grace," Mrs Lavigne said breathlessly, dropping into an obsequious curtsey, head bent so that her nose practically skimmed the floor. For a moment Izzy looked slightly taken aback, but I saw Max's hand settle in the small of her back – a tiny gesture of reassurance – and then her chin lifted.

"Mrs Lavigne," she said in her most dignified voice, and I had to hide a smile. Max, of course, needed no such support. Suddenly I saw why he had the reputation he did among the ton. He seemed taller, straighter; his face was set in firm, uncompromising lines as he acknowledged the Lavignes with a chilly formality that bordered on rude.

Far from looking put out by this cool reaction, the Lavignes seemed even more delighted. I understood at that moment precisely why Izzy and Max were behaving as they were – the Lavignes were more convinced of the duke and duchess's consequence than ever by this frigid greeting, and their contrasting warmth towards Oliver only underpinned the closeness Mrs Finch had hinted at. Mrs Lavigne in particular was starry-eyed, and I wondered if Mrs Finch was right, if this unsettling presence may knock the woman off-balance.

Helene, on the other hand, withstood the arrival of the Duke and Duchess of Roxton as if two ogres had waltzed into the house, determined to crunch on her bones.

"Y-your Grace," she managed, and for a moment it was hard to tell if she was curtseying or swooning away.

"Right, well, that's done then," Oliver snapped,

clearly impatient to get on with things. "Why don't I show you to your rooms? We have several hours before the guests will start to arrive and you will want to rest."

"Oh, yes," Izzy said, "and I hope Miss Bloom will join us. I am so excited to hear all about your engagement."

"Of course," I murmured, and the four of us made our way to the stairs, while Barker and several of the new, pleasantly muscular footmen began bringing in the Roxton's luggage, of which there seemed to be plenty. Mrs Lavigne hovered anxiously over the scene, directing everyone with that grating sense of authority that I couldn't like.

Izzy kept up a stream of inane chatter until we were well out of earshot of the Lavignes.

"How have you been?" she asked in a low voice, squeezing my hand.

"Fine," I said. "Though it feels like we've made little progress."

"Perhaps we can help with that," Izzy replied.

"Here we go," Oliver said without ceremony as we approached a door just down the corridor from mine and Mrs Finch's rooms.

He turned the handle, and as we all piled inside I let out a small sound of surprise, because Mrs Finch was standing in the middle of the room.

"We *just* left you downstairs!" I exclaimed. "How on earth did you do that?"

Mrs Finch only smiled. "I have my ways." Her attention turned at once to Max and Izzy. "So?" Her eyebrow arched and she dropped into the chair in front of the dressing table. "What news?"

"Plenty." Izzy stripped off her gloves, striding across the room towards the bed where she laid them down before setting to work unpinning her hat. "First of all, Maud and Winnie paid a visit to Dr Wright on Harley Street."

"The doctor the Lavignes consulted?" Oliver asked, leaning against the door frame.

Izzy nodded. "They posed as medical students and went to interview him for an article on brain injuries." A smile pulled at her lips. "Maud said that Win got a bit carried away and they ended up staying for three hours. According to them, his practice is legitimate, and from what we could discover, it is perfectly possible for a patient's memories to return after a period of several years or following another injury. Winnie had done significant research on the subject, and her discussion with the doctor apparently got quite … *technical*. Unfortunately" – here Izzy winced – "in layman's terms, it all seems to boil down to the fact that the human brain is deeply mysterious and there is much we don't know."

"So presumably a great many things are possible, though not necessarily likely," I surmised.

"Precisely." Izzy nodded. "However…"

"I do enjoy a good *however*!" Mrs Finch sighed happily.

"After they left the doctor, Maud went below stairs and spoke to some of Dr Wright's staff. It seems that your Mr Lavigne visited the doctor alone, without Helene or his wife."

"So the doctor didn't examine Helene at all?" I frowned.

"As far as we have been able to ascertain, after checking the passenger lists on the Channel crossings, Helene and Mrs Lavigne weren't even in the country at the time." Izzy said. "They arrived in England only days before they all came to Yorkshire."

Oliver frowned. "They told me they had travelled over from France together – why lie about such a thing?"

"And why did the doctor write a letter for Mr Lavigne if he hadn't actually seen Helene?" I asked.

"Thanks to a bit of help from Ash and Joe, we were able to discover that Dr Wright had some gambling debts that have now been settled." Izzy smiled, pleased with herself. "The man who settled them fits the description of your Mr Lavigne."

"So Lavigne paid off the doctor's debts so that he would write the letter for a patient he hadn't seen?" Oliver said slowly. "For God's sake, why? Especially if the contents of the letter are only what any doctor would conclude anyway?"

"I assume because there was some reason Helene and Mrs Lavigne couldn't come with him in the first instance, and Mr Lavigne was in a hurry?" Mrs Finch said serenely.

"You would be correct," Izzy agreed. "Upon greasing several of the right palms, we were able to trace Mr Lavigne's movements after he disembarked the boat. We were intrigued to find that, prior to his visit to the good doctor, Mr Lavigne had met privately with a rather senior assistant in the Home Office ... in a pub in Whitechapel."

Mrs Finch exhaled sharply. "Now that is interesting," she said.

"It seems that the gentleman in question is known in certain, shall we say, *less than legal* circles to be a dab hand at forging official documents, with the assistance of many of his influential friends."

"Which is when Izzy brought this to me," Max said, rubbing a hand over his face, which I noticed looked suddenly tired. "And our agency have begun work, uncovering a counterfeiting operation that we believe at this time may reach all the way up into the cabinet. It's a damn mess."

"*Your* agency," Izzy scoffed.

"Acting on the exemplary work of the Aviary, of course," Max added solemnly, though his eyes twinkled.

"And for which you no doubt took all the credit," Oliver grumbled.

"We are a *secret* organization, Oliver," Izzy pointed out fairly. "Credit really isn't our thing. And, believe me, Max is so foolishly honourable that it's more of a curse than a gift that he has to take the credit for all our good ideas."

Max scowled. "I'll probably get another promotion at this rate," he said dolefully. "That or a medal."

"Wait, wait," I said, bringing us back to the matter at hand. "So, Mr Lavigne had someone forge documents?" My mind flashed to the search of their room. "The travel documents!" I exclaimed. "And Helene's adoption papers?"

Izzy nodded. "Yes. It seems that after the forged documents were delivered, your Mr Lavigne travelled back to France, and then he, Mrs Lavigne and Helene returned using the travel papers in question before heading here. If anyone – say, Ellen's long-lost brother, for example – were to look at the crossing records, they would see only the three of them crossing all neat and tidy together."

"You keep saying *your* Mr Lavigne." Oliver frowned. "And I don't think it's by accident."

"No." Izzy shook her head. "I'm sorry, Oliver. Because we had investigated the doctor's appointment, we knew that Mr Lavigne must have been in the country earlier than records indicated. It took us a while to piece it together, but the man downstairs first travelled to England several weeks ago under the name David Brown. He visited the doctor and acquired forged documents, then returned to France. It was only the second time he entered the country that he arrived as Mr Lavigne, with his wife and daughter in tow."

I sat on the side of the bed with a thump. "So what you're saying is…"

Izzy's face was grim. "Whoever those people are downstairs, they are not who they claim to be."

CHAPTER THIRTY

It took several moments for the rest of us to absorb these words. Mrs Finch frowned into the distance, and I almost imagined I could see the cogs in her brain spinning wildly. Oliver's face was set, and he too seemed lost in thought. Izzy watched him, her expression worried.

"What do we do now?" I asked quietly, breaking the silence.

"I don't know," Izzy admitted. "Technically, it is Sylla who should decide, but we have been having some trouble reaching her in France – communications are moving too slowly to keep up with the information we are uncovering."

"So far we know very little about David Brown," Max offered. "It is a common name and there are many who have travelled to and from France through Dover and Folkestone over the last dozen years or more."

"There is only one thing we can do." Mrs Finch got to her feet, carefully smoothing her skirts. "Oliver, Mari and I must go to Paris."

There was a frozen moment as her words hit me.

"To Paris?" I choked. "Paris … *France*?"

Mrs Finch nodded. "It is the only course of action open to us." She began ticking off items on her fingers. "As Max has said, it is useless to try to gather information on David Brown here, when any record of him and his movements for the last decade are likely to be found across the Channel. The Lavignes have clearly lived in France for some time. We can confirm for certain that they travelled *from* France a fortnight ago. Any information on them will be there."

"That is true," Izzy said thoughtfully.

"Also," Mrs Finch continued, "the Lavignes – or

whoever they are – have given us a thorough account of how Helene came to be found. This was corroborated by the police reports in France. It sounds as though they were on the scene, at the very least."

"The accident at Le Pecq," I murmured. "The village they lived in, Herblay. They must have either lived there or known someone who did. The story would have to stand up to Oliver's scrutiny. It is obvious that any claimant would be investigated."

"That's why they needed the travel papers," Izzy agreed.

"And perhaps why Brown had to move quickly," Max mused. "If they saw the advertisement, they may have feared another young woman coming forward, or even that Oliver would give up and have Ellen declared dead."

"Let's revisit what we *know*, as opposed to supposition," said Mrs Finch. "A young girl was in an accident at Le Pecq. She was washed up along the river and taken in by a local family. She attended the Lycée Sainte-Geneviève. Helene, or whoever she is, has a Bible with the name of the school inside it, which she brought all the way to England." Her fingers drummed at her side. "The school is the key, I am sure of it. We can't wait for Sylla – not in light of this new discovery. Not in light of what this might mean for Ellen."

The name fell between us like a stone dropped in still water.

"Ellen," Oliver breathed, his eyes wide. "What does this... What does *any* of this mean for my sister?"

"It means one of several things," I said slowly, looking to Mrs Finch, who nodded in encouragement. "Either Helene really *is* Ellen and the couple we know as the Lavignes are using her for their own ends. Or..."

"Or?" he said, teeth clenched.

"Or," I said softly, "she is an imposter and at least one of those people downstairs knew Ellen well enough to be able to pull off this ruse. And if *that* is the case, then it may mean that Ellen is in France..." I swallowed. "Or..." I said again, only this time I found I couldn't finish the sentence.

"Or Ellen might really be dead," Izzy said gently, her eyes full of sympathy as they focused on Oliver, whose face was a frozen mask.

"At the very least she might be in danger," Mrs Finch

added. "Whatever the case, I think we can agree that, for Ellen's sake, the faster we move the better."

"And so we go to France." Oliver's voice was threaded with determination.

"And so we go to France," Mrs Finch confirmed.

CHAPTER THIRTY-ONE

"And what about the Lavignes? Helene?" I asked.

Mrs Finch smiled, a dangerous sort of smile. "We take them with us, of course."

"Take them *with* us?" I repeated.

"It will stir the pot nicely, I think." She chuckled, and if her smile was dangerous, then this laughter was deadly. "Oh yes, I think it will work very well indeed. They will scramble. They will make a mistake. And we will strike. Oliver can announce the trip tonight at the party. As a surprise for his newfound family."

"You can't imagine we will still be having the party?" Oliver growled. "I can't even look at those people."

"You must." Izzy jumped in. "Oliver, it is *imperative* that the Lavignes do not suspect you know any of this. Everything must be just as it was. It's the only way you will catch them and uncover the full truth."

At this, Oliver's jaw tightened, but he managed to incline his head in a small, sharp nod.

"Mari, you will write to your family," Mrs Finch said. "Let them know that your trip has been extended by a couple of days. I do not anticipate that we will be in France for long; I think that once the cat is set among the pigeons, a conclusion will not be far behind."

What the outcome of this conclusion would be, none of us knew.

"I will speak to Barker and make sure all the arrangements are in place for us to leave tomorrow. We can travel back as far as London with Max and Izzy," Mrs Finch said. "Izzy will inform Winnie and Maud, and they can follow behind. I will telegraph Sylla that we are en route."

I felt a moment of relief. Sylla, Maud and Winnie. The

whole charm together. Then I remembered we would be together in *Paris*, and my mind happily returned to panic as well as a tentative emotion it took me a moment to identify as anticipation.

"Good," Izzy said. "Now, with that all decided, we should start getting ready. It's not every day you attend your friends' pretend engagement celebration."

There was a knock at the door, and Oliver opened it a cautious crack, peering out before pulling it open more widely to reveal Barker standing at the threshold.

"Sorry to interrupt," Barker said, utterly unfazed by all of us crowded in secret conference in Max and Izzy's room. "I sent those parcels to Mrs Finch's room – the ones you asked for, Your Grace." He directed this comment at Izzy. "And if you're ready, the lads will bring the rest of your luggage up."

"Perfect, thank you, Barker." Izzy smiled, then she looked to Mrs Finch. "I visited Madame Solange as you requested and spoke to Iris."

The tension left Mrs Finch's face, replaced by a small, pleased smile. "Excellent." She turned her attention to me. "Mari was only asking the other day after my dressmaker. Now she will experience her talent for herself."

"You ordered me a gown?" My brows rose.

"Certainly." Mrs Finch sniffed. "It is your engagement party, Mari."

"I can't believe you found the time to organize such a thing," I said.

Mrs Finch looked affronted. "Marigold Bloom," she replied. "I may be a brilliant, singular mind managing a secret organization of exceptional women as we fight against the tyranny of an oppressively patriarchal society, but there is *always* time for fashion."

Hours later I gripped my glass of champagne, watching the couples swirling around the dance floor in front of me with a curious feeling of detachment.

Almost everyone in this room – and it seemed, suddenly, as though there were so *many* people, far more than the forty I knew had been invited – believed that this whole party was in celebration of an engagement that didn't exist, between me and the man who stood beside me, his posture rigid as he too watched the dancers.

Several people – whose names I had already forgotten – stood with us, and one man was opining on the subject of estate maintenance and the lack of good help available these days.

My eyes darted to where the Lavignes stood, deep in conversation with another couple, watching Helene dance gracefully with a man about her own age. It was hard to smile into their faces while knowing that they had lied and tricked their way into this house, into Oliver's family.

In a way, I had thought the party full of guests would be easier. Easier than lying to people I knew and loved, easier than maintaining a fiction over a period of days for the suspicious Lavignes. A sort of superficial level of dishonesty. But it wasn't easier.

Standing here, in the scrupulously cleaned and polished ballroom, surrounded by displays of fragrant flowers that I had arranged myself, candlelight flickering seductively over the scene, it was more like being shoved out on a stage in a gilded theatre – and I was no actress.

Then there was also the matter that those displays of flowers reminded me jarringly of this afternoon's scene in the flower room. If anything, I was trying very hard not to let my feelings for Oliver slip through, not to let them show. Perhaps that was a mistake because it would have helped us to appear more convincing as a couple, but I couldn't do it. I was afraid that if I looked up at him, then he would see the naked yearning in my eyes and realize that it wasn't an act at all.

I didn't have the luxury of falling in love with Oliver Lockhart, I knew, because something so foolish could only end in disaster. I wasn't prepared to deal with that sort of heartache. I had too many people who were depending on me, and right now one of those people was Oliver himself. I needed my attention to be on finding his sister, not on how nice he smelled, or how tall and strong he was, or how he looked when he smiled, or the way he had said *Bloom* earlier, as if I were something precious and wonderful.

"I think I need some air," I said, my voice tight. "Please excuse me for a moment." With that, I turned and edged round the dance floor, where I noticed Max and Izzy were dancing in perfect harmony, gazing at each other as though no one else existed. Max leaned down and whispered something in Izzy's ear, and she laughed, the sound a burst of pure joy.

I made my way through the crowds, nodding and smiling, and accepting the congratulations of people as I passed, until I was out in the cool quiet of the hallway.

I let my feet take me in the direction of the garden, greeting the chill of the air against my heated cheeks with relief.

It was a cloudless night, still as a tomb, and as I looked up I realized there was something else that was different away from the fog and smoke of London: spread over me like a taut length of midnight silk was the clear night sky.

I felt my breath catch as I stared. A riot of stars scattered carelessly across the black, each one a pinprick of pure silver light. There were thousands, and I could only stand, dazzled by the way they wheeled overhead.

"Pretty, isn't it?" a voice asked from behind me, and I don't know why I was surprised to find that Oliver had followed me – after all, he was probably more eager to get away from the crowds than I was.

"It's beautiful," I replied. "I have never seen so many stars. At home, they are hidden... I suppose it's silly, but

I didn't imagine there could be so *many*." It made me feel very, very small, but the feeling was not unpleasant.

Oliver came to stand beside me, and we both stood there, looking up for a moment.

"Are you cold?" he asked finally.

"No, not at all," I said. "It was too warm in there. Too many people."

"I know," Oliver huffed. "I swear Mrs Finch must have added another dozen invitations to the list without me noticing."

"At least," I agreed with a smile.

"How ever did she even get all these people up here?" He sighed. "It is supposed to be one of the benefits of living in the middle of nowhere that no one can get here at a moment's notice."

"I think she can do anything," I said reverently. "Part of me thinks she could have flown them here if she set her mind to it. She planned this whole thing, while running the Aviary, schemed all her schemes and still managed to remember to order a gown made to my exact measurements – which I certainly didn't give her." I broke off here, glanced around and leaned towards him. "I think she might have measured me in my sleep," I whispered.

Oliver huffed out a laugh. When he looked down at me, his eyes were warm. "Whatever her underhand machinations may have been, it was worth it. You look lovely."

"Oh, thank you," I said, thrown by the simple sincerity of his tone, no trace of his usual dryness. I ran my hands over the soft silk of my skirts. "I know we have much more important things to focus on, but I have to admit it was love at first sight for me. I've never worn anything like it."

The dress that Mrs Finch had pulled from between layers of thin tissue paper was a dream. Made in the exact tender green of spring, the neckline was cut in a broad arc, sitting wide on my shoulders. Cinched at the waist, but not at all restrictive, it fell out into a wide pool of silk that diffused into a darker green at the bottom. The elbow-length sleeves and the hem of the dress were embroidered with delicate spikes of pink heather, just like I had seen on the moors.

Heather. *Calluna*. Meaning: luck and protection.

With my hair pinned up in a loose crown of rose-gold curls threaded with matching heather-pink ribbon, I felt like a fairy queen, and hard as the evening had been, I had to admit that Mrs Finch was on to something when it came to the importance of clothes – this dress felt like armour. Even Mrs Lavigne had been stunned into silence when I had come floating down the stairs, confident that whatever other problems I had, worrying about looking the part was not one of them.

Mrs Finch, glorious herself in a gown of spangled navy tulle, had only beamed like the cat who'd got the cream, while Helene and Izzy descended into raptures over me.

"You look very handsome too," I said to Oliver now, running my eyes appreciatively over the fine black suit, his usual monochrome appearance broken up by the inclusion of a copper-coloured brocade waistcoat. His jacket fitted him like a glove, the tapered waist and tails emphasizing his tall, lean body, and his black tie was worn in a neat bow, as enticing as the ribbon on a present.

Looking at him properly was, I realized, a mistake, because suddenly my mouth had gone dry and my palms were clammy. My eyes swung away, towards the dark shadows of the garden in front of us, lit only by the light streaming from the house.

Oliver cleared his throat. "Perhaps," he began, unusually tentative, "we could … dance."

"Dance?" I squeaked. "I – I thought you hated dancing. Do you even know how?"

His eyebrows shot up. "Madam," he said grandly, "I *am* a gentleman."

"Well, I am no lady," I muttered, cheeks flushing. "I don't know how to do those fancy waltzes."

The music drifted softly through the open doors. The smile Oliver gave me was soft, secret.

"Ah, but the beauty of the waltz is that you only need the right partner." He held out his hand. "Follow me?"

Unable to resist, I watched my fingers touch his as though I had no control over them. His hand wrapped round mine; his other hand went to the small of my back, gently tugging me in towards him.

My heart seemed to be on a mission to beat out of my chest as he began to guide me in the steps. It took a minute or two, but I realized as I softened into his touch that he was right, that if I let the pressure of his hands guide me, then I *could* dance. Sort of. It was probably the worst waltz in the history of waltzing, but as I felt his fingers tight round mine, his shoulder, warm and solid under my touch, the heat of his tall body crowding my own, I didn't care. I was floating.

"You mowed the lawn," I said, if only for something to say, something that neither of us had mentioned. I hoped he wouldn't notice the huskiness in my voice.

He nodded. "Someone told me it was the best place to start, if I wanted to set the garden to rights."

"And do you?" I asked. "Want to set the garden to rights?"

He lifted the shoulder under my fingers in a shrug. "I think it's what my mother would have wanted. It would have made her unhappy to see it as it is now. Though I'm not sure I have the vision to do it justice. What would you do?" His eyes slid to me. "If it were yours?"

I tried not to look as if I had been thinking about exactly that since the first time I glimpsed it out of my bedroom window.

"Well, I suppose you could repair the pergola," I said

offhandedly. "Then train some plants over it. Wisteria is always magical in early summer, and then clematis as well. That would give you flowers all the way through to autumn." I nodded towards it. "You could have seats under there, in the shade. Somewhere soft and inviting to curl up with a book and enjoy the view."

As he spun us back towards the lawn, I continued dreamily. "Then you could reinstate the existing flower beds, but I would extend the one on the west side all the way down the lawn and then sweep it into a wide curve. It would soften everything and make it feel less formal. I'd focus on a pallet of purples, blues and whites, but with some deep pinks too. Nothing too structured, but a little wild-looking, tumbling, romantic – some lovely scented roses too, fat and pretty, with a bench to sit on and enjoy them." I briefly lifted my hand and pointed off to the side before returning it to his shoulder. "Over there I would put in a large pond with a water feature – there's nothing nicer than the sound of running water when you're sitting in a garden.

"I'd have steps going down to the back lawn and repair the wall so that it was a proper walled garden again. You could grow beds of flowers like a nursery there, fruit and vegetables too if you were interested. And then, most importantly, the greenhouse." I closed my eyes for a moment. "There is space for a huge greenhouse, and what you could grow in there ... well, the possibilities are limitless. You could grow rare tropical plants, propagate the most temperamental roses, and you could do it on such a scale..." I trailed off here and glanced up to find Oliver looking down at me with laughter in his eyes.

"It sounds," he said solemnly, "as though you have given the matter some thought."

"No! I... It just... You asked for my opinion!" I flushed, the words coming out defensively.

"I did," he agreed. "And I'm glad." His eyes drifted over the land in front of us as if he were picturing the scene I had described. "I like the way you talk about it."

"It's a joy, really," I said simply, as he spun me under the stars. "It all comes out of joy. Making something like a garden, it takes patience and hard work. You don't see the results at once; sometimes you don't see the results for years. It's an exercise in hope."

"You make it sound ... healing," Oliver said.

I beamed. "That is precisely what it is. If you ask me, doctors should be prescribing it. And you're so lucky, Lockhart ... all this *space*. Where I live there is no space like this. I know you have difficult feelings about the house, but for what it's worth, I think that if you wanted to you could make it something better than the story of its past. I think your garden could be part of that."

He was silent at that, but I saw the muscle in his jaw tic. The music swelled.

"I think perhaps you have already found a way to use your gift," he said finally, roughly, "to make the world a better place."

We looked at one another for a long moment, the air between us crackling with something that I was trying so hard to deny. Our feet had stopped moving. I pulled my hands away from him.

"Thank you for the dance," I said, though the words came out in a whisper. I had to stop this at once. All this *tingling*. It wasn't appropriate. It wasn't why I was here. "We should go back. You need to make your big announcement."

"Yes," he replied. "I suppose so, though standing up in front of that crowd and making a speech is far from my ideal way to spend the evening."

"I will be right there next to you," I said, and the words drew a small smile.

"Thank you, Bloom," Oliver murmured. "After you brutally accosted me the first time we met, I never dreamed those words would be so reassuring."

"I did not *brutally accost* you!" I exclaimed, taking his proffered arm as we turned and headed back to the house. "It was an accident, and actually I think you have been a tremendous baby about the whole thing..."

"A *baby*!" Oliver interrupted, clearly insulted. And the two of us bickered all the way inside.

I tried not to enjoy it too much.

Minutes later Oliver and I stood up at the front of the ballroom, everyone's eyes on us. Beside me, I could feel him almost vibrating with tension, could see the way he gripped his glass of champagne so tightly it looked as though it might shatter, and yet to the rest of the guests I knew he seemed the picture of commanding elegance. I felt my own spine stiffen with determination. If he could do this, then so could I.

"I would like to thank you all for being here on this happy occasion," Oliver said. "I had no idea that I had so many friends who could drop in at a moment's notice," he added dryly. "This is in fact a double celebration for my family. First of all, we are here to celebrate the frankly *unbelievable* fact that Miss Marigold Bloom has agreed to become my wife." Here, he looked at me, and I saw the glint of humour in his eyes.

"She is – as I'm sure you are all aware by now – not only beautiful but clever, determined and far too good for the likes of me."

The audience tittered good-naturedly, though none of the humour remained in Oliver's face. He looked at me for a long moment, his expression serious, and I felt something pass between us again, a throbbing echo of the feelings that had fluttered through me in the flower room. He cleared his throat and continued.

"The other reason we are here, of course, is because – as many of you may have heard whispers of – my sister, Ellen, has been returned to Lockhart Hall, thanks to the intervention of her adoptive parents, Mr and Mrs Lavigne." Now, all the attention moved to the Lavignes, where they stood near us, smiling and looking the picture of innocent delight. Helene, in contrast, appeared to be quite uncomfortable.

A murmur went round the room. Of course the news of Helene's arrival had become the juiciest piece of gossip in town days ago, but now that people could actually see her with their own eyes, there was a feverish edge to their interest. This was not so surprising given the wildly romantic story.

"In fact," Oliver continued, and I felt my heartbeat pick up, knowing what was about to happen, but not how it would play out, "my fiancée and I have organized a surprise for our honoured guests."

I was watching closely, so I noticed that there was a flicker of wariness in Mr Lavigne's face, but his wife betrayed no such emotion, only clasping her hands together, a greedy light in her eyes.

"Oh, Mr Lockhart," she demurred. "You have already given us the greatest gift imaginable, completing our Helene's happiness."

The smile Oliver gave then got nowhere near his eyes. "It is I who am indebted to you, and to that end I have arranged a trip to Paris for us all. We leave tomorrow."

The pleased smile dropped from Mrs Lavigne's face, but Mr Lavigne beamed broadly. "Paris, sir? Tomorrow? What a spontaneous adventure."

Oliver turned his attention back to the crowd, who were hanging on his every word. "I found that hearing tales of my sister's life in France made me want to visit for myself, to see where she grew up, safe and happy though we were apart." A murmur went through the room at this, at the emotion that had broken through Oliver's words. I knew that in that moment he was thinking of his sister, worrying about her, wondering if she really was standing in this room with him.

I moved so that the back of my hand brushed his own. So that he knew, as I had promised, that I stood there beside him.

He exhaled. "I have missed so much time with Helene," he said, steadier now, "and I think it is about time we started making some new memories together."

The Lavignes' smiles had a frozen edge; Helene's face

was bleached of colour. I looked into her eyes and could not begin to read the storm of emotions there, but she dipped her head in a nod, as though accepting Oliver's words.

"To new memories," Mrs Finch's voice cried out, and she lifted her glass.

"To new memories," the room chorused, and as the wave of chatter crashed over the room, and as both we and the Lavignes were swamped by well-wishers, my eyes met Oliver's.

It was time for us to solve this mystery ... once and for all.

PART FOUR

Paris
August, 1898

CHAPTER THIRTY-TWO

We were in Paris.

I was in *Paris*.

It didn't sound any less ridiculous the more times I said it in my head, or even – on several occasions – aloud.

"I know perfectly well where we are, Bloom," Oliver said bitterly. "There is no need for you to keep *announcing* it."

"But, Lockhart," I breathed, standing in front of the window of my room in the Grand Hotel Du Louvre, looking down over the bustling Place du Palais Royal, lined with its impossibly grand buildings, all sand-coloured stone and soaring colonnades, and classical sculpture. "We are actually *in Paris*. Paris! France!"

Oliver groaned into a cushion from where he was slumped into the red silk of the sofa – because not only was I staying in an enormous hotel with two hundred rooms, two steam-powered lifts, a famous artist in residence on the floor above us, and its own telegraph room ("That will come in handy," Mrs Finch had remarked), but my room was a suite, which meant it was actually several rooms full of glass chandeliers and oil paintings and antique furniture, and I had *never* seen anything like it.

I glanced at Oliver, flooded with sympathy. "Are you feeling *any* better?" I asked.

Oliver lifted his head at that. "I told you already that I am perfectly fine. I don't know why you have to keep asking. Between that and the constant ejaculations of 'Paris! Paris! Paris!' you are growing incredibly wearisome."

I decided to ignore this outburst because he was still pale and limp.

"Just let me know if you think you're going to cast up your accounts again," I said cheerfully. "I will have to try to find the least expensive-looking receptacle for you to vomit into." This would be tricky as everything in the room seemed to be made of solid gold.

"I did not *cast up my accounts*, you wretched woman," Oliver groused, closing his eyes. "So stop saying that I did."

It seemed Oliver had inherited his mother's aversion to travelling by sea, and he had spent the entire ferry journey across the Channel clinging to the side of the boat, green-faced and miserable.

"I don't care what you say," I chided, "as soon as the hot water we sent for arrives, you'll drink the tisane I'm mixing."

I moved to the coffee table and bent over the leather case I had unpacked, a gift from Mrs Finch when Winnie and I began our experiments. It was neatly divided into three layers of small, square cavities, housing glass jars filled with various dried and powdered plants.

"Ginger," I said, pulling out jars as I went, "and barberry and mint."

"Sounds revolting."

I fixed him with a hard stare. "You will drink it and then you'll feel better."

There was a knock at the door, and the arrival of the hot water (in an elaborate silver pot) coincided with the arrival of the rest of the Finches for our meeting to discuss our strategy.

Sylla eyed Oliver with distaste before dropping into an armchair. "Why do you still look so … clammy?" she asked in greeting.

"I am not clammy. I am perfectly fine," Oliver ground out.

"I'm making him a tisane," I said, and Winnie drifted over, eyeing my movements with curiosity.

"Barberry?" she asked, pushing her glasses up her nose. "I thought that was an emetic?"

"What is an emetic?" Oliver asked suspiciously.

"It causes vomiting," Winnie said sunnily.

"I knew it! You're trying to poison me!" Oliver exploded in outrage, while Sylla perked up, leaning forward with obvious interest.

"I am not poisoning you," I said calmly. "In *large*

quantities, barberry can cause sickness, but the amount I am using here will only soothe any stomach pain. It is all in the dosage."

"Fascinating," Winnie murmured. "Isn't it curious how often we have found that the same ingredient can cause problems *and* cure them?"

"Sounds like Bloom," Oliver grumbled. "First she gives me a headache, then she shoves tea down my throat to get rid of it."

"Just be quiet and drink this," I said, handing him the teacup, which was steaming gently and smelled pleasant, and therefore did not at all deserve the wrinkled look of disgust on Oliver's face.

"I have to say," Maud chimed in from beside the fireplace where she was poking at the various ornaments on display on the mantel, "that this hotel is a step up from our usual digs. I'm glad you invited Win and me along for this one."

"We have Mr Lockhart to thank for the accommodations," Mrs Finch said. "It is especially convenient that Sylla was already installed here and has several contacts working on the staff who could arrange things to our liking." Our rooms were all next to one another, and the rest of the rooms around us had been kept empty – providing us with a level of privacy that we needed.

"The Lavignes' rooms are two floors below ours?" I said.

"Yes." Mrs Finch nodded. "And I would say that any qualms they may have had about the trip were dispelled by the grandeur of the hotel. I believe they are starting to relax again, which is in our favour. We want their guards down." She turned to Sylla. "Perhaps you would like to update us all on your own progress?"

I knew that Mrs Finch had met Sylla in her room straightaway to share our news, but we had not yet heard what had been going on this side of the Channel.

"Certainly." Sylla reclined in her chair, picking an invisible speck of lint off her extremely fashionable sapphire gown. "I have been busy establishing the veracity of the Lavignes' claims – or lack thereof. You have since learned that Mr Lavigne has another identity all together, but I believe I can still provide several missing pieces of the puzzle." She leaned forward. "To put it succinctly, on the surface, everything the Lavignes have told you appears to be true."

"What?" Maud exclaimed. "How can that be possible?"

Sylla's shrug was liquid. "I can only tell you what I know. A Mr and Mrs Lavigne lived for over a dozen years in Herblay, most of these with their adopted daughter, Helene. Mr Lavigne was a merchant, and Helene was sent away to school – the Lycée Sainte-Geneviève. Most importantly" – she focused her attention on Oliver – "Helene was discovered as a child, wandering alone in the village with a head injury and no memory of her past."

"My God!" Oliver sprung to his feet. "It is true, then? Ellen is alive?"

"It seems likely that it was indeed your sister who survived the accident and was adopted by the Lavignes," Sylla conceded. "There were several *extremely* talkative characters in the village who couldn't wait to share the story with me – wildly embellished in places, of course. There was some speculation that Helene had been a lost princess, the secret descendent of the Bourbon line. However, I attributed this particular theory to the surprisingly good brandy on offer in the local tavern. What is also a fact is that your mother's accident took place in Le Pecq. The dates align perfectly. It is possible then, even probable, that the story the Lavignes told was true – that the young girl found in Herblay was Ellen. Whether she is also the girl in this hotel is another question. We know that the couple purporting to be her parents are certainly *not* the real Lavignes."

Oliver's legs went from under him, and he collapsed back into the sofa, all colour gone from his face. "I do not think I really let myself believe," he murmured. "My sister is truly alive." His eyes darted between us. "Is she also Helene, then? The Helene we know, I mean."

Sylla let out a noise of frustration. "There, I hit something of a wall. The Lavignes left Herblay around eight months ago, and no one seemed certain where they had gone or whether they took their daughter with them. Several people said that they had moved somewhere down south, but that Helene had not gone with them. One woman swore that Helene was living alone in Paris, and she had a good deal to say on the matter of loose morals and modern young ladies." Sylla's nose wrinkled. "Parochial attitudes abound in the suburbs."

"We must look into David Brown, I suppose," I said. "It seems to me that uncovering the truth about the Lavignes will inevitably lead to the truth about Helene's involvement."

"Yes," Sylla said approvingly, "and of course there is the school. I have managed to arrange an appointment tomorrow afternoon with the headmistress. From what I can gather, she has been there since the dawn of time, so she should be able to answer questions about Helene."

"Can we get Helene to go to the school with us?" I asked. "Surely then the headmistress will be able to identify her?"

"We cannot." Mrs Finch shook her head regretfully. "Such a suggestion would spring the trap too soon – Mr and Mrs Lavigne would certainly take to their heels, and with them would go the information we need about Ellen."

"I can sketch her," Maud said. "I have seen her several

times since we arrived at the hotel, and it would be easy to do. It is not perfect, but..."

Winnie nodded. "It is a good idea. Maud is an excellent artist," she added proudly.

"Yes," Sylla said thoughtfully. "Maud can do the sketch and then Mr Lockhart and Mari can take it with them tomorrow."

"Us?" I said. "We're the ones who are going to the school?"

"It makes sense," Sylla said. "Helene's history is well known; it will be natural for you to have questions about Lockhart's missing sister. You will tell the Lavignes you have wedding arrangements to make while you are here – that your wedding outfits are being made by Worth. I have already taken the precaution of making you an appointment that several dressmakers will swear you attended."

"What about the rest of you?" Oliver asked.

"Maud and Winnie will follow the Lavignes to make sure they are behaving themselves," Sylla replied briskly. "With any luck, they will lead us to more clues about their history if they believe they are unobserved, and as they have not met Maud or Winnie it should be a straightforward job." She fixed Maud and Winnie with a dark look. "As long as I can trust that neither of you will get *distracted*."

"Please!" Maud looked offended. "We are professionals." The picture of professionalism she was trying to present was slightly undermined when she added, "But is it too much to hope that they have an interest in seeing the can-can dancers?"

"Or skeletons. I'm longing to visit the catacombs..." Winnie said with a delighted shiver. "For science!" she added when several pairs of eyes turned to her.

"I will be looking further into the accident at Le Pecq," Sylla said, ignoring all this. "I have managed to track down one of the local police officers who was originally connected to the case."

"And I have several meetings set with contacts in the ... less *genteel* parts of the city," Mrs Finch said. "I have a feeling that David Brown might be well known there. All being well, we will reconvene at Café Fleur at four o'clock tomorrow to share information – we already know that the Lavignes plan to take tea at the hotel then."

"Good," I said, eyeing Oliver, who looked anxious and wan. "So we have a plan. But now I need some fresh air. Lockhart?" I gave him my biggest smile. "Would you care to take a walk? I don't know if you've noticed, but ... we *are* in Paris."

CHAPTER THIRTY-THREE

The hotel was directly opposite the Louvre, and – because I had no idea where we were – Oliver guided us under a cool stone passage and through to a large square, each side bordered by the grandest buildings I had ever seen. It was strange to be alone with him like this, but now that we were here, in another country, where not a soul knew us, it was suddenly easy to shed the restrictions of propriety and it felt delicious.

The size of the buildings around us was overwhelming. At the bottom, a covered walkway ran behind rows of graceful, symmetrical archways, each column topped with a statue of a man looking wise and dignified. The facade stretched up, hundreds of windows in neat rows, punctuated by monumental gateways, all topped with a grey slate roof that seemed to shine under the August sun.

I stood, frozen and gawping until Oliver chuckled. "Quite the sight, isn't it?"

I was relieved to hear him laugh. He had been tense and silent since we left the hotel suite, not that I could blame him. There was a lot to sift through.

"All of this is a museum?" I asked, dazed.

Oliver nodded, pulling me along through the milling crowds. "Stuffed full of art," he said, "but I think I know somewhere that *you* will find more beauty and artistry than any wing of that museum."

We walked towards an enormous stone arch, topped with a statue of a woman driving a chariot, flanked by two golden figures.

"It's a triumphal arc." Oliver gestured towards it. "Built by Napoleon, as a lot of these grand monuments were, to celebrate all his successes. Unfortunately for him, the statue on the top these days represents Peace in her chariot – celebrating his failure instead. Funny how quickly things can change."

We passed under the arch along a wide path, cut between perfectly manicured lawns, and down a set of shallow stone stairs.

"Oh!" I exclaimed softly.

"The Jardin des Tuileries," Oliver said.

"You brought me to a garden?" I was absurdly touched.

He shrugged. "It seemed the right thing to do."

And of course it was. The sun shone, dazzling overhead as we stood in the middle of the elegant gardens stretching out endlessly in front of us. "So much green," I murmured. There were avenues lined with trees leading down to a large pool with a tall fountain. Children were floating little boats with red sails across the surface in noisy races.

Beyond the trees I could see the rooftops I already recognized as being quintessentially Parisian with their soft blue-grey slate above straw-coloured stone. Standing to the west of us, somewhere in the distance was the Eiffel Tower, and I started at the sight. I had seen pictures, of course, but it felt so strange to see it in real life. The tallest building in the world.

And then, because I couldn't help myself, I pulled Oliver away from the path where fashionable couples were perambulating, the sensible ladies holding pretty parasols to protect them from the August sun.

I pulled him past the wistful, classical-looking statues of suffering women, and plunged towards the flower beds, which – even in this formal setting – were rioting, full of colour and texture that spilled over their neat borders.

"I might have known you'd be straight in the dirt," Oliver said.

I knelt down on the grass and brushed my fingers with delight against one of the fat apricot-coloured blooms.

"Just look at all these dahlias!" I exclaimed. "I've never seen such huge flowers. The French are actually at the forefront of many of the advances in our field. I was talking to Win about it the other day, and she said…" I trailed off, looking up at Oliver whose expression was almost fond. I cleared my throat. "These white ones too.

So beautiful, though I'm not sure of the variety. Fleurel, perhaps."

"Dahlias," he said with no sign of impatience at my enthusiastic rambling. "Let me think. Eternal love and commitment, wasn't it?"

The words were mild, but they set my pulse thrumming. It was that reminder of being in the flower room. The fact that we almost kissed but didn't ... and then we didn't talk about it. I'd be lying if I said that particular moment hadn't been playing on a loop in my head ever since.

"Mmm," I managed. "That's right." I forced my attention back to the flowers. "This planting is so creative; I see *amaranthus, leonotis leonuris...*"

"Leon-what?"

I grinned. "We call it lion's tail. It's this orange one here. And look at these beautiful salvia plants, the purple and the orange together... It's quite feisty for a public space, isn't it? So vibrant."

Oliver only made a slightly perplexed sound of agreement.

"Perhaps I was wrong about the colours you should

have in your garden," I mused. "A space like that could handle something bold, don't you think?"

"I think Lockhart Hall could certainly benefit from a bold presence." The touch of gravel in his voice had me looking up, though his face was in shadow under his hat, and I found it hard to read his expression.

He held out his hand to me, and I accepted so that he could pull me up to my feet. The instant our fingers touched I felt the now-familiar tingling that spread like a cold shock through my body.

I let go of him, brushing hastily at my skirt. "I have got myself all muddy again," I said, flustered.

He reached out, placing a finger underneath my chin and tipping it up so that I was looking at him. His eyes roamed over my face, and he stepped closer, whatever he saw there drawing a low rumble from his chest.

I felt dizzy. We were tucked away, out of view of the crowds, surrounded by flowers, and it was as if the surrounding noise and bustle dropped away for a moment. All that existed was the two of us. His hand on my face, his mouth so close to mine. I wanted him with a desperation that edged into pain.

In the end it was this realization that brought me to my senses.

"We – we can't," I stammered, the words wobbling. His hand dropped away as my own lifted to my chest, pressed over my heart, which was actually aching. "I can't... We shouldn't... There's too much..." I rambled, trying to think, trying to *breathe*.

"Of course," he said at once, taking a step back. "I apologize."

"No, you... I..." I tried again but got no further.

Oliver only gave a brisk nod. "Please," he said with enviable calm, his voice gentle. "You don't owe me an explanation. It was my mistake, and I would never want to make you uncomfortable."

"You – you haven't made me uncomfortable," I said, though he absolutely had, just not in the way he meant. My whole body felt like a lit firecracker, set to explode.

"Good," he said, clearly relieved. "I would hate that. Shall we return to the hotel? Mrs Finch will be wondering where we are."

And with that, we finished our walk in silence.

*

That evening Mrs Finch had dinner sent to me in my room – a luxury that I had hardly dreamed of. It had been a long day of travel, and I was grateful for the calm moment to reflect on my own emotional turmoil. I wasn't sure if that was why Mrs Finch had suggested we all have a quiet evening. I knew she saw far too much, and I hadn't missed her keen look when Oliver and I returned from our walk.

Still, I was not complaining when the waiting staff arrived at my door laden with trays covered in silver-domed plates. When removed, the domes revealed perfectly boiled eggs with swirls of creamy mayonnaise, chicken quenelles with cream and baby peas, a capon covered with a sauce I didn't recognize, something light brown and earthy and delicious, and a pastry called a mille feuille, which was an actual taste of heaven.

As I ate, I thought about the walk with Oliver, about the way we had almost kissed … again. About how much I wanted it, wanted him. I was a practical woman, I reminded myself. I was a *businesswoman*. I knew a little something about risk and reward, and I knew damn well that Oliver Lockhart was a risk I couldn't afford to take.

There were too many reasons we could never work, too many responsibilities between us and too many differences. He needed a grand lady, not a florist constantly covered in dirt who couldn't waltz and didn't know what a truffle was. (The waiter who retrieved my empty plates had explained that this was the mystery ingredient in the delicious sauce, in perfect English, because I didn't speak French – another thing that any woman Oliver Lockhart ended up with would undoubtedly do beautifully.)

It wasn't that I didn't think *I* was worthy; it was that I knew I wasn't from his world. I was acutely aware that Simon had thought I was below him socially and it had hurt. I thought about the pain I felt when he'd called off our engagement and I knew it was nothing to the hurt I would experience if I gave my heart to Oliver and it didn't work out. Safer, far safer, not to risk it. I could protect myself from heartache if I simply never fell in love.

And all this was before my responsibilities to the Aviary, and to Bloom's and my family were taken into account. Really, there was no question that stopping the kiss had been the only practical option.

I had almost talked myself into believing that pulling away had been for the best when there was a knock at the door, and I was relieved to find Maud and Winnie standing in the hallway, all dressed up and grinning at me with mischief in their eyes.

"Come on, Mari," Maud said. "We're taking you out on the town."

"Oh, but Mrs Finch said..." I began.

Maud cut me off with a wave of her hand. "Mari, we're in *Paris*! And a girl I know works at Maxim's. She might have information about the Lavignes or David Brown. It's practically *work*."

"Please, Mari," Winnie chimed in, her cheeks pink. "It will be so much fun."

How could I resist? Honestly, a distraction was very welcome, and fun was just what I needed.

"Come in while I change," I said, and the pair of them squealed.

Maxim's, it transpired, was only a short walk from the hotel, and it was a nightclub for the wealthy and famous. We were, of course, neither, but Maud's friend let us in through the back door with a wink and a warm greeting and we were soon lost in the crowd.

The place was ... *red*. That was the first thing that struck me. The carpets were thick and red; the walls were scarlet, with crimson silk drapes. The room was lit by lamps covered in red silk shades, casting a warm and somehow decadent glow across the scene.

And what a scene it was. A bar and dining room crammed full of beautiful people in fashionable clothes talking animatedly at a hundred miles an hour in a language I didn't understand. The red walls were lined with enormous, gilt-edged mirrors that reflected the crowds making the place feel even busier. The air was full of perfume and the smell of tobacco. On a small dance floor, couples whirled to the music being played by a small house orchestra in natty red-and-gold uniforms.

"This place is perfect," Maud said, looking about herself with pleasure.

"Nothing worries her, does it?" I asked Winnie as we were shown to a corner table with plush red velvet seats and Maud began chatting with the waiter.

"Maud can fit in just about anywhere," Win said with a proud smile.

"Where did she learn French?" I asked.

"Oh, I taught her." Winnie beamed. "Maud has a wonderful ear for languages."

"Perhaps you could teach me?" I said tentatively. It hadn't ever seemed necessary before, but the Aviary was expanding my world in so many ways.

"Of course," Winnie said. "I'd be happy to. Though Maud might be more help."

"More help with what?" Maud asked.

"Mari wants to learn some French," Win replied.

A wicked grin lit Maud's face. "Oh, yes, let's have the first lesson now."

The next few minutes passed in fits of helpless laughter as Maud taught me an absurd number of rude words in French, and the waiter delivered us tiny glasses of milky green liquid that tasted like liquorice that had been set on fire.

"Go steady with that." Maud smirked. "Absinthe is not for the faint of heart."

"So, Maud." Maud's friend, Eloise, stopped by our

table, an empty tray in her hand. "What are you doing in Paris?"

"We're working," Maud said brightly.

"Ah." Eloise nodded in a way that made me believe she knew at least some of the truth about the Aviary. Her eyes moved to Winnie and I. "You must be Win," she said, smiling. "Maud told me so much about you when I was last in England."

"Yes." Win's eyes were soft as she glanced at Maud. "And this is Mari, our newest recruit."

Eloise and I greeted each other. "So – not that I'm not glad to see you – but is this just a social call?" she asked after some small talk about Paris.

"Yes and no." Maud twirled her glass between her fingers. "We needed a night off, but I did think if there was information worth having that you might have it."

"And what sort of information might you be looking for?" Eloise asked, raising her brows.

Maud pulled some bank notes from her pocket and slid them across the table. Eloise picked them up and stuffed them in her apron with a practised nonchalance.

"We're looking for a couple called Lavigne and their daughter, Helene," Maud said.

Eloise shrugged. "Never heard of them."

"What about David Brown?" I asked. "An Englishman."

Eloise pursed her lips at that. "David Brown," she said softly, the name sounding musical in her French accent. "There was a man by that name a couple of years ago. A con man based out in Ménilmontant near the cemetery, I think. Ran with a bad crowd." She tilted her head. "Cheated some dangerous people. I thought he was dead, actually. I'm sure that was the story."

"Nothing else?" Maud pressed.

"I heard he left England in the first place because things got too hot for him there, but he went back and forth using an alias. Maybe more than one." Eloise tapped her fingers against her skirt, her face screwed up in concentration. "Yes," she said thoughtfully. "That was right. I remember because Hugo... You remember Hugo?" she asked Maud with an arch of her brows.

Maud chuckled. "Oh, I remember Hugo."

Eloise sighed, pressed a hand to her chest and grinned at me. "Broke my heart."

"Was that before or after you stole his family silverware?" Maud scoffed.

Eloise primmed her mouth, though her eyes still danced. "I don't know what you are referring to."

"Fine, fine," Maud said. "But back to David Brown..."

"Ah, yes." Eloise nodded. "It was Hugo who knew him a little. Said he had a line on the best forger in England. *Real prime stuff*, as you would say. Meant he could more or less come and go as he pleased. But that was a while ago. If he's not dead, I don't know where to find him. He could well be using a different name."

"Any idea who he might call upon if he found himself in the city?" Win asked.

Eloise shook her head regretfully. "No, I'm sorry. I don't have much to do with those people any more."

"It's fine," Maud said. "It all helps. Thank you, Eloise."

While Eloise sashayed back to work, the three of us sat in thoughtful silence.

"It's not much we didn't know already," Maud said finally.

"It fits," I said. "A career con man. Dangerous. It's another puzzle piece. If it's the same man."

405

Winnie shivered. "It must be the same man, surely?"

"There are too many damned moving parts in this mess," Maud grumbled. "Still." She seized her glass and lifted it in the air. "That's a problem for tomorrow. For tonight we are young and lovely, and drinking in Paris. Let's enjoy ourselves."

"I'll drink to that," I agreed, and the three of us clinked our glasses together in a toast.

CHAPTER THIRTY-FOUR

The next morning, Sylla had a note sent asking me to meet her early in the hotel lobby. I was actually feeling a trifle worse for wear after the night before. Maud had been right about the absinthe, and I felt rather green myself.

"I see you had an entertaining night," Sylla huffed. Naturally, she looked immaculate.

I dragged a hand over my hair, trying to tidy it, but the curls kept springing out at wild angles. "We got some information," I said quickly.

"Yes, I know." Sylla crossed her arms. "Winnie and I had breakfast with Mrs Finch."

Last time I had seen Winnie she had been weaving towards her room in the early hours, singing a song of her own composition made entirely of rude French words, so I found this information surprising.

"David Brown is a con man," Sylla said. "It would make sense. Mrs Finch will include Ménilmontant in her excursion today. Perhaps track down this Hugo fellow and see what he knows about his old friend."

"So why did we need to meet this morning?" I asked.

"You are still in your training period," Sylla said impatiently. "We are not here on holiday, Mari. There is work to do and we should absolutely take advantage of the opportunity this trip has provided."

"Of course." I nodded, chastised. "What did you have in mind?"

"We're going to plan an art heist," Sylla said serenely, and she led me out of the hotel towards the Louvre.

This time we went inside the building, and I thought my brain was going to explode. We passed through room after room, each one heaving with masterpieces. The ceilings were high, gilded, often painted. There was one long gallery, called the Gallery of Apollo, that was like stepping inside a jewellery box – every single surface covered in gold and paintings and sculptures. It was an apt comparison because it housed the French royal jewels. I trailed around after Sylla, trying to pay attention to the lecture she was giving me on the jewels' history while my magpie eyes were being distracted by each new shining object.

As we moved into another gallery, Sylla came to a stop in front of a handful of paintings.

"Da Vinci," she said reverently.

I regarded the paintings. I knew almost nothing about art, but I was enjoying Sylla's lesson.

"In our line of work, at least a little knowledge in art and antiquities will always come in handy," she had said. "One never knows when one will have to forge something or steal something or hit someone over the head with an oil painting." This last one I thought was a touch specific.

"Now, let's talk about stealing a Da Vinci," Sylla said, instead of delivering the lecture I had come to expect.

"You want to *steal* a Da Vinci?" I whispered.

Sylla rolled her eyes. "Well, not at this precise moment, obviously, but it's always nice to have a plan in place. This is part of your training; you need to be able to formulate solutions to potential problems." She stared wistfully at the paintings. "It has been too long since I needed to pull off a good heist."

"Fine," I said. "So, we're stealing a Da Vinci."

Sylla straightened. "Yes. First of all, tell me which one you're going to take."

I observed the wall of priceless paintings. "Um, that one." I pointed to a painting of the Virgin Mary holding the baby Jesus, who was holding a squirmy-looking lamb.

"Hmmmm." Sylla tipped her head thoughtfully. "Possible, but not the most practical option." She pointed to a picture sandwiched between two of the larger canvases. It was small and muted, a portrait of a dark-haired woman looking enigmatically out from the canvas. "This one would be better. It's smaller, and the space it would leave is more easily overlooked. Now" – she clapped her hands together – "how would you steal it?"

I looked at the painting. I turned my head to look around the room we were in, noting the number of visitors, the single guard. For a moment I went over increasingly outlandish ideas in my mind. I tried to think about what I had learned so far, from the plans we had put in place with the Aviary. I thought about the fact that the best plan was often the simplest.

"A cleaner or handyman would be best placed," I said finally. "Someone who works for a few weeks or months, preferably under a false name. Someone who the guards stop noticing." I swung my head to where a pale man in a red jacket stood near the door looking bored. "They would come in early on a day that they aren't due to work and hide somewhere – in a cupboard, perhaps. They would know the comings and goings of any guards. Then, after the museum closes, they could simply unscrew the painting from the wall and walk out with it under their jacket. It's small enough to be easily concealed, as long as it were winter and they wore a bulky coat. People don't tend to worry about people getting *out* of a museum after hours; it's the getting in that's hard."

Sylla looked at me in surprise. "That is actually ... a good plan," she said.

I beamed, feeling less queasy than I had all morning. "Well then," I said, "at least you've finally made a master criminal out of me."

"Don't go getting ahead of yourself." Sylla sniffed. "It's one thing to steal it; the real trick would be selling it without getting caught." Nevertheless, I thought I saw her lips twitch into a smile before she turned away.

"Now," she said, ambling further down the gallery. "There was another reason I wanted to get you away from the hotel. Why don't we discuss the matter of you and Oliver Lockhart?"

My heart sank. "Wouldn't you rather tell me off some more for going out last night?" I said hopefully.

She fixed me with a hard stare. "I just want to be certain that this little romance of yours isn't going to become a problem. We have an important job to do, Marigold, and that must come first."

"There is no romance," I said firmly, though the look Sylla gave me made me think I hadn't been convincing.

"Nothing will interfere with the work." A promise to her and to myself.

After a moment, Sylla gave a brisk nod and carried on walking. Another minute or two passed and I thought the matter was closed.

"For what it's worth," she added, and the words were reluctant, "most of the men we encounter in this business are terrible. Oliver Lockhart is ... the exception."

I came to a halt. "What does that mean?" I asked.

Sylla scowled. "What do you think it means? I'm not going to organize your personal life for you – even though we all know I *could* and that I would do a much better job at it. I've said all I have to say on the matter and now it's up to you." On this surprising note, she stomped off, muttering under her breath.

I stood, frozen for a while. It was possible, I thought, just possible, that Sylla actually ... *cared*.

CHAPTER THIRTY-FIVE

Later that afternoon, Oliver and I set off with a hired horse and buggy for Lycée Sainte-Geneviève. Oliver drove and we sat up behind the horse together, enjoying the view and the warm golden sunshine.

Over the course of the day, I had become increasingly anxious about this trip. How would Oliver and I handle spending time together after what had happened (or almost happened) the day before? Fortunately, Oliver seemed utterly his usual self. Bad-tempered, grumbling, secretly amused by me. I was relieved, after worrying he would be stiff and polite, worrying that I would be too bright, too awkward. Perversely there was also a part of me that was … disappointed? Why had the encounter been so easy for him to brush off when I still felt jangled? I tried to push the feeling aside. It was good that we could be normal. It was good that we could concentrate on what needed to be done. I had promised Sylla, hadn't I? Nothing was going to interfere with the work.

And with that in mind, a giddying sense of freedom descended on me as we rode through the city in the open air, every sight and sound completely new. I managed to keep myself from rhapsodizing aloud again, but clearly I wasn't doing a good job at hiding my excitement completely.

"Bloom…" Oliver sighed, concentrating his attention on the road. "I can feel you *quivering*."

We drove through the Place de la Concorde, where the towering obelisk covered in ancient hieroglyphs stood tall between two burbling fountains, down on to the Champs-Élysées – that wide road fringed with the tall green canopies of horse-chestnut trees marching tidily down the sides. In contrast, the traffic wheeled around, a bustling crowd of carriages of every size, winding about each other with seemingly little order at all. At the end of the road, the Arc de Triomphe loomed over everything around it, more traffic circling round and round it at a frantic pace, like a bizarre carousel.

"But just ... look!" I exclaimed, gesturing with my hands at ... *everything.*

Oliver said nothing, but I saw the smile pulling at his lips.

The school was about five miles outside the city in a pleasantly green suburb. It must have once been an old manor house: a large, stoic-looking building hunkered into the landscape, made of white stone with a shining blue-black roof. Girls in neat blue smocks, with short, matching capes tied round their shoulders milled about the grounds, full of happy chatter.

I felt something loosen in Oliver's posture at the sight. I think part of him had feared finding out his sister had been sent away to live in a bleak Dickensian parody of a boarding school, but that was not what this was at all.

We drew up a long, gravelled driveway, and Oliver brought the buggy to a stop, jumping down and handing the reins to a waiting groom while the horse tossed his head. Oliver came round to help me down from the high box, holding his hand out to me.

I placed my fingers in his and felt the warmth of his touch all the way through our gloves. When my feet hit the ground, our hands seemed to cling for a moment longer than was necessary. I looked up at him from beneath the wide brim of my straw hat, and the sunlight gilded the lines of his handsome face. I felt my heart flutter pathetically.

He cleared his throat, then dropped my hand. "Shall we?" He gestured towards the school.

I looked up at the building. "There are answers here," I said. "I know there are."

Oliver exhaled slowly. "Then let us go and find them. I have had quite enough mystery and intrigue."

I smiled. "A little intrigue can be good thing."

"I will agree to a sprinkling of intrigue. No more." With that, he tucked my hand into the crook of his arm and sauntered towards the school, the picture of composure.

Inside, we were greeted by one of the teachers, a

woman who introduced herself as Madame Boucher, sweet-faced and smiling. She guided us to the office belonging to the headmistress.

She knocked once, and a voice called, "*Entrez donc!*"

Madame Boucher pushed the door open for us and then slipped away. Oliver and I entered the office to find an elegant woman in her seventies standing behind a beautifully polished walnut desk.

"Monsieur Lockhart, Madame Lockhart, welcome," she said in delicately accented English. My composure almost slipped at her words, but I remembered that, to simplify matters, Sylla had written that we were a married couple. "I am glad to see you found us without any problems. I am Madame Moreau." She leaned across the desk and shook hands with us both. "Please." She gestured to the pair of chairs. "Sit."

"It is a pleasure to meet you, Madame," I said, sinking into the chair. "You have a beautiful school here."

An affectionate smile lit her face. "Ah, yes, we are certainly proud of it, and of the young ladies who come here for their studies. We hope that the world finds them – how do you say? – a credit to us."

"I'm sure," I murmured.

"Madame," Oliver broke in, and it was clear that he was holding on to his patience by a thread. "Do you know why we are here?"

She nodded. "Your associate wrote to me that you have questions about your sister, that you have reason to believe she was a student here – Helene Lavigne?"

"That is correct," Oliver said. "From what we have been able to piece together, my sister – Ellen – suffered an accident in Le Pecq and lost her memory. She was then taken in by a couple called Lavigne and we believe she was sent here to study."

Madame Moreau tilted her head. "Helene Lavigne was a student here, from 1890 until 1894, and you are quite right that she had suffered a loss of memory in her early childhood. She was a charming girl, bright and engaging. Unfortunately, Monsieur, I do not know where she currently resides. When she left us, I believe she returned to her parents in..." She frowned here, tapping the edge of her desk. "Herblay?" she said finally, then she shrugged. "But whether she remains there or not, I cannot say." She smiled. "I think perhaps *not*, because

Helene was always full of plans. Not all our girls keep in touch, you understand, though I would love to help you." She held up her hands in a gesture of defeat.

I pulled the sketch that Maud had done of Helene from my pocket. It was a good likeness, I thought, even capturing some of Helene's bashfulness. "Madame, does this sketch look like Helene?"

The headmistress took the paper from my hand and then placed a pair of small silver spectacles on her nose. She examined the picture closely, her lips pressed together.

"Hmmm," she said finally. "It could be her, I think. It is hard to say, and of course it has been over four years since I last saw her." Oliver slumped in his seat, and Madame Moreau turned her inquisitive gaze on him. "This sketch. This is your sister?"

"I—" Oliver began, and then hesitated, rubbing a hand across his brow in a weary gesture. "Truly? I don't know. It is complicated."

Madame Moreau looked down at the drawing again, making another thoughtful humming noise. "But, of course, the easiest thing to do would be to show you the photographs, *non*?"

Oliver and I both froze. "The – the photographs?" I managed finally, squeezing the words out.

She nodded, standing and moving to the bookcase behind her that held a shelf full of fat leather-bound albums. "We take a class photograph of all the girls at the end of the year," she said, pulling on one spine after another until she located the one that she wanted. "The parents like it, and we have been doing it for over twenty years." She smiled at me here, hefting one of the albums from the shelf. "We are a very modern establishment." Again she sounded proud.

She laid the album on the desk and carefully leafed through the pages, each one a thick board separated from the next by a sheet of tissue paper.

"Ah!" she said. "Here. Our most senior class in 1894. This will be the most recent picture that we have of Helene." She laid the photograph out and took a step back, allowing Oliver and myself to lean over, and search the image, scanning the rows of neatly dressed and smiling young women. My heart was thundering in my chest.

Then, as Oliver let out a quiet gasp, I saw her.

"She is here!" I whispered, my finger moving to point. "Helene! She is right here. It really is her."

There in the front row stood a girl who, without question, was Helene, the girl we knew, the girl who had been staying at Lockwood Hall and had travelled with us to Paris. A few years younger, yes, but still her. We had found her. We had really found Oliver's sister. And she had been under our noses the whole time.

Madame Moreau leaned over, looking at where I pointed. "Oh no, my dear," she said. "I'm afraid you are mistaken. That is not Helene Lavigne."

It felt as though all the air was leaving my lungs. "It's – it's not?"

"No, no," Madame Moreau said placidly. "*That* is Lucy Brown."

I looked over to Oliver, stunned, but he was only staring wordlessly at the photograph. He lifted his hand, and I saw that it was trembling wildly. He pressed his finger gently against the picture, softly touching the face of the girl beside Lucy.

"Ellen," he whispered, and the word was choked with emotion. "It is Ellen."

CHAPTER THIRTY-SIX

Madame Moreau beamed. "*Oui, d'accord!* This is Helene. Helene Lavigne."

I looked at the girl in the picture. Side by side with Lucy, the two of them could be sisters. The images of their faces were small, a little grainy, and yet in Helene's face – the real Helene – I would swear that I could see some of that mischief, that furious energy that I had seen in the portrait of her as a child.

In contrast, the girl I now knew was Lucy Brown smiled out from the photograph utterly without guile, eyes wide and innocent. *Well*, I thought, fury coming rapidly to the surface and humming through my veins, *looks could be deceiving.*

Oliver crashed back into the chair behind him, and I sat too, realizing that my own legs were shaking. But I needed to remain calm. Oliver was clearly in no state to ask questions, so it was up to me. I tried to consider what Mrs Finch would do.

"Madame Moreau," I said finally. "Can you tell us more about Lucy Brown?"

"Lucy?" Her eyebrows lifted as she returned to her own seat. She rested her elbows on the desk, steepling her fingers. "Lucy was a sweet girl. Shy, quiet, nervous, but a good student. She was extremely diligent, with an eye for art and a beautiful singing voice."

"And she and Helene," I asked, "were they friends?"

"Oh, yes. Those two were as close as sisters." Madame Moreau smiled fondly. "Such different personalities, but the best of friends. I believe the other girls called them *les jumelles* – the twins."

Here, finally, was the piece we had been missing. The Helene we knew was a fraud. In reality, she was the real

Helene's childhood friend ... and it would seem that she was David Brown's daughter.

"What about Lucy's parents?" I asked. "Did you know much about them?"

Madame Moreau's nose wrinkled in distaste. "I should not say it, really, but the Browns were not precisely ... *respectable*. Lucy attended the school for six years, and I do not believe she returned home for a single holiday during that time. In fact, she spent many of them with the Lavignes. It is my understanding that the Browns moved around a lot... Something to do with Mr Brown's business. They showed scant interest in their daughter and their account with us was almost always overdue. Sad as it was, this school was her only home, and I hope that in these walls she found some of the security she was missing from her family. Lucy was a good girl."

I had to keep myself from scoffing at that. It seemed to me that Lucy Brown had tripped along quite happily in her parents' criminal footsteps, after all.

"We have to go." Oliver suddenly jerked back to life, shaking off some of the daze he had been in, and he was already on his feet.

I jumped up after him. If Madame Moreau was startled by Oliver's abruptness, she covered it behind her immaculate manners.

"Of course," she said. "I am sorry I could not be more helpful. I wish you both luck with your search. Helene is a special girl. I would be glad to think she had found the part of her history that was missing."

"Thank you," I replied, shaking her hand. "You have been more help than you can imagine. I am sure now that finding Helene cannot be far away."

We left the school in silence; Oliver set a pace so brisk that I had to scurry to keep up.

"So, now we know," I said when we were back in the buggy and pulling away. "Most of it, anyway."

"But not where my sister is," Oliver said through gritted teeth.

"We'll find her."

"Oh, I know we'll find her." Oliver smiled without humour. "Because I'm going to tear pieces off David Brown until he tells me where she is."

"As tempting as that sounds," I said, "it is not likely to be our best plan."

Oliver made a noise that could only be described as a snarl. He was driving so fast that we bounced furiously down the road, and I gripped the side of the buggy hard enough to hurt.

"It explains why Lucy knew all about Helene," I said. "The girls were like sisters. She would know the childhood stories, she would know about the scar…"

"What did they do with her?" muttered Oliver. "What have they done with my sister?"

"It is entirely possible that Helene knows nothing of all this," I said soothingly. "That she has never been involved or placed in danger. That she is simply somewhere living her life. David Brown may not *know* where she is. He just saw an opportunity and took it."

"Only one way to find out," Oliver said with steel in his voice.

"That is not true either. If anyone has information on Helene it will be Lucy, and if you start using your fists on her father I doubt you'll get very far. Stop a moment. *Think*."

With that, we finally began to slow down. I peeled

my fingers away from the side of the buggy with a sigh of relief.

"So what do you suggest?" Oliver asked, turning to look at me. It seemed that Sylla was right, and I was going to have to start making my own plans sooner rather than later.

"We must separate Lucy from her parents, and deliver her to the Finches, of course." I pulled my watch from my pocket. "It is gone three o'clock. If you drop me back at the hotel, I will find some pretence to get Lucy to come to my room alone. You go to Café Fleur and wait for the others. Get them back to the hotel as soon as possible. The sooner we question Lucy Brown, the better."

"Fine." Oliver nodded. "But if that doesn't work…"

"If that doesn't work, we can take it in turns punching David Brown in the face."

His eyes slid to me. "I haven't seen this side of you before, Bloom," he said. "Bloodthirsty. I like it."

"Every rose has its thorn, Lockhart," I replied coolly. "The Aviary is no ladies' social club, after all."

CHAPTER THIRTY-SEVEN

Back at the hotel, I headed immediately for the salon, where I knew the Lavignes were due to take tea but found no sign of them. Spotting one of Sylla's contacts working on the reception desk, I drew her aside and she informed me that the Lavignes had gone upstairs to their room twenty minutes ago. Winnie and Maud had entered the hotel right behind them, and seeing the Lavignes – or rather, the Browns – settled they'd headed out to our rendezvous at Café Fleur. I had just missed them.

Thanking the young woman, I made my way straight

up the stairs for Lucy's room. This, I thought, might work to my advantage. Lucy and her parents had separate rooms, and hopefully catching her alone would make it much easier to lure her up to my suite. I hadn't quite worked out how I was going to do that, but I'd think of something. Perhaps something to do with wedding gowns... After all, she *was* posing as the sister of the groom.

Another stab of anger struck. It might have been my job to keep Oliver calm and focused, but beneath my cool demeanour I was burning up. I knew what Oliver's mother and his sister had meant to him, especially growing up with his father, and the fact that these people had taken something so pure and good in his life and twisted it for their own gain made me feel sick inside.

I moved down the thickly carpeted hallway, towards Lucy's room, and knocked softly on the door. I didn't want to alert the Browns in the next room of my presence. There was no answer.

"Helene," I said quietly. "It's Marigold. I need to talk to you." When that produced no response, I tried the door handle, which turned easily.

I gave the door a gentle push and was met by the sound of raised voices. I froze in the doorway for a moment before my brain made sense of where the sound was coming from. There was a connecting door between Lucy's room and her parents'. The three of them were clearly next door, locked in a ferocious argument.

Slipping into Lucy's room as soundlessly as possible, I edged towards the connecting door, which had been left slightly ajar.

Heart pounding, I took hold of the handle and slowly, slowly widened the crack until I could peep through to the other side.

Lucy stood in the middle of the room, tears running down her face as she faced her parents.

"I won't let you do it!" Her voice was high, breathless. "You swore no one would get hurt! You said it was a victimless crime. But it never was. Never!"

"Don't be hysterical," Mr Brown responded coolly. "What do I always tell you? We might have to get our hands dirty now and then, but everything your mother and I do is for you. For our family."

"Family!" Lucy spat. "What would you know about

family? Oliver Lockhart cares more about family than you ever did, and I won't let you hurt anyone. I won't!"

"Lucy, darling." Mrs Brown's voice was soothing. "This one thing, this one small thing, and then we'll be set for life. We will finally be able to give you everything you deserve. A life of luxury, a place in society, a husband and a family of your own. And no more worry. Never again. No more penny-pinching. No more jobs. A clean sweep." She set her hand on Lucy's arm. "You know how much your father and I love you."

The look in Lucy's blue eyes was anguished. She turned her back on her parents. "I heard you," she said, determination in her voice. "Just now. I heard what you have planned, and I won't be a part of it. I'm going to tell them everything. If you want to avoid prison, you should gather your things and go – get out of here before it's too late."

"Lucy, sweetheart," Mr Brown began, but then Lucy made a soft sound of surprise and crashed suddenly to the floor.

For several seconds nothing moved. I stood with my hands pressed against my mouth to stop myself from calling out as Mrs Brown stood over Lucy's prone body, arm raised, a small gold ornament in her hand.

"Joan!" Mr Brown sighed. "Was that really necessary?"

With a terrifying cool, Mrs Brown leaned over Lucy and checked her pulse.

"She's fine, just knocked out," she said shortly. "We must get on with it before she comes to."

Mr Brown eyed Lucy narrowly, and the speculative expression on his face made my heart sink and my stomach churn. "What if she tells them the truth after she wakes up?"

I braced myself to intervene. Surely the man couldn't mean to murder his own daughter?

Mrs Brown scoffed. "She won't have the stomach after the thing is done. She's soft; she won't want to see us arrested. And once the threat is gone, she'll be living in style. Money can make a person far more amenable to telling a lie or two, I've found."

"So we just leave her here?" Mr Brown said, eyebrows raised.

"I told you: she's perfectly fine," Mrs Brown huffed, already striding to the door that led out to the hallway.

"Now come on – there is much to do."

With that, they both left. I waited for a handful of painfully loud heartbeats until I was certain they had really gone.

I yanked the door open and flew across to Lucy, gently turning her face and brushing the hair away from her forehead. Her chest rose and fell, but she was horribly still.

"Lucy!" I patted her cheek, panic lacing my words. "Lucy, can you hear me?"

After a few terrible seconds, her fingers twitched in mine.

"Lucy?" I said again, and relief rushed through me as her eyelids fluttered.

"Wh-what happened?" she asked, her voice shaky, as I gingerly helped her up into a sitting position.

I hesitated. It seemed impossible to tell her what had happened ... that her own mother had knocked her down with such icy ruthlessness.

I didn't need time to find the right words, however, because her eyes widened in sudden understanding. "My parents..." she said dazedly.

I nodded.

Then another realization spread across her face. "You called me Lucy," she murmured.

"I did," I agreed. "Can you stand, do you think? We should get you to the bed. Someone should come and have a look at your head."

Lucy lifted her fingers to the back of her skull and winced. "Just a bump," she said, as we levered her up from the floor. She swayed for a moment, but then seemed to gather herself and moved back through to her own room, sitting on the edge of the bed with a sigh. She kept my hand in hers.

"I am glad," she said quietly, "that you know the truth. I have hated every moment of this deception. I was a fool to let them talk me into it. Foolish and weak." She closed her eyes briefly and a tear leaked out. "How did you find out?"

"I am not Mr Lockhart's fiancée," I said. "Mrs Finch and I work for a ... detective agency of sorts. Mr Lockhart and I went to your school. We spoke to Madame Moreau."

"Madame." Lucy's smile was sad. "She was always

kind to me." She looked at me inquisitively. "You are not really engaged to Mr Lockhart? It was ... an act?"

"Yes," I said. "An act. Though that part is not important now. Do you want to tell me about it?" I asked carefully.

Lucy nodded. "Of course. You deserve the truth. You all do." She let go of my hand and looked down at her own fingers. "Helene and I were best friends," she said. "As close as you can imagine. Closer than sisters. We called ourselves twin souls. The day she started at Sainte-Geneviève's was the most fortunate day of my life. We were inseparable from that moment on. When my parents left me at school over the holidays, she would take me home to the Lavignes in Herblay."

Reaching under her pillow, Lucy pulled out the Bible we had found at Lockhart Hall. Opening the pages, she pulled out the piece of embroidery and spread it gently over the bed cover.

"HL," I said, the truth dawning. "Not Helene Lavigne at all. Helene and Lucy."

Lucy nodded, tears in her eyes. "Helene made it for me when we were about fourteen." She gave a watery chuckle. "She always was terrible at embroidery."

"But what about the scar?" I asked. "The one on your hand. It is just like Helene's."

Lucy lifted her palm. "It is the same as hers. We did it not long after she arrived at the school with a penknife. It was Helene's idea – to make us blood sisters, she said. A silly sort of ritual that we imagined was filled with binding magic. It bled like the devil, and we had to hide the evidence from Matron. Helene always seemed to be dragging us into scrapes … and then dragging us back out again."

"How did the plan to impersonate Helene come about?" I asked, and the question jarred us back to the present. Any lingering happiness fled Lucy's eyes.

"It was my fault, really," she admitted. "I should have known better than to let anything slip to my parents. I saw the advertisement that Mr Lockhart had placed in the paper – we always have the London papers delivered for news of home – and I realized when I saw the name that it was about Helene."

"Helene knew Mr Lockhart's name?" I asked. "She remembered who she was?"

Lucy bit her lip and nodded. "The story about losing her memory was true, but it didn't last long. Helene began to remember everything while we were still at school, but she never told a soul except me. She was happy in France – and she was so afraid, you see, of her father. Of being sent back…"

I nodded slowly. "So you saw the advertisement…" I prompted her.

"Yes. When we finished school, Helene tried to get me to go with her, but my parents had some scheme running in the south of France, and they swept me along." She bit her lip unhappily. "Then when that went wrong, it was on to the next town and the next. Helene and I stayed in touch by letter, and I clipped the advertisement to send to her." She closed her eyes for a moment. "I mentioned it over breakfast to my father, that Helene's brother was looking for her. Silly of me."

"And they realized there was a scheme to be hatched?" I guessed.

"Exactly." Lucy's sigh was weary. "Later that day they both confronted me. They had opened the letter and read the full contents, and they saw an opportunity to claim Helene's inheritance for themselves. You don't know what they're like," she said, eyes wide as she gripped my hand again. "The way they bully and belittle and wheedle until I hardly know what they're saying. They said that Helene had hidden from her family all these years, and clearly didn't *want* to be found. All that money was only sitting there; it was a victimless crime. Mr Lockhart would be happy to have his sister back and we'd be able to stop moving around, stop running. I would finally have a normal life, and we'd be *protecting* Helene, helping her to keep her secret. They made it sound…" She hesitated here. "Almost … reasonable.

"Only once we arrived in England, things seemed different. Mr Lockhart was so kind, so obviously concerned about his sister. Not what I had expected at all. I couldn't stand it. And then Mother began all that talk about marrying me off to someone with a title and I realized that I would be trapped in this lie for ever, that Lucy Brown would fade away and I would have to pretend to be Helene to a husband, to children, for the rest of my life…" Her words were tight, breathless, pain written in every line of her face.

"Lucy," I said quietly. "All that is done now. But I need to ask you … do you know where Helene is?"

"Helene?" Lucy repeated. "Of course I do. She is here in Paris."

"She's here," I breathed, but I was cut short by Lucy, who leaped suddenly to her feet, her face transformed into a mask of fear.

"Oh God, Helene!" she cried. "I forgot… My head… I was distracted… I can't believe…"

"Lucy," I said again as calmly as I could manage. "What is it? What's wrong?"

"It's my parents!" Lucy choked out, already halfway to the door. "I overheard them. Making plans. They said they wanted to *eliminate any threat to the plan.* Marigold!" Her eyes met mine, wide with panic. "They're going to kill Helene!"

CHAPTER THIRTY-EIGHT

"I was in my room and the door was ajar," Lucy told me breathlessly, as we waited for the doorman to hail us a carriage.

I had checked, but there was no sign yet of Oliver and the rest of the Finches. I considered leaving them a message, but what would I say? *I've found your sister, but she's about to be murdered, so couldn't hang about and wait for you??* It seemed better just to go and deal with the situation as swiftly as possible.

"I heard them talking," Lucy continued. "Mother

said that being here in Paris was too risky, and there was a good chance we'd be discovered. Father mentioned a package from the chemist and that no one would taste it mixed in with coffee. *Then* Mother said it was good that they *were eliminating the threat*, and that perhaps this trip to Paris had been a blessing in disguise. She said, with Helene out of the picture, nothing would stand in their way."

My own pulse thundered in my ears as we clambered into the carriage, and Lucy gave the driver Helene's address in Montmartre.

"Do you think we're too late?" she asked tearfully.

"I don't know," I murmured, my thoughts turning painfully to Oliver, who had only just found out that his sister was really alive. Now it was possible he was going to lose her all over again. I willed the carriage to move faster as we wound through the busy traffic.

"I will never forgive myself if anything happens," Lucy whispered. "Never, never."

"We don't know that anything *has* happened yet," I snapped, nerves frayed. "Yes, they were ahead of us, but not by so much."

We pulled up to an apartment building in the 18th arrondisement and jumped down. I flung money at the coach driver, and the sound he made led me to believe I had handed over far too much.

The building was on a quiet, cobbled street – tall and grey with shutters on the windows and one or two cheerful window boxes full of flowers on the sills. There was no one about, no sign of the Browns at all.

Lucy climbed the stairs and began frantically ringing the bell. There was no answer.

We waited. Lucy tried the bell again. The minutes crawled by.

"What do we do now?" Lucy asked.

"Now we break in," I said grimly, opening my leather bag and pulling out the shiny lock picks that Mrs Finch had provided me with.

I set to work on the lock. It was not a complicated security measure, and Izzy would have had it open in the space of a deep breath. Unfortunately, I was not the talent that she was when it came to breaking into things. I tried to remember all our lessons, carefully manipulating the picks until I felt the pins inside the lock move.

It took two tries, and my hands were clammy, but finally the lock gave with a satisfying click, and we had the door open.

"It's the top floor!" Lucy exclaimed, already running for the spiralling staircase that seemed to stretch up to the heavens.

"Of course it is!" I sighed, chasing after her.

By the time we reached the top we were both winded, pink and panting.

"Helene!" Lucy shouted, banging on the door. "Helene, it is me! It's Lucy!"

There was no answer. Cursing, I readied the lock picks again.

"Lucy?" A voice came from behind us, and both Lucy and I swung round to see a young woman standing at the top of the stairs, looking at us in shock. She had the same build as Lucy, the same brown eyes, but her hair was darker, pulled ruthlessly back into a tight knot, her features sharper. She wore a narrow dove-grey skirt and matching waistcoat, a white shirt and a black tie. She was the picture of a fashionable, modern Frenchwoman.

"*Helene!*" Lucy cried, and she threw herself into Helene's arms.

Three things became instantly obvious: first, we had found Oliver's sister; second, she had not been murdered; and third, Helene and Lucy were far more than friends.

"Lucy, Lucy!" Helene said through muffled laughter. "What are you doing here?"

"I thought you were *dead*!" Lucy buried her face in Helene's neck and burst into tears. Helene's round eyes looked over the top of her head to where I stood frozen, still holding my lock picks, with every appearance of breaking into her apartment.

"Hello," I said with a weak smile. "I'm Marigold Bloom. Perhaps we can talk inside."

Helene blinked, her arm tightening round Lucy's waist for a second. "Of course," she said finally, in an English accent that still held a faint trace of Yorkshire. "Why don't I make some tea?"

Twenty minutes later, we were sitting in Helene's sunny kitchen, steaming cups of tea in front of us as Lucy and I explained the whole story.

Helene's face was pale. "You've been pretending to be me?" she asked.

Lucy nodded miserably, her hand tightening in Helene's where they were clasped on top of the table. "Yes. I'm so sorry. My parents…"

"Your parents" – Helene's face darkened – "should be locked up."

"And this time they will be," I said calmly.

Lucy made a small sound of distress, but Helene nodded firmly. "It's time, Lucy. They've gone too far. But I don't understand their plan," she said. "They really want to kill me? So that Lucy can inherit in my place?"

"It seems to be the case," I said, though I too was confused about the Browns' plan. They had left the hotel some time ago – so where were they now? How exactly did they plan to poison Helene? I shook my head. "But it doesn't matter any more. We have found you, this place is locked up tight and you know their plan. You are safe from them now, and there is absolutely no reason for us to hold off from turning them in any longer. I expect once they realize that we've tracked you down, they will try to make a run for it. There is nothing for them now that you disprove Lucy's claim."

"I can't believe my brother is here in Paris," Helene said, her eyes drifting to the window.

"Will you see him?" I asked.

She looked down at the cup of tea in front of her. "Miss Bloom," she said, her voice steady, "may I ask you a question?" When I nodded, she hesitated before finally speaking again. "Oliver... What sort of man is he?"

"What sort of man?" I asked, confused.

"Yes." Helene's gaze sharpened. "When I last spoke to him, he was eleven years old. In the three years before that I hardly saw him at all because he was away at school. I know the boy he was, but after our mother..." She paused, swallowed hard. "After our mother passed away, he was left alone to be raised by our father – a man who was cruel and brutal. So, I am asking you, what sort of man is Oliver Lockhart?"

I blinked. "He is ... a bad-tempered recluse with a healthy dislike of people," I said at last. "He is grumpy and stubborn and ferociously loyal to the ones he cares about, and he cares deeply. He is handsome, funny, generous. He can be charming. He is clever and creative. He is kind. I think under it all he might be the kindest person I've ever met."

"You are in love with him," Helene said quietly.

"Oh, no!" I blustered at once, taking a hearty sip of my tea. "I – I have only been playing a part."

"Very convincingly too," Lucy added with just a hint of mischief.

I shifted uncomfortably in my seat. Helene smiled. "He sounds like the brother I knew." She exhaled. "I'm glad. I'm so glad. Yes, I will see him."

I felt something in my heart crack wide open. "Is that why you didn't come home?" I asked curiously. "After your memories returned, I mean. You were afraid that Oliver might be like your father?"

Helene took a moment to consider it. "You have to understand," she said finally, "when I remembered who I was, my father was still very much alive. I knew I would be sent back to him, and Mother had given everything – had ended up giving her *life* – to get us away. I was ten years old and my only thought was that I couldn't go back. The Lavignes had taken me in, and from the beginning they loved me as their own. It didn't take long for me to return that affection. They have been parents to me, the best of parents, and I wouldn't leave them. By the time I found out my father had passed away, I was living here in Paris." She gestured around the flat. "I have built a life here; I have a job that I love, working as a journalist. Everyone believed Ellen Lockhart was dead. It seemed foolish to stir up the past unnecessarily – particularly when I didn't know how Oliver would react to the news I was alive, or that I had stayed away all that time."

Here, she fiddled with the brightly patterned tablecloth. "I always felt guilty. That I had left Oliver there alone. With him."

"You should talk to him about it," I said gently. "But I know that he doesn't blame you. He said that he wanted you to leave."

Helene's eyes shone with tears. "Mother was going to send for him," she said. "When we were in Spain. I don't know the details, but she told me he would come. She wouldn't have just left him. Not like I did."

"You were a child," I insisted.

"What more could you have done?" Lucy grasped

her hand again. "It is a miracle that you survived at all. Now the two of you can be reunited. The story will finally have a happy ending. Your mother would be proud."

The three of us sniffled then.

"This is… This is very nice tea," I said, clearing my throat.

Helene gave a watery chuckle. "I buy English tea. I can't help myself; I never did learn to like coffee."

I looked at Lucy, something tickling at my mind. "Ah, so that was part of your Helene backstory?" I asked. "Don't tell me you actually *do* drink coffee?"

Lucy winced. "I couldn't be sure what Oliver knew or remembered, and Helene always hated coffee."

"Horrible, bitter stuff," Helene agreed.

"What a poor Frenchwoman you are," Lucy said fondly. "I will be very glad to go back to drinking it."

"Coffee," I murmured, still reaching for the idea that refused to come quite into focus. "But … didn't you say…"

I sat up suddenly, sloshing tea into my saucer. "Coffee!" I yelped.

Helene and Lucy were both looking at me with obvious concern.

"Lucy," I managed. "Didn't you say that your parents were going to poison Helene's *coffee*?"

Lucy frowned. "I suppose that *is* strange."

"They knew she didn't drink coffee because you made such a point of it. Why would they say that?" I asked.

"I don't know," Lucy said. "Perhaps my father misspoke?"

"But how were they planning to poison Helene's drink, anyway?" I said slowly. "It doesn't make sense. They're not even here. It's such a strange plan…" I looked at Lucy, her expression one of wary confusion. "Tell me again what they said," I demanded. "*Exactly* what they said."

"Um…" Lucy squinted, clearly trying to remember. "Father said, '*Now that we have the packet from the chemist, we shouldn't delay.*' He said the coffee would mask any taste." Lucy's face scrunched up in concentration. "Then Mother said, '*Perhaps this trip to Paris was a blessing, after all. Now we have the opportunity to eliminate any remaining threat far from home and prying eyes.*'"

"But England isn't their home," I said slowly. "Or Helene's. Go on," I encouraged her. "Say the rest."

"I don't remember," Lucy said. "I think then Mother said something about a document that I didn't understand."

"What about a document?"

"She said that their man over here was almost as good as the contact back in England anyway, so it didn't matter about the authorities being on to him."

The forger, I thought, the pieces tantalizingly close to fitting together. The one who had forged the Browns' papers had the authorities breathing down his neck, thanks to Max. That must be who they meant, so perhaps they had another man in Paris who could do something similar. What sort of papers would they need forging now?

"What else?" I demanded.

"That's it. Then they said that with Helene gone nothing would stand in their way, that I would be the only heir."

"You're sure?" I said, gripping the edge of the table. You're sure they said with *Helene* gone?"

"I..." Lucy hesitated. "I don't know... No ... perhaps not. But who else stands in the way of me becoming the only heir?"

A buzzing noise filled my ears, and I swayed in my seat. "It wasn't Helene they meant to kill at all. It is Oliver," I whispered. "They're going to poison Oliver."

CHAPTER THIRTY-NINE

By the time we reached the hotel again, I thought my heart was going to burst, the relentless hammering of my pulse the only sound I could hear. Helene and Lucy were right behind me as I ran through the doors into the opulent lobby, heads turning in our direction as we flew past, unheeding.

A thousand images flickered in my mind. Oliver, lying on the floor, a shattered coffee cup beside him. Dead. Dead and gone. The pain of it was so sharp that I felt my vision turn white at the edges. I had to remind myself to breathe, breathe, breathe, as we sprinted down the hallway towards my room.

I flung the door open, and it smashed against the wall with a tremendous bang. Inside the room, five astonished faces turned in my direction.

Oliver. He was alive. He was standing there, alive. Then I noticed the coffee cup in his hand.

"Bloom!" he exclaimed. "What—" The words died on his lips and his eyes widened as he took in the women crashing into the sitting room behind me. "Ellen!"

But before he had a chance to move forward, I was charging into him, smashing the cup from his hand, knocking him to the ground, where I tumbled on top of him.

"Oof!" Oliver made a breathless, winded sound.

I peered down at him, our faces so close together that I could count every one of his ridiculously thick eyelashes. I scanned his face in concern, as his arms came up round my waist, holding me steady. His eyes, so dark that they were almost black, looked into mine, and his mouth softened, pulling up into a half-smile.

For a tiny moment I melted into him, felt the blissful warmth of his body sink into my bones.

"Bloom?" He arced a brow at me. "Not that I'm not enjoying myself, but may I ask … is there any particular reason why you have tackled me to the ground?"

"How much coffee did you drink?" I asked urgently.

Oliver frowned. "Have you suffered some sort of head injury?"

I clambered off him, barely taking in the baffled expressions on the faces of my friends. I ran to the coffee cup, which had spilled on the floor, a small pool of liquid already soaking into the plush carpet. I grabbed the pot. Half of it was gone.

"How much did you drink?" I asked again frantically.

But Oliver wasn't paying attention to me; instead he had struggled to his feet and was slowly approaching Helene. "Ellen," he said softly. "It is really you."

"Yes." Helene took a step towards him. "Oliver... I..."

"OLIVER! HOW MUCH COFFEE DID YOU DRINK?" I yelled then.

Oliver turned to me slowly, his eyes narrowing. "Bloom, I do not know what your obsession is with my coffee-drinking habits, but is this really the time?" He gestured towards his sister. "There are more important things happening, you know."

If the coffee didn't kill him, I might. Fortunately, Mrs Finch stepped forward. "He drank about half a cup," she said quite calmly. "I suppose it is poisoned?"

"Poisoned?!" Oliver exclaimed.

"With what?" Winnie's voice held mild interest.

I ran to the bedroom and reappeared with my leather case. "I don't know." I began desperately grabbing at the glass jars. "Lucy didn't hear that part."

All eyes swung to Lucy.

"And what *did* Lucy hear exactly?" Sylla enquired, piercing Lucy with an interrogative glare.

"They... They only said they had something from the chemist," Lucy stammered. "That you couldn't taste in coffee."

"Strychnine?" Winnie mused.

"Maybe cyanide?" Maud suggested.

"My money is on arsenic," Sylla said dispassionately.

"I'm sorry," Oliver said acidly, "are you about to start taking bets on how I have been *poisoned*?"

Sylla shrugged. "Who among us hasn't ingested a little poison here and there?"

"The fact that you are still alive is a good sign," Mrs Finch said reassuringly. "You hardly drank any of the coffee."

"You're all mad," Oliver snapped. "Thankfully, I feel fine." On that note, he suddenly staggered, grabbing on to the side of the table. "Just dizzy." He looked at me, and I saw alarm flare in his eyes.

"Drink this now." I thrust a glass of water at him. I had emptied the entire jar of dried barberry into it.

Thankfully, he didn't question me, only knocked the water back, then sat heavily on the sofa. "What now?" he asked.

"You're not going to like it." I summoned a quavering smile for him.

Mrs Finch emptied the heavy gold coal scuttle into the fireplace and brought it over, holding it out to Oliver.

"What's that for?" he said suspiciously.

"It's for your vomit," Winnie said, peering into the

coffee pot with interest. "I should take a sample of this for later," she said.

"For my—" Oliver didn't get any further with that outraged exclamation because he was too busy retching into the coal scuttle.

"So, you're the sister, I take it," Sylla said, as we all politely ignored him.

"Yes, I'm Helene Lavigne," Helene said. She and Lucy looked rather dazed. "Um. Nice to meet you."

I poured Oliver a glass of water, as Sylla performed a round of introductions, and then I helped him lie back on the sofa. He was pale, but I put my fingers to his wrist and felt the strong, reassuring flutter of his pulse.

"Well, will I live?" he asked me, dry as sand.

I sank to the floor beside him, my knees well and truly giving out, and gently brushed a lock of dark hair away from his forehead. "I think you should be fine. You didn't drink much of the coffee, and now that you've purged so quickly…"

"*Purged!*" Oliver groaned. "Let's not talk about purging any more."

"I'm so sorry, Mr Lockhart." Lucy appeared at my

side, looking down at him, her eyes wide. "This is all my fault – my parents and I..."

"Yes, *Miss Brown*." Oliver's eyes narrowed. "I'd be very interested to hear about your parents."

"Oliver, don't be angry with Lucy," Helene said softly, rounding the sofa herself to take the other woman's hand. "If anyone knows how difficult it is to live with parents who are far less than we deserve, it is you and me."

A sigh moved through Oliver's body. "I suppose so," he said grudgingly. He looked at his sister. "I am sorry that we are reuniting like this. Ever since I found out you were still alive, I imagined it would be ... well, different."

"Different from you being poisoned and then vomiting repeatedly into a coal scuttle?" Helene said, and when her mouth pulled up at the corners, I saw the resemblance between her and her brother.

Helene held out her hand, and after a moment Oliver took it in his own. They only looked at each other for a long while.

"There is much we need to talk about," Helene said finally.

"We have time," Oliver replied softly.

My eyes filled, and Oliver's gaze shifted to me. "Good grief, Bloom. Don't go telling me you need my handkerchief again. For someone who claims not to cry very often, you are a veritable watering pot."

"Don't worry," I sniffled, reaching into my sleeve. "I have one." I dabbed at my eyes with the handkerchief that Oliver had given me on the moors. When I looked back at him, he was watching me with a reluctant fondness.

Mrs Finch cleared her throat. "While Oliver and his sister may have all the time in the world to catch up, I'm afraid the issue of the Browns is a touch more urgent. Marigold, I assume that with this turn of events the Browns have managed to get their hands on more forged documents?"

I stared at her, stunned. "Yes! But how on earth did *you* know that?"

"I followed your lead to Ménilmontant. One of my contacts there knows of a very good forger – I have even used his services myself a time or two – and she had heard whisperings about a job that he had taken on." Mrs Finch nodded her head towards Winnie and Maud. "These two followed the Browns all day and saw them stop in at the watchmaker's, which is a front for his more illegal practices. The Browns must have worried that being in France would soon lead to the discovery of their deception, so such a step makes perfect sense. Oliver had already presented Lucy to all the guests at his party as his sister. If he suffered a tragic accident, then who would question Lucy's right to inherit everything if she also held a new will drawn up in her favour?" Mrs Finch hummed with something close to approval. "Quite a tidy plan, actually."

"Oh yes, very tidy," Oliver scoffed. "Especially the part where I am got rid of."

"Thankfully they did not reckon with Marigold Bloom." Mrs Finch smiled.

"Thankfully they did not reckon with the Aviary," I corrected her.

"I'm sorry," Helene jumped in. "But if the Browns have, in fact, attempted to poison my brother and presumably believe him to have keeled over by now" – Oliver gave a muttered protest here – "then ... where are they?"

The question hung in the air.

"I suppose," said Sylla, "that they are in their hotel room, waiting for the tragic news to be delivered."

"Then, by all means," I said, getting to my feet and dusting off my skirts, "let us go and give it to them. I for one have several things I should like to say to them before the police cart them away."

"Wait." Mrs Finch held up her hand. "We do not all need to go. Winnie, Maud, you split up and find Celeste, the head housekeeper. Tell her that I sent you. Tell her we will need some of those muscular henchmen the hotel employs. Miss Lavigne..." she began, but Helene cut her off.

"I am going," she said. "After what they did to Lucy? To my brother? I want them to see *me*."

Mrs Finch smiled. "I was going to suggest you stay here with Miss Brown, but as you feel so strongly about the matter..."

"I can come with you..." Lucy started, but Helene took her hands gently between her own.

"She is quite right, Lucy. You must stay here. You don't need to go near those two again. I won't have it." Her voice was firm.

Lucy bit her lip, nodded. "I – I suppose. If you think it best."

"You must call a doctor to check on Mr Lockhart," I said to Mrs Finch.

Oliver sat up at this. "Absolutely not." His feet hit the carpet. "I am coming with you."

"Don't be absurd," I snapped. "Five minutes ago you were almost *dead*."

Oliver waved an airy hand. "Who among us hasn't ingested a little poison here and there?"

Sylla made a sound of approval.

"This is ridiculous," I said as he struggled to his feet, teeth clearly gritted. "You are *green*."

Oliver reached out and took my hand. The look he gave me was heart-melting. "Bloom, didn't you promise me that we were going to take turns punching David Brown in the face?"

"*So romantic*," I heard Winnie murmur dreamily to Maud.

"Fine," I bit off, flustered and annoyed. "But if you fall over and knock yourself unconscious, don't expect me to rescue you. *Again*."

"And I shall accompany you three in a supervisory capacity," Sylla said primly. "After all, Mari still hasn't

464

technically completed her training. This will be her first time confronting the villain."

On that note, we all filed out into the hallway. Sylla, Helene, a queasy-looking Oliver and I made a strange party to confront the Browns, but we certainly had the element of surprise on our side.

When we reached their door, I didn't knock, only turned the handle and walked inside.

Mr Brown stood by the fireplace with a drink, his wife sat in an armchair, leafing through a periodical. My blood ran cold at the fact that they believed Oliver was dying downstairs by their hands, and they somehow managed to give the appearance of an illustration in a domestic magazine.

When Mrs Brown glanced up and caught sight of us, her face paled. Mr Brown took one look at Oliver and his brandy glass fell to the hearth and shattered.

"M-Mr Lockhart," he managed.

Oliver's smile was terrifying. "Mr Brown," he murmured. "I don't believe you've met ... my sister?"

Helene took a step forward, and I heard Mrs Brown's breath catch.

My eyes locked on her and she in turn was staring at Oliver. "I thought you were … you were supposed to be…"

"Dead?" Oliver said. "I'm afraid not."

"Oh, Mr Lockhart," Mr Brown's voice held a smile, and I heard a chilling and familiar click. "I wouldn't be so certain about that. The night is still young." In his hand was a gun, and it was pointed straight at my head.

CHAPTER FORTY

"What exactly do you think you are doing?" Oliver asked coldly, as Mr Brown stepped closer to me.

"What am *I* doing?" Mr Brown's smile stretched wide. "*I* am threatening the life of the woman you love. So *you* will do exactly as I say."

"It wasn't real," I said quickly. "Our engagement. It was a cover so that I could investigate you. I'm not his fiancée. I'm nothing."

Mr Brown's smile didn't falter. "Interesting. Is that right, Mr Lockhart?" he asked. "Is Miss Bloom nothing to you?"

Oliver's jaw tightened. His pitch-dark eyes were filled with a rage I could not have imagined him capable of. "Step away from her," he said quietly. "I will not ask you again."

I needed to do something; I needed to think of a plan. He had a gun. He had a gun, and he was moving closer to me. I was going to die. He was going to shoot me and everyone else.

"Or what?" Mr Brown smirked.

"Goodness," Sylla said in bored tones. "What a lot of unnecessary drama."

This produced a startled silence.

"And who exactly are you supposed to be?" Mrs Brown sneered, confidence clearly returning at the sight of her husband brandishing a deadly weapon.

Sylla's eyes ran over her with a haughty disinterest that had the blood rushing to Mrs Brown's cheeks. "Who I am is of no great importance at the moment," she said. "It is who I work for that you should be worried about." Her eyes locked with mine, and it was as if a jolt of electricity had been fired into me.

The roar of panic dulled in my ears, and in that

moment of relative calm I remembered who I was. I wasn't just Marigold Bloom any more. I was a Finch. And that meant that I wasn't afraid of a man with a gun, because I knew precisely what to do. Hadn't Sylla trained me for this herself?

"That," Sylla added, "and the fact that there are several of the more burly members of the hotel security on their way up here, along with the police, I should think."

"Well then." Mr Brown took another step towards me, and I felt the cold muzzle of the gun pressing against my temple.

"Don't—" Oliver choked, taking a half-step forward, terror in his face.

"Oh, I wouldn't do that if I were you," Sylla said coolly.

"Listen, you little brat," Mr Brown spat, "my wife and I are about to walk out of here with your friend, and if *anyone* tries to stop us, then you'll be cleaning her brains off the carpet. Is that dramatic enough for you?"

Sylla's eyes flicked to mine, and I could have sworn there was actually amusement there. "What do you think about that, Mari?"

I assessed the situation. Mr Brown had his eyes narrowed on Sylla. He was not at all concerned with me because he expected nothing from me, no resistance, no sort of fight. In my head, I heard Simon's voice telling me that I should make myself small, that I wasn't clever enough or pretty enough or ladylike enough, knowing I would never stand up for myself or fight back. I thought about Scullen standing over Scout in that dingy alleyway.

Just like those men, Mr Brown utterly underestimated me and, like every member of the Aviary, I knew this to be my greatest advantage.

Taking a deep breath, I moved before I could think about it too much, my body only shifting in the way it had been relentlessly drilled to do over the last six months. I grabbed Mr Brown's wrist, pushing it in a smooth motion so that the end of the gun swung away from me; a loud bang rang in my ear as it discharged, the bullet flying wide.

Wrapping my other hand round the barrel of the gun, I pulled sharply down, hearing the horrible crack as I broke Mr Brown's finger, still on the trigger. (I could have sworn I also heard Sylla chuckle.) He screamed, and I twisted his arm towards his back, the gun falling free of his hand and skittering over the floor, where Sylla stopped it by resting her slippered foot on top. My other elbow lifted up, hitting Mr Brown hard in the face, and I spun round, applying my knee with great force between his legs. He made a rather inhuman noise and fell to the floor in an untidy heap. *Writhing*, I thought. Sylla was right. Watching it really did get the blood pumping.

The whole thing happened in the space of a few seconds, and I found myself breathing hard, standing over the prone body of my attacker.

Everything was utterly still.

"Good, Mari," Sylla said finally, picking up the gun and checking the remaining bullets. "A touch slow on your first move; remember you want to swing the gun as wide as possible. I suppose your ears are ringing?"

I nodded, feeling slightly dazed.

Sylla turned the gun almost absently on Mrs Brown. "The mistake, you see, is in getting too close," she told me. "There is no need to press the gun to your victim's head for dramatic effect. I am perfectly capable of killing Mrs Brown from this distance."

Mrs Brown sank back into her chair, her head in her hands. On the floor, her husband let out a low moan.

"Yes, I see," I replied, my voice thankfully calm. I turned my attention to Helene and Oliver who wore matching expressions of surprise – eyebrows raised, mouths slightly open. It was enough to bring a smile to my own face. They really were brother and sister.

"That was…" Helene trailed off.

"Extraordinary," Oliver breathed, and the way he looked at me made me feel like a goddess. "Bloom, you are extraordinary."

"She certainly is," Helene agreed with a grin. "I hope you will show me how to do that?"

"Have you ever considered any investigative work, Miss Lavigne?" Sylla asked, her tone thoughtful. "Perhaps the Aviary might benefit from a French branch."

Oliver moved to the far wall where the bullet from Mr Brown's gun was buried in the plasterwork. He ran his fingers over it. "You could have died," he said slowly. "You could have died right in front of me."

"*You* could have died right in front of *me*," I said. "So I suppose that makes us even."

"I think I have lost several years off my life today." Oliver pressed a hand to his chest. "And I realize there are some things I need to say as soon as possible. I—"

This interesting speech was cut short by the door slamming open. Mrs Finch and several very tall, very broad footmen appeared on the threshold.

"Oh, good," Mrs Finch said, her eyes travelling from Mr Brown's crumpled body, to Sylla, holding the gun trained on Mrs Brown. "I see you have everything under control."

"Perfectly," Sylla replied, as the footmen set about tying up the Browns. Once Mrs Brown was secure, Sylla checked the pistol was disarmed and placed it on the mantelpiece. Her eyes flicked to me. "I believe we can safely say that Mari's training period has concluded. Her performance was…" She hesitated here. "Satisfactory."

"Satisfactory?!" Oliver interrupted hotly. "She was *magnificent*."

Sylla ignored this utterly. "Are the police on their way?"

"It transpires that Mr and Mrs Brown are wanted for several crimes both here and in England under a variety of different pseudonyms." Mrs Finch pursed her lips. "They're to be held at the hotel until various officials have fought it out among themselves. Either way, they're both bound for a cell."

"I told you this was too risky!" Mrs Brown screeched at Mr Brown, who was busy staring daggers at me, his left eye already turning an unpleasant shade of purple. "Now look what you've done! Look what has become of us!"

"This was as much you as it was me," Mr Brown growled. "More! *You* were the one who decided we had to marry the girl off. You were the one obsessed with a title."

"Yes, yes," Mrs Finch said pleasantly. "There will be plenty of time to portion out the blame when the prosecution has you in the dock."

"I should go and check on Lucy," Helene said, casting a dark look at the Browns. "*Someone* should be concerned about what happens to her."

"Nothing will happen to Lucy," Oliver said. "I will make sure of it."

I realized then that he was leaning quite heavily

against the wall, and that his face was almost completely drained of colour.

"You need to lie down," I said, rushing over and pressing my hand to his forehead, which was thankfully still cool to the touch. "*And* see a doctor. You were almost killed half an hour ago."

"You were almost killed five minutes ago," Oliver said stubbornly. "And I don't see anyone fussing over you."

"Mari is quite right," Mrs Finch said, and she smirked at me. "Take Oliver down to his room; the doctor should be on his way soon. I already called for him."

"Thank you," I said, and when I slipped my arm around Oliver's waist, taking some of his weight, he didn't protest beyond a brief mutter of disgruntlement, which I knew meant that he was feeling worse than he'd admit.

Moving slowly, we left the Browns in Mrs Finch's capable hands, and I returned Oliver to his room, a perfect copy of my own. "At least sit down on the sofa," I said, and he did, slumping into the cushions and looking increasingly bad-tempered.

"What can I get you?" I asked. "Some tea? Do you feel warm at all? Or cold? A blanket, perhaps…"

"I am not an infant," he snapped crankily. "I refuse to be *coddled*."

I ignored this, rearranging the cushions around him so that his head was better supported. "The doctor will be here soon, and then we'll be sure that there are no lingering effects from the poison. Fortunately, you seem to have absorbed very little; you'll probably just feel weak as a kitten for a few days."

"A kitten?" Oliver glared at me. "I am not a kitten."

"Of course not, Lockhart," I said solemnly. "You are definitely not a kitten. You are the picture of strength and vitality. I meant to say weak as a lion."

"You are making fun of me when we have important matters to discuss," Oliver huffed.

"Important matters?"

"Well, I don't know if you'll consider the fact that I am in love with you to be an important matter, but I certainly hope so," Oliver said, in the same tone one might use to comment on the state of the weather.

"In love with me?" I repeated, stunned.

"Yes."

"*You*," I said, pointing at him, "are in love with *me*?" I gestured at myself.

"My God," Oliver groaned, his head dropping back and his eyes closing. "This is to be *we are in Paris* all over again, isn't it? You are an intelligent woman, so I know you understand the words I am saying. Yes, *I* am in love with *you*."

It was this very cranky, very Oliver declaration that finally broke through to me. "I think I need to sit down," I said distantly.

"Oh, by all means." Oliver gestured to the armchair behind me, and I sank into it, my head a whirr as joy and panic crashed together in a wave that threatened to upset my sanity.

"Well," Oliver said after a moment, "is there anything you would like to add to this conversation?"

I looked at him and saw that, despite his offhand tone, he was watching me, his expression decidedly nervous.

"I—" I began, but there was a knock at the door.

I leaped to my feet. "That will be the doctor," I said, rushing to the door and letting him in. "I will give the two of you some privacy."

And then, coward that I am, I hurried out into the hallway.

"This conversation isn't over, Bloom," I heard Oliver call after me. I couldn't decide if it was a promise or a threat.

CHAPTER FORTY-ONE

Rather than returning to my room, I headed out to the gardens again, a place where I could be alone and try to untangle the events of the last few hours in my own mind.

It was … rather a lot, I thought as I wandered aimlessly through the crowds. There had been several attempted murders; we had reunited Oliver with his long-lost sister *and* apprehended two dangerous criminals. Yet the thing that had me utterly off-balance was Oliver's declaration.

He was in love with me.

"He is in love with me," I said it aloud, as if testing it

out. The words were like honey, sweet and golden on my tongue. "*Oliver Lockhart* is in love with *me*."

As I let the idea sink in more fully, I began to appreciate what it meant. Oliver didn't care where I was from. Or maybe that was wrong; Oliver did care, and he *admired* it. Oliver wouldn't break my heart or leave me for a better prospect. He said that he loved me, and I knew that it must be true. Not only because Oliver wouldn't lie, but because he was so careful about admitting that he cared for other people. That was no surprise really, given his past, but it meant that his grudging declaration felt, to me, as demonstratively romantic as a lengthy sonnet. More so, actually, because I would have no patience at all for a man spouting poetry at me. Daisy would be disappointed.

Daisy. I came to a halt in front of the fountain.

Just like that, the dreamy smile was wiped from my face. What about my family? I could hardly leave them behind to fend for themselves. And Oliver Lockhart of Lockhart Hall wasn't going to want to take over a flower shop on Oxford Street. Our lives were utterly incompatible.

Then, of course, there was the Aviary to consider. They had invested six months in training me. I cared about them, and I believed in them. I could hardly leave them. I didn't *want* to leave them.

Dropping on to a bench, I tipped my head back and closed my eyes. The sun was warm on my face and left shadows dancing behind my eyelids.

Someone sat down beside me. "I had a feeling I would find you here," Mrs Finch said.

Opening my eyes, I found her observing me with steady amusement. I was glad somebody was having a nice time.

"I wanted to check on you," she said, "now that everything has been tidied up and our adventure is at an end."

"Thank you, but I am fine," I said, while she spread her skirts out neatly.

Mrs Finch fixed me with a piercing look. "I can only assume that Oliver Lockhart has just declared his intentions."

I started. "Have you really inherited gifts of clairvoyance?" I asked. "How do you know these things?"

Mrs Finch laughed, the picture of relaxation. "In this case, I'm afraid one doesn't need to be clairvoyant to see what is happening between the two of you. It is – I hate to inform you – patently obvious to everyone with eyes. The boy adores you." Her eyes narrowed. "And you adore him too. So I wonder why you look as though you are about to attend a funeral."

I fidgeted in my seat. "I have obligations," I said finally. "To my family. And" – I lifted my eyes to hers – "to you."

"I see. Well, I cannot speak for your obligations to your family, but as far as your commitment to the Aviary, I do not see why that must be any great impediment."

"You don't?" I managed.

Mrs Finch considered me. "No, I do not. First of all, none of the women who work for us are *obliged* to do so. They choose it."

"But I want to do it," I said desperately. "I *want* to choose it – that is precisely part of the problem."

Mrs Finch only smiled. "Well, in that case, the Aviary has agents all over the country – soon to be all over the world if Sylla has anything to say on the matter. Unfortunately, women in need are not neatly confined to the borders of London, however much we may be tempted to view the metropolis as the centre of the world."

"No," I said slowly. "I suppose not. It sounds silly, but I have only recently really thought about just how limited my experience of the world has been. The Aviary has opened my eyes to a lot of things."

"I find that to be a great compliment, Marigold," Mrs Finch said with a pleased smile. We lapsed into a thoughtful silence. On the pool in front of us a handful of little red toy sailing boats drifted by.

"I had an interesting conversation with Oliver the other day," she said, breaking the quiet. "About Lockhart Hall."

"Oh?"

Her tone was innocent, but I knew her better now, knew what her face looked like when she was scheming. And she *definitely* had a scheming face now.

"Yes," she continued, smooth as glass. "It seems that in recent weeks he has been giving a good deal of thought to the legacy he has been left with. He believes that there is a chance Lockhart Hall could be – how did he put it? – *something better than the story of its past*."

I started at the repetition of my own words. Mrs Finch pressed her lips together as if to hide a smile.

"He wants to turn Lockhart Hall into a retreat," she carried on. "For women who need … sanctuary."

I stilled. "A retreat?"

Mrs Finch nodded. "We have several already, though nothing like the size of Lockhart Hall. It is perfect, of course – so out of the way and secluded. And the place is literally a fortress, so it should inspire a feeling of safety in those who need it most. I have to say I am delighted with the plan."

So was I. It was perfect. It was the perfect way to use Lockhart Hall; it was the perfect way for Oliver to honour his mother. It was the perfect way to bring that house back to life. It could be warm, I knew. I had seen it. It could be warm and safe and welcoming.

"Of course, we would probably need someone there who worked for the Aviary to run things. One could hardly leave taking care of people up to Oliver." Mrs

Finch smiled fondly. "Anyway..." She got to her feet and dusted herself off. "Just something to think about."

And on that earth-shattering note, she left me alone.

It was a couple of hours later that there was a knock on my door. I knew it would be Oliver, and I hadn't decided if I was prepared for that or not. I had sat in the park for a long time, turning over Mrs Finch's words. Funny, I thought, how all this had started in a different park six months ago, how wildly different my life was now.

When he strode into the room, he was more subdued than usual. I felt that same nervous energy coming off him, and for some strange reason that helped me to feel calmer. Perhaps it was because I realized I wasn't in this alone.

He looked much better than the last time I saw him. His colour had returned and, though he looked tired, he had also clearly taken the opportunity to tidy himself up. His hair was brushed back neatly, his face cleanly shaven, his suit impeccable. I felt touched by it, even as I knew that I liked him best when he was rumpled and untidy.

He stood awkwardly in the middle of the room. "Bloom," he began gruffly.

And that was all it took. Every objection flew out of my head as I saw him standing there, looking at me with his heart in his eyes.

I crashed into him, pulling his head down until my lips met his. He made a small noise of surprise, and then his arm looped round my waist, pulling me tightly against him. He kissed me as though I was something rare and lovely. He kissed me as though he loved me and wanted me, and would never, never get enough.

And I kissed him back, poured my own feelings into every soft touch of my mouth, into the way I gripped the lapels of his jacket, pressing into him almost desperately.

It was a warm, breathless dream of a kiss, and when we finally broke apart, I looked up at him. Dazzled.

Fortunately, he looked equally affected. His hand moved, almost nervously to his tie. I was pleased to see that his hair was thoroughly rumpled, and that his well-kissed lips and lust-blown pupils all contributed to a very delicious, decidedly discomposed picture.

"I am in love with you too," I said.

He blinked. "I think I need to sit down," he replied, his voice rough as sandpaper.

I burst out laughing, and his own mouth pulled up. "I deserved that," I said.

"And more, I'm sure," Oliver agreed. And then he bent to kiss me again. Softer, this time. His hands cradling my face.

"I have something for you," he said when we finally parted. Reaching into his pocket, he pulled out a small black leather jewellery box.

"What is this?" I asked, taking it from him.

"Look and see," he said, nervous again.

I opened the box and gasped. Nestled inside, on a bed of black velvet was a ring. Its delicate gold band was made of two entwined vines, and they wrapped around a flower made of glittering yellow stones. "You … made this?" I managed. "You made this for me?"

He nodded, colour high on his cheeks. "I know in the language of flowers that marigolds mean grief, but I have to agree with your mother on this one. I think they are the loveliest thing in the world. To me, Marigold means only joy."

There was a lump in my throat, and my eyes glazed dangerously.

"Don't you dare," he murmured.

I blinked hard. "I don't know what you mean," I sniffled. Then I found myself being thoroughly, ruthlessly kissed once more.

"Oh," I said breathlessly. "That is certainly one way to make me stop crying."

"I shall have to remember that," Oliver said. "So that I never run out of handkerchiefs." He looked down at the ring box still in my hand. "Well, Bloom?" He quirked a brow. "Shall we stop pretending to be engaged and just get married?"

"What a romantic proposal."

He smiled then – the full, dazzling smile that made my head spin. "Marigold Bloom," he said, taking the box and pulling out the ring. Casting the box aside, he took my hand in his, slipping the ring on to my finger where it fitted exactly. "I don't really like anyone. But I love you. Will you marry me?"

"Perfect," I whispered, and then his mouth was on mine, and I didn't say anything else for several very interesting minutes.

"We have a lot to talk about," I said afterwards, as we sat side by side on the sofa.

"I know," Oliver said. "Your business, your family…"

I swallowed, nodded. "I have an idea that I would like to discuss with you." I cleared my throat, suddenly nervous. "Mrs Finch told me about your plans for Lockhart Hall."

"And do you approve?"

"Wholeheartedly. I thought about what you said about gardening being healing. I wondered if there was a way to make the garden an important part of this sanctuary: a place to heal, emotionally and physically."

"I like that." Oliver nodded. "I like that very much." His fingers twined with mine, his thumb brushing lightly across my knuckles.

"And about my family…" I hesitated. "We will have to find a solution."

"Together," Oliver said firmly. "We will make this work together. We can talk to your family and find an answer that suits everyone. I promise you that we will not leave them in the lurch; I promise you that the business you built will not suffer. I am not here to hold you back, Bloom. I am here to help you grow. We are going to be partners in this. Partners in life. That is what my mother and father never had, but I won't have anything less between us."

It was the best thing he could have said. "I would like that," I murmured, resting my head on his shoulder. I smiled. "You know, I think I can tell you the exact moment I fell in love with you."

"Oh?"

"Yes." I turned, peeped up at him through my lashes. "I believe it was the moment I first saw your horribly overgrown gardens."

And Oliver Lockhart threw his head back and laughed.

EPILOGUE

"What if they hate me?" I asked nervously as Oliver and I stood outside Bloom's two days later.

"Of course they won't hate you," Oliver scoffed.

"At least the shop is still standing," I said, looking up at the familiar facade. "Though who knows what disaster awaits inside."

Oliver nudged me. "Only one way to find out."

"Right." Pulling my shoulders back, I pushed the door open. The familiar sound of the bell rang out and I steeled myself.

But instead of disaster, I was met by only blissful tranquillity.

The shop was immaculate. The flowers displayed to perfection. Several customers browsed happily.

"What—" I began, but I was cut off when Daisy looked up from her place behind the counter, and shrieked, "Mari!"

I found myself with my arms around my sister who had thrown herself at me, dancing gleefully from foot to foot.

"You are back!" she exclaimed. "We weren't expecting you until tomorrow."

"Oh, well, we had some news to share, and I thought—"

Again, I was cut off as Daisy ignored me completely, darting towards the back room and shouting. "Mother! Grandfather! Mari is back!"

I watched in astonishment as the two of them came rushing in. My mother was wearing my dirt-covered apron. They pulled me in for more embraces. Then Grandfather pumped Oliver's hand enthusiastically and slapped him several times on the back.

"Delighted to see you," he said. "Delighted!"

Politely ushering the remaining customers out, Daisy turned the shop sign to "CLOSED" so that we were alone.

"Will Mr Lockhart be joining us for dinner?" Mother asked.

Oliver's eyes slid to mine. "Thank you for the invitation, but no. I'm afraid I am catching the train straight back to Yorkshire where I have business matters to attend to. But first I needed to come... I wanted to come ... to ask you..." He cleared his throat nervously.

"We're going to get married," I blurted desperately.

To this enormous announcement, my family barely blinked.

"Well, yes – that's wonderful, of course, darling," Mother said finally. "But we already knew that."

"I— What?" I managed.

Daisy looked in confusion between Oliver and myself. "You told us that before you went to Yorkshire."

"I – I told you we were *considering* possibly *becoming* engaged," I stuttered.

Grandfather chuckled. "Naturally, we realized you were simply trying to prepare us for the inevitable as gently as possible."

"It's so like you, Mari!" Mother beamed. "Always thinking of others. But it was clear to us the moment we saw you together that you were meant to be. And of course Mrs Finch told us all about it."

"Mrs Finch," I murmured, dazed. "Told you all about it."

Daisy nodded. "And when we got her telegraph about placing the announcement in *The Times*, of course we were so pleased."

"In *The Times*?" Now Oliver was the one repeating things.

"It looks very handsome," Mother said with satisfaction. "*The engagement is announced between Oliver, son of Richard and Violante Lockhart of Lockhart Hall, Yorkshire, and Marigold, daughter of Rowan and Rose Bloom of London*. I bought three copies!"

"And I took great satisfaction in thinking about Simon Earnshaw reading it over his breakfast!" Daisy smirked. "I hope he choked on his toast, that disgusting pig-worm."

At this, Oliver made a sound of agreement.

I wondered then, almost wildly, if Mrs Finch had somehow planned this, planned *everything* knowing all along that Oliver and I would end up here. It was silly, impossible really, and yet ... if anyone could bend the universe to her will, it was her.

"But you're not ... upset?" I asked.

"Upset?" Grandfather frowned. "Why should we be?"

"The shop!" I exclaimed. "The letter I had from Daisy made it sound as though the place was falling down."

Now it was their turn to look shocked.

"Of course there will be an adjustment period," Grandfather said slowly. "Just as there was when you took over the running of the place, Mari." He twinkled at me. "Or are you going to pretend you never made a mistake, because I still have a surplus of extremely unfortunate brown ribbon that would beg to differ. I mean, for heaven's sake, I made dozens of near-catastrophic errors when I first opened the place, but your grandmother and I muddled through."

"And truthfully, with you away, we all realized that we had come to rely on you *far* too much," Mother said.

"But you left everything so well organized that the place almost runs itself," Daisy put in.

"Daisy is being modest." Grandfather smiled. "She has taken to the business like a duck to water. It's obviously in the blood."

"I love it!" Daisy grinned, and I saw – in an instant – that she did.

"Well," I said, unable to even begin to sort through what I was feeling. "That's ... wonderful."

Grandfather clapped his hands together. "I think we should go upstairs and toast to your happiness, Mari."

"Yes," I said dimly. "Wonderful. I will just say goodbye to Mr Lockhart."

"Of course." Grandfather winked bawdily. "You young people take your time."

"I can't wait to discuss wedding plans!" Daisy squeezed my hand. "Do you think I should wear pink or yellow?"

By the time Oliver and I were alone, my head was spinning.

"So," he said, eyeing me cautiously, "that was easier than we expected."

"Yes," I said blankly. "It is wonderful."

"You already said wonderful," Oliver pointed out. "Several times. Would you like to tell me what you're really thinking?"

"They don't need me at all!" I burst out, indignant.

Oliver laughed. "Poor Bloom," he said, winding his arm round me and pulling me close. "Will it help to know that *I* need you?"

"You do?" I said, looking up into his wickedly handsome face, enjoying the secret grin that he saved only for me.

"I do," he said.

And then he kissed me. And I found it did help, actually. It helped a lot.

ACKNOWLEDGEMENTS

Thanks as always to Louise Lamont and Gen Herr, my personal dream team and the best people to make a book with.

Thanks to everyone at Scholastic who played such an important part in creating the book you are holding in your hands. Special thanks to Cathy Liney and Lauren Fortune for their editorial insight, thanks to Harriet Dunlea and Kiran Khanom for all their hard work in publicity and marketing, to Sarah Dutton and Wendy Shakespeare who polished this book up until it shone.

Thank you to Emily Landy who has been so kind, and who is determined that the Aviary achieve global domination! Thank you to Jamie Gregory and Mercedes deBellard for creating another beautiful cover.

Thank you to Sarra Manning, Sophie Irwin, Katherine Webber and Louise O'Neill who said such kind things about *The Agency for Scandal* and helped so many readers find the funny, fearless women of the Aviary. It's because of you all that I got to write this book, and to spend more time in a world I love so much. I appreciate you!

Thank you to my deeply charming, and fantastically good-looking family and friends who are an extremely patient source of support when I am deep in the pit of writing despair. (It happens every. Single. Book. Aren't they lucky?!) Especially to Paul and Bea who are actually forced to inhabit a shared space with me during the trying times. I love you so much! Now the book is finished I will be an absolute delight to live with until the next one starts (imminently).

Biggest thank you to my precious readers, old and new. I am so grateful for you. Let's do this again soon, yes?

MARIGOLD'S GUIDE TO THE LANGUAGE OF FLOWERS

Anemone (*Anemone*) ~ forsaken love

Aster (*Symphyotrichum*) ~ daintiness

Calla Lily (*Zantedeschia*) ~ magnificent beauty

Camellia (*Camellia*) ~ longing for you

Clematis (*Clematis*) ~ ingenuity and cleverness

Columbine (*Aquilegia*) ~ foolishness

Cornflower (*Centaurea cyanus*) ~ be gentle with me

Crocus (*Croceae*) ~ youthful glee

Daffodil (*Narcissus*) ~ unrequited love

Dahlia (*Dahlia*) ~ eternal love or commitment

Edelweiss (*Leontopodium*) ~ courage and daring

Forget-me-nots (*Myosotis*) ~ I will miss you

Foxglove (*Digitalis*) ~ riddles and secrets

Heather (*Calluna*) ~ luck and protection

Hydrangea (*Hydrangea*) ~ boastfulness and heartlessness

Lady Slipper Orchid (*Cypripediodeae*) ~ sudden and unpredictable attraction

Laurel (*Laurus*) ~ victory, success

Lilies (*Lilium*) ~ you were beloved

Maidenhair Fern (*Adiantum*) ~ secrecy

Marigold (*Tegetes*) ~ grief

Peony (*Paeonia*) ~ the promise of good fortune

Petunia (*Petunia*) ~ anger or resentment

Poppy (*Papaver*) ~ I am not free

Rose (*Rosa*) ~ passionate love

Sunflowers (*Helianthus*) ~ false riches

Tansy (*Tanacetum vulgare*) ~ hostility

Tulip (*Tulipa*) ~ declare my love for you

Violet (*Viola*) ~ wisdom and hope

Yellow Pansy (*Viola lutea*) ~ thinking of you

Laura Wood is an academic and writer. She loves Georgette Heyer novels, Fred Astaire films, travelling to far-flung places, recipe books, Jilly Cooper, poetry, new stationery, sensation fiction, salted caramel and Rufus Sewell's cheekbones.

Other achingly romantic stories from Laura Wood: